RETRIBUTION

Jill

editors

RETRIBUTION

BEVERLEY ELPHICK

Matador
9 Priory Business Park,
Wistow Road, Kibworth Beauchamp,
Leicestershire. LE8 0RX
Tel: 0116 279 2299
Email: books@troubador.co.uk
Web: www.troubador.co.uk/matador
Twitter: @matadorbooks

ISBN 978 1789015 812

British Library Cataloguing in Publication Data.
A catalogue record for this book is available from the British Library.

Printed and bound in the UK by TJ International, Padstow, Cornwall
Typeset in 11pt Aldine401 BT by Troubador Publishing Ltd, Leicester, UK

Matador is an imprint of Troubador Publishing Ltd

MIX
Paper from
responsible sources
FSC® C013056

For Martin, Elle and Alex

Author's Note

The excerpts at the head of each chapter come from a variety of sources. Spellings and punctuation are as depicted at source. I have endeavoured to reproduce the original copy except in the case of the local newspaper where early editions used the letter 'f' to signify 's'.

The difference in punctuation, style and spelling does not detract from the information contained which illustrates the conditions found in the late eighteenth century.

***

I would like to thank the following people for their assistance in the creation of this novel:

Catherine Stewart whose care and advice in editing Retribution resulted in a better book; Alison Green and Amanda Deadman who helped in many ways; Darryl Wratten, Julie Windless and Lyn Hayward, all dear friends who insisted on there being a sequel to *Three Round Towers*, as well as the many others who encouraged me.

I would also like to thank all the people who bought *Three Round Towers*, read it and demanded to know more of Esther Coad.

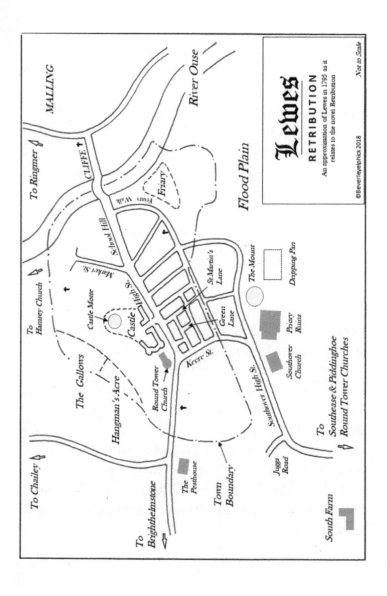

Lewes

RETRIBUTION

An approximation of Lewes in 1795 as it
relates to the novel Retribution

©Beverleyelphick 2018

Not to Scale

Part One

May 1796

Chapter One

On Sunday last a respectable tradesman was going to his accustomed place of worship, when some rude fellows (who throng Cliffe Corner at these times) were throwing at each other, and a handful of garbage struck the individual referred to, and whose expostulations were grossly insulted for daring to be offended. Where are the police on these occasions is the question demanded by the ratepayers? I am, Sir, yours faithfully. AN INHABITANT

Sussex Weekly Advertiser and Lewes Journal 1750/1806

We wanted to be married with the sun on our backs, gladness in our hearts and no shadows from the past to haunt us. Wilf and I counted the days to our summer wedding as we prepared the cottage that Farmer Elwood had offered us, a place suitable for a married land agent and his wife - me, Esther Coad, spinster of the town of Lewes with a child, Beth, who had been born in tragedy but lived in love.

Beth was the illegitimate daughter of my best friend Becca and our employer Farmer Coad. Becca had been violated by this evil man who was, I am ashamed to say, a member of my distant family. We had both worked together as servants at Coad Farm, Hamsey, near Lewes. Becca had been unable to bear her shame and the cruelty of the family and after birthing alone in the nearby church she drowned herself in the river Ouse above Lewes.

Following a period of great distress, I had been made Beth's guardian. Farmer Coad had been fined heavily for his sins, which included an attempt to implicate me in her death. At the direction of the court, he was forced to give me a sum of money for her upkeep. With his wife and three sons, he still lived at Hamsey and I did everything I could to avoid meeting them. The horror of the days when I had been falsely accused and jailed for Becca's murder still hung heavily on me but, with the help of some good, kind people, I had overcome my sorrow and was raising Beth to be a happy, beautiful child who lived in comfort, surrounded by laughter as well as love.

Most evenings Wilf and I tried to meet up at our new cottage and do our best to make it homely. Cecilia, Farmer Elwood's wife and my closest friend, had opened her linen chest for me to pick some fabrics and offcuts from her old gowns and linens to make into a colourful warm bedspread. With coins I had saved from my work with Dr. Grieve, I bought cheap plain cotton for window curtains before embroidering a border for decoration. We had glass in our windows but there were still draughts and most of all I wanted us to be warm and snug. Wilf was honing his carpentry skills on the bed his parents had left him; the thick oak board at the top now had our initials carved into it and a surrounding garland of oak leaves – that, with my pretty spread and curtains, was enough to make it home.

We giggled every time I felt it necessary to try the softness of the bed, and when he wanted to try it more thoroughly I was hard pushed to fend him off. Beth loved the cottage and wanted to stay every night; we planned to bring the little truckle bed from South Farm for her to sleep on and there was just room in the one good-sized upper room for all of us. There were two smaller box rooms for when she grew bigger and, perhaps blessed with little ones of our own, we thought we could build on to the back of the cottage, making another bedroom. We were fortunate to have so much room.

It had been a glorious spring, so I was able to harvest some early sweet-smelling herbs and grasses before they bolted to seed, and it was these that I stuffed our mattress with. Luckily, I still had plenty from last year for the floor. I dried the new fresh ones in the sunshine ready for our wedding night and put the remainder in one of Farmer Elwood's barns until the cottage was ready. I sprinkled some of my store of lavender in amongst last year's crop; I didn't want to overpower the grasses, but lavender in small quantities has a freshness about it and discourages the bugs.

The cool spring evenings had been perfect for digging and planting our garden; I had already located some herbs that were not easily found in the hedgerows and replanted them for later medical use. Mr. Jenkins, Dr. Grieve's gardener, had supplied me with many young plants and some saplings and they were all growing well. I used my papa's apothecary notes to remind me what to plant and how to prepare and harvest although, essentially, I seemed to know just what to do. I clearly remembered my mother's teachings, but it was good to refresh my knowledge and read his neat hand again.

Life felt good and one evening when Dr. Grieve called at South Farm, it got even better because he asked me to resume my old employment as a midwife and nursing assistant. When Cecilia had been due to have her baby, I had returned to South Farm to be her nurse, companion and friend but young Frederic was strong and healthy now and I hankered for my work and the fulfilment it had given me. I had given up all nursing while caring for Cecilia and Freddie as I had little spare time for outside work, so I was enormously happy to return to my daily duties in the doctor's home and to ride Flossy regularly again.

'You really can't wait, can you?' Cecilia smiled at my efforts to contain my joy. 'What about me, Freddie and Beth? Are we to be left to the ministrations of Mrs. Fisher?'

She laughed at the guilt on my face. 'Oh, Esther, I am only teasing, though I think I will rely on Mary-Jane and Cilla to be nursemaids rather than Mrs. Fisher.'

I couldn't resist rushing around to the stables to tell Flossy my news and it was while I was whispering into her velvety ears that Wilf came upon us. He certainly wasn't pleased to hear my plans.

'I can't see why you be going back to Dr. Grieve. You be a married woman soon and will 'ave more than enough to do in our own home.'

A chill struck my heart as he grumbled on. 'Why can't he employ someone proper, like?'

'What do you mean, proper?' I asked as anger surged through me.

'Someone suited: an apothecary.'

'I am proper. I am his apprentice; he teaches me,' I declared.

He looked straight at me, his face stiff with suspicion, which angered me even more.

'And why is that, Esther, why you?'

'I can't believe you're saying this, Wilf, let alone thinking it. What about the money I earn - good money that will make us more comfortable?'

'I earn enough for the all of us, and I don't want my wife trailing around after another man.'

I was dumbstruck for the minute, especially as I recalled a barbed comment from the workhouse overseer who had taunted me with being the doctor's fancy woman when I had criticised him some months previous.

Flossy tossed her head and I caught her eye before I rounded on Wilf.

'I have a job, I am good at it. Dr. Grieve values me for that reason alone and I have no intention of giving it up, so, if you think I will, then let me remind you – I am a nurse, and in due course I intend to be a midwife. If you can't abide it then perhaps you should say so now, afore we wed.'

I left him there, his face bearing that shut-down look that it has when he is cornered or angry. Fuming, I went back to the house and ran up to my room. I splashed my face with water from the jug, glancing in the mirror as I did so. My colour was high and I felt so angry at Wilf's jealousy and expectation that I would be just another homely wife. Most women were not taught to do anything other than tend their own hearth, raise their children and have a meal on the table but I was being trained up, and I didn't want to stop learning or putting my skills, particularly my herbal knowledge, to good use. I was more than capable of running our home, raising Beth and any other children that might come along and becoming - what I wanted most of all - a good midwife.

I caught sight of my friend Becca's comb and clutched it to my breast as hot angry tears coursed down my face. Becca had been dead and gone for a while now but this, her most prized possession, still had the power to comfort me. Thinking of her was enough to remind me that her child,

Beth, needed me to be strong and capable. I would not be trammelled by men, even good men like Wilf. If he didn't like it, he would have to put up with it or there would be no wedding and I would be sore sorry about that for I loved him, most of the time; but not when he was taken by his darker mood.

I drew the comb through my ruffled hair and with a bit of prodding and fixing with pins I saw my face return to its normal colour. I liked to think of Becca's spirit nearby; she soothed me. I dried my tears and pinched my cheeks to fetch some colour before going up to the nursery and the noisy prattle of Freddie and Beth who were running Mary-Jane ragged.

The next day I was wakened early by the birds chirruping their chorus into the thin pale dawn. Having roused Beth and completed our toilet we stood at our window watching a shy sun soften the garden with pastel light. Later, I left Beth at her breakfast with Cilla and Mrs. Fisher before Mary-Jane came to take her up to the nursery to join Freddie. Mary-Jane had stayed on at South Farm after Beth was weaned; she helped in the kitchens or wherever she was needed. Fortunately for me she was very good with both babies and toddlers and Cecilia trusted her to act as nursery maid. She'd got rid of the nits, and her mother took care of her own little boy who was much too old to nurse. It was a good arrangement for her as she had a better and more reliable income than being a wet nurse whose milk could dry up at any moment.

Once I was certain they were all settled for the day, I rushed to get Flossy from the stables. She was tacked and waiting with a bright gleam in her eye and as I stroked her quivering brown nose she whickered with pleasure. I used the mounting block to clamber onto her broad back. It wasn't very graceful, but I was becoming quite adept. I didn't ride as Cecilia did; I put my legs firmly astride which was much easier for me and my limpy leg. Gathering the reins, we turned out from the yard and trotted toward Lewes and Dr. Grieve's house. He lived just behind the castle and I loved going there. I couldn't help humming a little tune as I admired the beautiful day developing around me.

The doctor's workroom was in a state of complete disarray, so I spent a deal of time sorting medicants, bandages and instruments which had been sterilised but not stored as I liked. In short, I had to tidy up before I could begin to transcribe the pile of notes and add them to the patients' particulars. By the time Dr. Grieve returned from his coroner's duties in the town, Mrs. Jenkins was ready to serve a light lunch. We sat together, just as we used to; it all felt so familiar and right.

'It is good to have you back here, Esther,' said the doctor. 'We have all missed your good cheer and industry. I hope we can continue like this?' He raised an eyebrow, looking deep into my eyes and hopefully not seeing Wilf's mean suspicions lurking there.

'I am that pleased to be back and I can't wait to get on with some proper nursing. Perhaps I could come with you on your rounds?' I suggested eagerly. 'I can catch up on the notes later, at home.'

'In that case, since you are so keen, you can come with me to see Mrs. Thomas. She is having her first and presenting with some difficulties. We might need to better position the baby if it hasn't done so naturally by now; it will be good experience for you.'

As I pulled off my work apron, I couldn't help thinking of Wilf's previous sweetheart who had died in childbirth because her baby was positioned wrong and no-one had gotten help for her in time. I didn't remind the doctor how I had accused him of ignoring patients who couldn't pay. Perhaps my angry words had had some small effect because he had changed his ways a little since that horrible day. Wilf had been quite unkind to the poor girl who had begged him to help her. I later found out that she had taken up with a travelling carpenter sometime after Wilf stopped seeing so much of her. The carpenter had disappeared as soon as there was a child in the offing. Molly was one of the reasons I was so determined to become a good midwife. I had been deeply upset by the tragedy of her plight – two lives lost but for the care she should have received. The lazy drunk who oversaw the workhouse and who left her to die should have been held to account.

Mr. and Mrs. Thomas lived near the rectory in Glynde and as we pulled up in the trap, I saw someone at the window. The door was opened almost immediately by a pink-faced girl in a grey uniform.

'I be that glad to see thee, Doctor. Missus is awful pained, and I didn't rightly know what to do to 'elp her, like.'

'Where is your master, girl?' he asked as he gave her his hat.

'He went off to stay at 'is brother's house. He told missus she would be better off with all women about her. I don't rightly know when 'e'll be back. There's only me and cook 'ere and whilst she be sure to know what to do, having six of her own, I don't know naught about birthing.' The poor girl looked as if she was about to cry, so I patted her arm and suggested that she prepare some water for the doctor's hands and make some of my own herb tea. I gave her several twists, each containing a measure of a restorative brew. She couldn't stop chattering and told us she thought the master would not come home until it was all over, and cook was doing her best, giving the missus some of his best brandy.

Dr. Grieve grunted but made no comment as we mounted the stairs.

Mrs. Thomas was not easy in her bed. She cried when we arrived, cried throughout the examination and cried when the doctor reassured her by saying that the baby was fine and only a little poorly positioned.

The girl, Sarah, reappeared with the tea for the mother-to-be. Cook was following on behind and she insisted on giving the doctor her advice until he silenced her with a look.

Gradually, we were able to calm our patient and I put my arms around her shoulders as Dr. Grieve prepared to manipulate the child in the womb. I nodded to Sarah and cook to leave us and Sarah, at least, looked only too ready to escape, whereas the cook clearly thought the good doctor wasn't as experienced as she!

'Get out, woman,' he snapped.

I held on to Mrs. Thomas tightly and reassured her calmly as Dr. Grieve gently, but firmly, manipulated the child's position inside the womb. At length, we women were exhausted by the concentration involved, even though the movement was tiny. Our patient sank into her pillows, looking pale and frail but a little calmer than when we had arrived. I thought it wonderful to see such skill and desperately wanted to understand it. The doctor had allowed me to feel the baby's movement for a few moments.

Sarah brought more water and clean towels for the doctor and me as he explained what to expect in the coming days until the baby was ready to be born.

'Where do you think Mr. Thomas is staying?' he demanded of Sarah as we went out to the trap. 'He belongs here with his wife. I will seek him out.'

'Oh, don't do that, Sir. He'll be awful mad if he thinks I blabbed.'

'He won't think you gossiped, girl. I have eyes in my head.'

Poor Sarah didn't look convinced as she described the house where Mr. Thomas might be found.

'Man's a brute, leaving his wife alone like that. Did she say if there is family nearby?' he asked me.

'She has a sister near Rodmell. I suggested that she send for her. Is the birth going to be difficult?'

'Mrs. Thomas is not one of those women who can churn out their babies one after another. She is delicately formed, and her pelvis is small for what appears to be a big baby. She needs to be kept calm and if her husband cannot oblige, then we need someone other than a servant to help her.' He was concentrating on the rutted ground as we started off before turning to me and saying, 'I might have to call on you, Esther, to step in as soon as things get underway. The baby's head is now better positioned to drop into its rightful place for a normal birth. In the meantime, I will seek out this husband of hers and he will be made to recognise his responsibilities to his wife and child.'

I didn't doubt it for a moment. Dr. Grieve was an important man in Lewes and he would soon send the father scuttling back.

Chapter Two

As I travelled around and about Lewes in the next few days I became aware of sullen looks and muttered words thrown in my direction. I had faced down the disapproval and animosity of Lewes people before when I had been wrongly charged with Becca's murder, but this time I had no idea what I had done that would cause such malice. I mentioned it to Cecilia, but she couldn't enlighten me, so I sought some answers from my old friend Billy-alone.

'Nobody 'urt you, did they, Miss? I'll sort 'em if they 'ave.'

'No, Billy, I just seem to see a lot of whispering and muttering when I pass by and one man shouted at me yesterday.'

'What do 'e say?'

I couldn't bring myself to repeat it but gave Billy the gist without using the hateful words.

'Thing is, Miss, after the smugglers' gang was broke up, a lot of the people who had an understanding with they found themselves out of pocket, like.'

'Understanding, what do you mean?'

'There be lots of people involved,' he replied. 'Not just the smugglers themselves but ordinary folk who made a penny or two greasing their path, like. There be lookouts, carriers, buyers - and pretty well everyone comes under that group. Some'll be missing their brandy and tea, as well.'

Thinking back, I remembered Mrs. Makepiece getting salt to cure the meat and there was always a drop of brandy for special occasions, as well as tea, every time I visited.

'So, people blame me for breaking up the gang?' I asked, dreading the answer.

Billy nodded. 'A lot of they relied on the extra pennies to feed their family and themselves.'

It all fell into place: the huge demand for drink, as well as luxuries, without taxes being levied on them. The smugglers had a secret network of workers who helped them transport the goods. I had seen a lot of them that dreadful time when I was moved from the barn where my wounded cousin had lain as I had tried to heal his terrible injuries. These carriers and lookouts would make their way by stealth or just turn a blind eye, and all would be rewarded in cash or kind. My part in the whole sorry affair was small but well known locally after the trial; and I could see it was easier to blame me than the excise men and the soldiers who had gone back to their camps.

I said, 'What can I do? I don't want children to go hungry because I helped break up the gang.'

'Naught, Esther,' said Billy. 'The gang is already regrouping, just not in Southease no more. When a person disappears there alus be someone to take 'is place. The Hawkhurst lot in Kent will be looking to take over this patch. Lewes be rich pickings. Just ignore them, Miss, it will soon be blowed o'er and everything back to normal.'

Billy's advice made sense and though I didn't want to remember that my mother's relations, her sister no less, were the leaders of the smuggling gang who had taken me and Beth, I couldn't forget the horror of our captivity and eventual rescue, when so many had died or suffered injury. No mercy had been given by the Revenue. They had been made fools of too many times, and both my cousins died on that fateful day, the day I was to be forceput in marriage to my cousin Sam with the connivance of a corrupt priest who was terrified of the family. My aunt, the leader of it all, had escaped death but had been imprisoned and sentenced to transportation. The past was still the present in my dreams but by keeping myself busy and hopeful of a better future, I had to keep reminding myself that I had not been the cause of all the trouble but someone who was just caught up in it.

What truly horrified me was that all my wider family had gone to the bad and only my mother had escaped their clutches and turned her life around once she took up with my father.

Dr. Grieve and I settled back into our routine and it was some days later that we called upon Mrs. Thomas again. Her husband had been encouraged to return to the family home by a short, I imagine, caustic visit from the doctor when Mr. Thomas would have been left in no doubt of his family responsibilities. Very few men, no matter how high and mighty, would ignore the town's coroner. The doctor wasn't a majestic man. In fact, he was a little portly and had some grey hair, as well as piercingly blue eyes, but it was his manner and powerful voice that made you notice and listen to him. He was very much a gentleman.

We were again admitted to the house by Sarah who looked a lot tidier and happier. She showed us upstairs to our patient who was sitting at a small desk by the window. Apart from a high colour she seemed remarkably well considering the distress of our previous visit. Once again Dr. Grieve examined her and pronounced all to be satisfactory, with the baby's head now in the birth position. I asked Mrs. Thomas if her sister would be coming to stay and was very happy to hear that she was due any day now and would be on hand for as long as she was needed. I told her that I would be available to help with the birth and to make her as comfortable as possible. She looked greatly relieved.

As we were about to leave, Dr. Grieve commented on the likelihood of Mrs. Thomas feeding her own baby rather than adhering to the fashion of employing a wet nurse.

She replied, 'I don't see the point of having a child if one is not to look after it in every way. Besides, I am not a fashionable sort of person. My husband, however, would prefer the services of a wet nurse so we can get back to 'normal' as quickly as possible.' She reddened as she looked up and asked, 'What do you think, Doctor?'

'I should disregard your husband if I were you, Mrs. Thomas,' was the curt reply.

I heard Sarah swallow a giggle which she barely covered with a cough and we all left the room. Mr. Thomas did not show his face, neither did Dr. Grieve send his compliments.

On our way home to Lewes I told the doctor what Billy had said about the smugglers reforming.

'Billy is right, Esther,' he said, after a pause. 'I too have heard that the smugglers are regrouping but no-one is saying where they are based, nor who is calling the shots. The Hawkhurst gang are probably behind it but they will need locals to restart the network, someone who knows the routes, the people to trust and those they can put pressure on.'

'Am I safe from them or will they be looking for revenge?' I couldn't help asking.

'You should take sensible precautions Esther. Always take Billy with you when you are likely to be alone. Don't go out at night - or even in the afternoon - unless you know you can return in daylight, even with Billy. He might be wiry and energetic but both you and he could easily be overpowered, particularly as ...' he pulled up the horse and looked at me intently. 'I am sorry to have to tell you this, Esther, but your aunt, she has escaped Newgate Prison, and no-one knows where she is or who enabled her to get away.'

My stomach lurched at this terrible and unwelcome news.

'I can't believe it,' I said. 'Is she likely to be near here?' I felt sick with terror at the thought of her approaching me, let alone wishing me and Beth ill.

'She is being sought and, as yet, there are no clues as to where she is hiding but such as she are masters of melting into the background. She will have many who will aid and keep her sordid secrets. However, there is a large reward and it is possible someone will give her up. Money talks in that world.'

We rode the rest of the way in silence. I worried at the vengeance she might seek on me and knew I would always have to look over my shoulder. In my mind, often in the depths of night, I constantly relived the day when her sons - my cousins - had been killed along with other members of her smuggling gang. Many had been taken prisoner and their families surely hated me as the instigator of the chain of events. Before I came into the district, they were secure in the knowledge that bribery and corruption could smooth over their dishonesty. I often wondered if I should have just let things be. If only I hadn't sought my family out. None of us would have been any the wiser and there would have been no deaths.

Over the next few days I told all my good friends and anyone who might look out for me about my aunt's likely return to the district and the possible resumption of trade under her direction. Having told my tale a number of times, her power over me seemed to lose its bite and though I took precautions and sought never to be alone, I did not feel quite as fearful as when the doctor first informed me of her escape.

Fortunately, my work days were fulfilling and I was able to be present to help Mrs. Thomas give birth to a beautiful baby boy. On one of our visits to the house before the birth, Mr. Thomas was surprised in his library where he tried to ingratiate himself with the doctor, though he ignored my presence entirely, not even acknowledging me. His manner seemed to irritate Dr. Grieve and at one point he turned sharply to him, saying, 'This is my nurse, Esther Coad. She will be with your wife for the birth and I want you to ensure that every civility is extended to her whilst she performs her duties. I will, of course, attend when I am called by Miss Coad. You have a boy who can ride to Lewes with a message?' he questioned.

Mr. Thomas did not look pleased to have to acknowledge a lowly creature like me nor to be lectured on behaviour, but the doctor stared him out and forced him to show civility and accept my part in the proceedings. It was very satisfying, and I couldn't help smiling to myself.

Mrs. Thomas' delivery was long and very hard on her but between us we managed a happy outcome. Even Mr. Thomas unbent a little, offering the doctor a tot of brandy to celebrate, and he did manage a wave in my direction as he gave his thanks. The child was to be named Charles and he was a fine bonny lad.

Chapter Three

On Thursday last the wife of James Piercy an industrious labouring man at old Brentford, was brought to bed of three boys; who were christened by the names Matthew, Mark, & Luke who are likely to live. It is remarkable that that day eleven months before the above woman had three boys and one girl at a birth.
Sussex Weekly Advertiser and Lewes Journal 1750/1806

Wilf did not sulk for too long after our sharp words and thankfully no further obstacles were put in my way, so, apart from the worry of my aunt and whether Mary-Jane could cope with Freddie and Beth on the days when I went out to work, it was a happy time for us.

One day, Beth and I went to visit Mrs. Makepiece and Beth's maternal grandfather, as well as the Jenkins. It was overcast with layers of banked clouds threatening rain so we all met at Keere Street and I spent a lovely afternoon telling them my news, Beth's achievements and hearing their doings as well. I had fallen behind in the hemming of linens for our new home, but both the good ladies gave me some of their own. I resolved to try and embroider our initials on the fine materials.

Beth's grandfather, though he never mentioned Becca, clearly saw his daughter's likeness in the child and I thought I detected a tear as he stooped down to play or simply hug her. He seemed so proud as she called out to him in a piping but demanding voice, 'Gwanda, Gwanda, stop talking and play with Beth,' she would say, and he did.

I took the opportunity to invite everyone to our wedding breakfast to be held at Cecilia and Farmer Elwood's home after the service at Southover Church on the 24th day of the next month, June. I had been greatly touched when Cecilia offered her home and hospitality as a wedding gift to me and Wilf, and although we wouldn't have large numbers of guests, it would have been too many for our little cottage. Wilf and I both commented on the fact that many of our guests would be the Elwoods' employees and I couldn't help thinking that Cecilia's mother would greatly disapprove of all this mixing with the 'lower orders'; and there were probably many in Lewes who would be equally disapproving. Our wedding would take place during the late afternoon, allowing everyone to do their work and then come to South Farm for the celebration.

'And what be your gown like, Esther?' asked Mrs. Makepiece, knowing full well that I hadn't got one. 'Reckon you should be concentrating on getting something suitable. You want your Wilf to be proud of his bride - and your best dress is not going to cut the mustard.'

'Cecilia and I are going to visit her dressmaker this week with a picture she saw in her periodical,' I replied. 'I have some money put by and she has given me some lace for a collar and cuffs.'

She nodded mysteriously, 'Aye, and you can rely on me to find you something special as well, though I won't say just yet what that be.' Beth's grandfather wasn't to be outdone and wanted to provide some flowers for me and Beth to carry as we walked down the aisle.

May slipped away and the month of our wedding was upon us before I was ready, but the dress was ordered and mostly made up. My poor worn boots would have to do with a bit of blacking. Cecilia had offered me some dainty slippers to wear but I wanted to walk as straight as possible and I could only do that with my boots on. Over the months previous, Dr. Grieve and I had worked on strengthening my weak leg muscles. The wood and sheepskin insert he had fashioned for me to fit into my boot was a boon, and my once obvious deformity was all but disguised. If I was on my feet for too long, it could still be painful and I had to keep up the exercises he had developed for me. Flossy helped in her way by giving me full and long mobility and the strengthening of my lower leg muscles and knees was helped by my having to use them to direct her. We were a fine team and there wasn't a day went by when I didn't remember how awkward I used to be and I thanked heaven, Dr. Grieve and Flossy in equal measure for my new appearance and comfort. It brought joy to my heart.

Chapter Four

Sometimes when you wake up in the morning you have no thoughts or cares as to how things will be by the time the sun sets, and today was to be one such day. I had awoken to a cloudless sky, a warm breeze and no known fear or challenge to my happiness other than Aunt Tilly and where she might be.

I was working from Dr. Grieve's house and his early consultations had finished in good time, so when he called me into his room, I went with a cheerful smile.

'Esther, it is not long now to your wedding,' he began, 'and I want to talk to you about your prospects.'

'Prospects?' I said. 'I'm sorry, I don't take your meaning, Doctor?'

'Perhaps that is not the right word, my dear, but I feel I must speak - before it is too late.'

I sat down. A nub of anxiety had crept into my mind and suddenly I was fearful. 'Too late for what?' I asked.

'This alliance you are about to make with John Elwood's agent, or whatever it is he calls himself, his farm hand…' His tone was disparaging and for a minute I wondered who he meant and why would he have that tone of voice.

'Wilf, you mean Wilf?' I said, trying to bring some sense to this strange conversation.

'Yes, him. This young man cannot offer what you deserve, Esther, and I can't continue without speaking my mind.' He pulled up a chair near me and sat down. 'You are a clever, resourceful young woman and, with the right care and tuition, you could have great opportunity and certain fulfilment.'

I didn't understand what he was trying to say but it all became clear as he continued in this forthright fashion.

'Marrying this young fellow will hold you back and tie you to a life that, though it might provide some short-term happiness, will end in frustration and drudgery. In short, you will become the domestic chattel of a short-sighted and overbearing husband who will prevent your personal development and, more than likely, saddle you with enough children to keep you at home.' He paused, as if to let his words sink in, and then said, 'Is that what you really want, Esther, because I think there is more to you than that?'

Dr. Grieve scraped his chair nearer mine and reached for my hand, which I didn't withdraw. I felt stunned and was quite speechless.

His voice dropped in tone and softened, 'I want to give you a better life, Esther, one that will stretch you and give you continuing happiness, as my… as my closest companion.'

'Companion?' I echoed. I felt a warm flush seep up my neck as I tried to work out what he meant. Was this an offer of marriage? He had never said before that he was interested in me but, in the past, he had made some comments that I had been doubtful about as to their meaning. I felt an unexpected rush of excitement, I couldn't deny it.

'I plan to take a sabbatical in Europe, my dear,' he went on, 'probably for a year, maybe more. I would like you to come with me, and bring Beth, of course. Once away from England's conventions, we can travel and live together as husband and wife, our own little family, all the while taking the opportunity to develop your skills and for you to enjoy my patronage and protection.'

'Your companion, but not marriage?' I asked, mortally embarrassed, and confused.

He sighed, 'It is not possible, my dear, for someone of my standing in the community to marry a young woman with no family or connections and of a class so far beneath mine - but we could enjoy all the benefits of being together if we were away from here. On the Continent, we would be as if married.'

His hand was warm and pressed mine before he rose and pulled me to my feet, clasping me to his chest. I wondered if he could feel my heart pounding.

'And what would be the consequence of such an arrangement, were we to come home to Lewes?' My voice sounded distant to my ears, but I had to know.

'When we return from this tour, which would be greatly advantageous to you in broadening your education and being the recipient of my care and love, why, then, we could do what most other men do. You would become my trusted 'housekeeper', my resident housekeeper. It is a system that works well for many men, married or not.'

Works for many men, I thought, but what about the women?

I pushed myself away from him and walked to the window, my neck and face still burning with embarrassment – or perhaps it was humiliation, I could not say. I felt stifled. I couldn't stay in the room a moment longer. I turned to him. 'I thank you for your confidence in me, Dr. Grieve. I must beg some time to think what to do.'

I swiftly left the room, unable to look at him.

I gathered my belongings and, avoiding Mrs. Jenkins, slipped out to the stable. Flossy welcomed me with a toss of her head. In no time I was riding, riding for all I was worth, back towards Southover, but then onwards, onwards and up to the top of the Downs.

I flung myself off the pony and dropped to the grass. How could I have been so blind as to think that I was valued just for my skills and intelligence when all along it was exactly as Wilf and even the workhouse overseer had said? I was just an object, an object he wanted to bed but not marry or be given the protection of marriage. I felt such a fool, a naïve and stupid fool. He thought me of a class too low for him, but I knew my father had been an educated man, much respected in the Kent village where we had lived before my family were wiped out by the great sickness.

As always, the wide sky and majestic Downs brought me perspective and comfort, but I confess not for some time. I sat on the tufted grass and tugged at it angrily for a good while, reliving his words, feeling again that strange surge of excitement – that heat in my body which had reacted, unbidden, to my heart and not my head – followed by the painful reality of Dr. Grieve's proposition and the knowledge that men, Wilf and others, could see it but I hadn't. I tried to go back through our many conversations. Had I led him to believe that I would welcome his attentions? I pictured him sitting at his desk, his great dignity, his noble looks. Half of his female patients were in love with him, but they never saw the pomposity which he undoubtedly possessed and which he covered with mannerisms that were ever polite, sometimes excessively so. He was not an old man, but his hair made him appear so, having a deal of grey intermingled with a rich brown. I believed him to be younger than Farmer Elwood, but he looked older.

Eventually, I calmed my thoughts and lifted my face to a tender breeze before deciding how I was going to cope with this. What had really upset and shocked me was that my body had responded to Dr. Grieve's proposition when I thought it had meant marriage; never mind that I was about to be wed to an attractive and personable young man of my own class whom I thought I loved. Should I give up all thoughts of marriage to Wilf if my emotions were so fickle as to run from one to another if it was advantageous; or did I not love Wilf as much as I thought? I had clearly relished Dr. Grieve's attention; did I care too much for him? But, he was older than me and he should have known better than to treat me like a whore. His housekeeper indeed! Surely, I merited better treatment than that. Were his physical needs so strong that he could cast me in such a light, against all the conventions of society, and thus effectively ruin me in the eyes of the community and beyond? Did he really think that people like Cecilia or Mrs. Makepiece would be so easily fooled or was it that I was too simple in the ways of the world to know what passed for normal behaviour amongst the upper classes? Was every housekeeper a mistress? I knew that to be wrong. Mrs. Jenkins would die to be thought of in those terms. And, what if I were indeed to take up his offer and become 'resident housekeeper' what would happen to Mr. and Mrs. Jenkins?

My head ached as I went over and over all these thoughts. I went through every emotion but the one I ended up with was quite straightforward: I was angry, very angry, and hurt. It was so painful and degrading.

Until this point, I had held Dr. Grieve in high regard. Perhaps I did have feelings for him which were unacknowledged, but from this time on, I would have to keep any such feelings suppressed. How dare he trample all over my good name and expect me to lay down at his bidding? What to do? I asked myself. I didn't want to lose my work, but I didn't see how we could carry on working side by side with such a chasm opened up between us. On the way home, I decided to sleep on it and make up my mind tomorrow. Somehow, I managed to slip into the house and retrieve Beth from the kitchen without having to talk with anyone. Wilf would be waiting for me at the cottage, but I wasn't going anywhere.

The following day I saddled Flossy and rode into Lewes, going straight to Dr. Grieve's house. My head was aching and I felt dreadful. What little sleep I managed had been tormented. I knew I had to speak to him and kept turning over in my head what I was going to say:

…The conversation we had yesterday was, I am sure, a mistake. I am hurt that you hold me in such contempt that you would allow me to be humiliated in the eyes of everyone of good name. I have no feelings for you other than professional respect and I don't wish to discuss this ever again. I am happy to continue in my role as nurse on that basis. If you are not, then we must part company today…

28

That was what I intended to say but when I got there, the doctor was not in his surgery. A letter was waiting for me on his desk. I shut the door and sat down in his chair before breaking the seal and as I read the first few lines, my heart sank.

My Dearest Esther

Your reaction to my heartfelt proposition was very clear to see and, on that basis, I must assume you do not wish to accompany me on my sabbatical. I am going to London today to finalise arrangements for temporary cover whilst I am away. I will return shortly and if you change your mind then please leave me a letter saying so, clearly and unequivocally. I will be spending the next few weeks in London whilst I await my ship. I will suggest that my replacement, Dr. Crabbe, employ you, but you will have to finalise that with him. He is a good man but a trifle bumptious and his wife is not capable of acting in a nursing capacity. I wish you every goodwill, Esther, and if my proposition was distasteful to you then I sincerely apologise. It was not my intention to insult you. We will not meet again unless you leave me word and I hope that life will be good to you and happiness yours. I do not know when I will return but be assured I will not embarrass you further.

Esther, I do remind you to be careful of your aunt's vengeance. My sources tell me that she is likely to be in Kent.

I am respectfully yours, dear Esther…

PS I have asked Dr. Crabbe to allow you sight of any printed periodicals that are sent to me. I do hope you will continue with your studies.

I groaned aloud as I read, my self-righteous anger plunging instantly into sorrow; deep sorrow to have so suddenly lost the company of a man I held in high regard even if I could never demean myself by becoming a mistress (though a part of my mind nagged wilfully at me that I *could*). Once again, my heart reacted before my brain, and it ached. There was nothing I could do but go home to South Farm. I stuffed the letter into my pocket and ran out of the house.

Setting off to return to Cecilia and the children, I wondered what on earth I could say. The doctor's declaration had been so shocking to me, but had others been aware of his interest? Had Cecilia or Farmer Elwood interpreted a look whilst we talked round their supper table? Did they see any overly long holding of my hand when we met? Wilf was jealous of him - but wasn't that based on jealousy of any man who saw more of his woman than he did? As I rode back to South Farm all I could think of was the gulf that was opening around me: possible loss of my employment, loss of a man whose advice I often sought, loss of his presence in the town and visits to South Farm. I regarded his home as my second place of safety, I loved riding up through the castle archway when I visited; I had my own room there, Beth was constantly there. What would Mr. and Mrs. Jenkins think? Did they know of his inclinations towards me? Farmer Elwood would be sorry to see his friend go and I hated to think how he would take it if he found out that I was the cause of his leaving so abruptly. Was there something in my nature that caused upset all around? Flossy picked her way slowly as if sensing my mood and sharing it with me. For the first time ever, I didn't want to go home.

Chapter Five

ESCAPE Lewes May 28 1800 BROKE OUT of the HOUSE OF CORRECTION, at Lewes on Tuesday the 27th day of May instant.

Richard Teeling, the younger, late of stock-ferry in the Parish of Piddinghoe, near Lewes aforesaid who at the last General Quarter Sessions for the Eastern Division of Sussex, was sentenced to be confined until he could find sureties of the peace towards THOMAS CARR, of Beddingham, Esq., the High Sheriff of the County of Sussex, for the space of two years.

The said Richard Teeling is a tall thin man of the age of 30 years or thereabouts, light complexion, light brown hair which he wears loose and long, slender made, formerly in the Sussex Militia and has lately followed the trade of huckster in buying ...at the sea side retailing then in the country – is well known to smugglers on the coast, whomsoever will apprehend the said Richard Teeling and lodge him in any of the Counties gaols and give information thereof at the House of Correction at Lewes shall receive a reward of TWENTY POUNDS. William Cramp Keeper.

Sussex Weekly Advertiser and Lewes Journal 1750/1806

Dr. Grieve's departure was a surprise to everyone in Lewes and there was much speculation as to his motives but, as always, the gossip dropped away as other local issues came to the fore. Mr. and Mrs. Jenkins were anticipating the arrival of Dr. Crabbe and his wife and just assumed that I would continue in my role within the household, so it came as a great shock to all of us when I called upon the new doctor and found that my services were not only unwelcome but were, in fact, abhorrent to this bigoted man.

He was tall, very thin and his hair was greased into a severe pin at the back. I noticed immediately an arrogance, or perhaps it was just the way he looked down his long and bony nose. His lips were compressed into a straight line and I could see no kindness there. I wouldn't want to be ministrated to by him! Dr. Grieve had described him as a little 'bumptious' but clearly had been deceived into thinking that he shared Dr. Grieve's enlightened views in employing first and foremost a woman, and then teaching her to become a midwifery practitioner in her own right. I had called the third morning after their arrival and the door was opened by a woman who I at first took to be a servant. She wore a dowdy gown with an untidy apron and cap that looked far from clean. Whilst I waited for Dr. Crabbe to appear, she stood nervously beside me, her mouth puckering and her hands constantly moving. I tried to engage her in conversation, but her voice was so low that I couldn't follow her replies to my enquiries. I gave up the effort and we both stood silently waiting.

Dr. Crabbe appeared from the direction of the library and my overtures of friendship and welcome were immediately rejected as he declined to take my hand.

'Young woman, I do not know what possesses a man of Dr. Grieve's stature to employ an untrained woman as his assistant,' he said, 'but I do not hold with such liberal views and will have no use for your services. Should my wife here,' and he indicated the woman at my side, 'be unable to meet my needs then I will seek out a trained male apothecary, as is the norm in our noble profession.'

My mouth must have dropped open in astonishment as he continued, 'Dr. Grieve might have commended you to my employ but I don't believe it is appropriate for women to step out of their proper role and I must ask you to leave and not attempt to continue any treatment of those who you might previously have had access to. I am the physician appointed and I will not tolerate interference.'

He tilted his head to his wife and she immediately sprang to open the door. I was outside within seconds, the door closed firmly behind me. I made my way around to the stable where Mr. Jenkins was waiting. He had not unsaddled Flossy, as he would normally have done, so he must have had an inkling of what my reception would be. His kindly face said it all and I was unable to stop a tear creeping down my cheek.

'Ee, lass, don't take on, he is not worth it,' he said, putting an arm round my shoulder.

'But my work, I love my work. How can he be so rude to me, he doesn't even know me nor what I am capable of? It is so unfair.' I sat abruptly on some hay as I saw my future life unfold without Dr. Grieve and without a role, other than wife.

'Mrs. Jenkins said to tell you that she hopes to meet up at Mrs. Makepiece's. We don't want to lose your company, Esther, but it is best if you do not come here,' he said. 'She feels that Dr. Crabbe could make life unpleasant for you.'

So, not only had I lost my friend and my work but I was to be shut out of the house that I regarded as a second home.

Mr. Jenkins bent his knee and knelt at my level. 'Come lass, you have had more to bear than this small setback. You will rise above such meanness and find your place again and remember you have many who support you in this town.' He patted me on the arm and I tried to smile through my tears at his gentle sympathy.

'Aye, you are right,' I said finally. 'I will do as you say and hopefully meet Mrs. Jenkins soon, and you too, my friend.'

'Can I help you up onto Flossy?' he asked as we both got to our feet.

'No, I can manage if I use the standing block. Flossy is so good I can even get on without.' She spirited me away a good deal quicker than normal, as if she knew we were not wanted.

We had not gone very far when I heard someone running behind me and calling my name. 'Miss, Miss Esther, wait up, can 'ee.'

I heard the familiar voice and turned; it was Billy. Flossy didn't need me to tell her to wait. She had already turned and was standing still, waiting for Billy to catch up.

'I been calling you.'

'Sorry Billy, I was thinking and didn't hear. Are you alright? You look a bit anxious.'

'I called in to see Pot at the doctor's house,' he said, out of breath, 'and Mr. Jenkins told me what 'appened, like.'

'Oh, Billy, you always seem to be nearby when I am in trouble.' I smiled down at him and then went on. 'I wasn't expecting such a thing, it's all such a shock.'

'You should send to Dr. Grieve and tell 'im. He won't like it, will 'e?'

I shrugged, lost for words and unable to explain that Dr. Grieve was lost to me.

'Why don't 'ee, Esther?' He repeated.

'I don't know where he is, Billy. His ship has probably sailed, and he wouldn't want to be bothered with petty things like this anyway. After all, taking a sabbatical means giving up your current life for another.'

'I don't rightly knowed what that word is,' said Billy, 'but I do know 'e won't like to see thee mistreated. Mrs. Elwood likely do know his whereabouts.'

'Dr. Grieve has gone, Billy, and there is no more we can do or say.' I took up the reins again. 'Now, I must get back. Do you want to climb up behind me? Are you visiting Cilla?'

He blushed as he flicked the hair out of his eyes. 'No, Esther, Miss, I be just worried about thee.'

'Billy, you are the truest friend and I don't want you to worry about me. I have lots to do. The wedding is coming up fast and I still haven't finished sewing for my bottom drawer. Why don't you come around to the cottage tonight and see what we have done to make it homely? You could ask Cilla to come with you.'

'Ask her to walk out with me, you mean? Don' know 'bout that, Miss, people might talk.'

'Let 'em, Billy, let 'em talk. You think well of her, don't you?'

'Aye, I do that, but walking out is a bit open, ain't it, and she might not want that.'

'You won't know unless you ask, Billy.'

'I'll think on it,' he said. 'You get 'ome safe now.'

It wasn't until I got back that I wondered why he had said that: *you get home safe now*. Did he know something I didn't? I would have to ask him; perhaps he had heard more of my aunt's movements. After all, Kent was not so far away and news travelled between smugglers and their support networks very fast indeed. I shrugged it off. Billy would have told me if there was something important. He was probably just being protective of me. He was such a kind lad.

Chapter Six

The inhabitants of the Parish of Battle having come to a resolution to put out their Poor on Midsummer's Day next, to some careful person who is willing to undertake to maintain and employ them; hereby give Notice that the Overseers will, in the meantime, receive proposals for this purpose, from anyone who may chuse to apply.
Sussex Weekly Advertiser and Lewes Journal 1750/1806

I found it very hard to tell everyone about my new situation, or lack of one, and even harder was it to cope with their well-meant indignation. But most people seemed to produce their own answers to my loss. It varied from 'you're better off without,' to 'you'll be married soon and won't have time.' I had very little of my own to add beyond such stoic comments as, 'I can manage,' and 'I will find some other way to occupy my time,' which was an untruth because time seemed to stretch out endlessly before me with very little to fill it.

I tried to plan for the future: making our home, creating a garden of herbs and vegetables, possibly a few fruit trees – some apples, maybe a pear and definitely plums. For a while I toyed with the idea of calling off the wedding but, after a few days, and seeing how joyful Wilf was as we filled the cottage with our bits and pieces, I realised that I did love Wilf; and even if I did harbour warmth for Dr. Grieve, it did not mean that I should have to give Wilf up. What would be the point?

After all, surely there was enough love to go around. When parents had children, their love for them wasn't divided and shared. Perhaps that was a lesson I must learn, even though I didn't think it was actually *love* that I felt for the doctor. It was all so confusing.

Billy-alone and Cilla visited us at the cottage and we were so pleased to see them together. I felt very motherly towards Billy and it did my heart good to see him so happy and striving to present himself as a good prospect to Cilla. They sat side by side on the window seat and blushed mightily when Wilf asked if Billy had approached Cilla's father for permission to walk out together.

'No, course I ain't, but I will, like, if Cilla be willing?'

Cilla rolled her eyes at me and we all laughed.

It was really enjoyable showing them around the cottage and pointing out all the improvements we had made, and Beth was very proud of her little bed alongside ours.

'Cor, did you do that carving, Wilf?' asked Billy. 'You could be a chippie if you wanted.'

'I'm quite happy with the job I got, Billy,' replied Wilf. 'But I do like to do a bit of whittling in me spare time. My pa taught me, and I got 'is tools when he died.'

Cecilia and I got very caught up in dress fittings for me and new accessories for her and it was all great fun especially when Beth tried on her new dress and spent hours in front of the big mirror in Cecilia's bedroom. All in all, my time was taken up and it was a great surprise to me that I could be fully involved in domestic life and preparation for our big day without missing my nursing; which is not to say that it would always be like that, but I would work to ensure that I always had plenty to do.

A week before the wedding, I was sitting in the kitchen

with Cilla, showing her how to steep borage into a useful preparation for lifting people out of lethargy when a knock came on the half-opened door. A young woman asked to speak to me and hoped that I would accompany her to her mother's house. She was a comely girl and I thought I recognised her but couldn't quite place where from.

'My ma's time has come, and she be straining for an awful long while, but the babe is not coming. Can you come and help her, please, Miss? She said you would know what to do.'

My heart did a skip and I grabbed my bag and rushed to put on my working dress before I came upon Cecilia. I explained to her what I was about and wondered if I would be in trouble if I went to this woman's aid.

'Nonsense, Esther,' she said instantly. 'What would have happened to me if you had not come to my aid? I'd likely be at the bottom of the well. If you can help this woman, then do so. I don't suppose for one minute she would be a paying patient of Dr. Crabbe, so what trouble can he make for you? Go, and go quickly, and we will pray on a good outcome for her.' As she turned to go, she added, 'One thing, Esther, I will ask Cilla to prepare water for when you return. You don't know what condition this woman lives in. I will take Beth up to help Mary-Jane with Freddie's weekly bath. I know she thinks she is chief bather!'

Flossy had been saddled for me and I clambered up with the young girl behind me. She directed me into Lewes and, as we turned down North Street, I suddenly remembered calling with Mrs. Makepiece to a ramshackle cottage down there. She had wanted to take some food to the family as the husband had been forced away from home by the activity of the press gang and the further risk of being taken up for poaching. When we visited previously, I had almost run into the eldest Coad boy, the nastiest of the three, which had upset me greatly.

'I remember you,' I said to the girl, who was now well grown. 'Mrs. Makepiece brought me to your home a while back. Is it your mother we are going to see?'

'Aye, that be so, Miss.' she replied. 'She don't see pa much but when 'e come, she nearly always gets in the family way. There were eight of us but we lost the youngest, Edie, last summer to a sickness. He just wasted away, like.'

'Your ma has done well by you all if you still have six brothers and sisters,' I reassured her.

'Things is easier now,' she went on. 'Pa is near a place called Hawkhurst in Kent and sends money home when he can, and me and my oldest sister, we do washing for some of the prisoners in the gaol. Mrs. Makepiece alus keeps an eye out for us and gives us eggs when she got some spare, like.'

We pushed open the door and were plunged into darkness as the window openings were covered by paper and dark rags. 'I will need some light, my dear,' I said. 'Can you let some in, or have you a candle? Natural light is best, and candles are so expensive.'

Mrs. Higgins was lying on a pallet on the floor and was very flushed. I asked to examine her and she grunted agreement, unable to speak to me. The contractions were rapid and her pulse fast. Fortunately, the baby was in the right position and would likely soon arrive. I could feel its head. As I talked endlessly, trying to encourage the poor woman and help the birth along, I was aware of lots of pairs of eyes watching me. Not one of the children made a sound and it crossed my mind that if anything happened to this brave lady, then all these kiddies would be thrown on the mercy of the parish.

After what seemed like an age and much pushing from his mother, who had taken heart with my encouragement, a healthy boy was born. He had a good lusty cry. I breathed a sigh of relief at having delivered my first baby with no supervision or oversight from Dr. Grieve. I was careful in cleaning my patient. Fortunately, she was not torn and May, the daughter who had called for me, dried the boy, wrapping him in a cloth before giving him back to his exhausted and thankful mother. I had looked around and was happy to see that there was food in the house and that the two elder girls were very capable. I had noticed a big urn outside where they must do their washing work and was pleased to see it full of grey water; there must be a well near-by, or perhaps they got it from the river.

'You have done really well in caring for your ma,' I said to May. 'I will call on Mrs. Makepiece now and tell her about the latest arrival. I am sure she will come by and check on you all.'

As I mounted Flossy, I looked at all the children peering up at me with such trusting eyes and said, 'If you have worries, then send someone for me and I will come immediately. Now, try and coax some small ale into your mother and then the milk will flow and she will be able to feed the little chap. She needs plenty of liquid as well as nourishing food, but he is a strong lad and should do well.'

May was white with relief and clasped my hands in her own. 'We can't thank thee enough, Miss. I don't think ma would have made it without your help, we thought she was giving up, she were so tired. We 'ave no coin to give you but when pa sends some, we will pay 'ee for your work today.'

'Don't worry about that,' I said. 'I am glad to have been useful. Your ma knows what she is doing, and she stands a good chance of getting through the next few days when the risks are greatest. Watch out for fever, pain or too much bleeding. She needs a deal of rest so try to ensure she stays on her pallet, with a clean cloth between her and the straw. If she is at all worried, then come for me as soon as ever you can.'

May, her sister and all the little ones waved me goodbye, telling me not to worry about going to Keere Street as it was getting dark. She would send one of the younger children to tell Mrs. Makepiece the good news.

I must have been at the cottage for hours, for it was full dusk by the time I left and trotted Flossy back towards Southover, throwing quite a few backward looks over my shoulder. The shadowy trees were thrashing in a steady wind, their upper branches clacking together and the lower seeming to whisper. I felt anxious and wished I had found Billy-alone to accompany me.

As I clattered into the yard, my worries disappeared. I was so happy at having a live birth to my name that I couldn't wait to tell everyone. I rushed into the outhouse and changed out of my work clothes, scrubbing myself down before bursting into the kitchen with my news. Wilf was there and looking none too pleased.

'Where you been all this time, Esther?' he demanded, rising from his chair. 'It be full dark, you shouldna' be out on your own. You could've fallen and where would we 'ave begun to look?'

I wasn't about to be told off when I had such joy in me. 'I've just delivered my first baby boy and it was wonderful,' I cried. 'The mother might've died if I hadn't been there! You'll just have to get used to me being out and about, Wilf, but I promise I will ask Billy-alone to accompany me in future, I won't ride alone in the dark again.'

He muttered something about Dr. Grieve.

'What's that you're saying? If you've got something to say, then say it out loud!'

'I hoped all this nonsense would come to an end,' he muttered, 'now your doctor friend 'as upped and left.'

Cilla and Mrs. Fisher were both in the kitchen as we had words, our voices rising above each other. Cilla's mouth hung open in astonishment and at that moment Cecilia walked in; with raised eyebrows she demanded to know what was going on. 'I can hear you in the dining room!' she protested.

I apologised and explained that Wilf was cross that I had come home alone in the dark.

'Well, perhaps he has a point, Esther, dear. You should be more careful of your safety,' she said. 'But now we have agreed on that, tell me what happened. Did the mother have her baby?'

My spirits lifted immediately as I told everyone about the birth, my first unaided.

'Mrs. Higgins had been in labour long before I got there, but I was able to help her along. She has had eight children already, so it was a bit surprising, but she produced a lusty boy who yelled the place down and I hope she will recover quickly,' I gabbled away in my excitement. 'She has two good girls to take the load off her. They are friends of Mrs.

Makepiece who, I am sure, will make every effort to help them.'

Gradually, the black gloom lifted from Wilf's face and I did my best to help him see how happy this birth had made me, and by the time he left he was back to his better self. Later I was sorry that I had spoken so sharply to him. He had lost his father to the smugglers and had a lot of responsibility on his young shoulders. It was more than reasonable for him to voice his concerns about my safety.

Chapter Seven

Wednesday morning executed facing the debtor's door, Old Bailey, were ten convicts including: George Mawley for escaping a second time from his place of confinement aboard the hulk, where he had been ordered to hard labour cleaning the Thames etc. They all behaved with that decency and propriety that became their wretched end.

Sussex Weekly Advertiser and Lewes Journal 1750/1806

Our wedding day was wonderfully warm, with a blazing summer sun and clear blue skies and I felt like the sun was shining for our benefit alone. A shower overnight had helped everything look fresh and vibrant. Beth and I were both so excited we could barely contain ourselves. We were welcomed down into the main dining room for a special breakfast with Cecilia, Farmer Elwood and Freddie. Beth wouldn't eat, and it took a deal of persuasion to make her do so.

'The service is not until late this afternoon and you will be needing your food now and at lunchtime, otherwise you might not be able to go,' I threatened.

All morning people arrived to wish us well and some left small gifts: vegetables, preserves and some lovely brown eggs. Beth's grandfather came early with a pretty collection of colourful wild flowers, leaves and grasses. There was a special posy for Beth, as well; he must have got up at dawn to find so many fresh flowers. We had invited his wife, Becca's stepmother, to the wedding but she maintained her stance of no interest in her husband's family. She probably still bore a grudge that Becca had stolen her special comb even though she, a Methodist, had forsworn personal adornment. Becca had taken much pleasure in thwarting her stepmother, so I wasn't put out that she wasn't coming. We would have a much better time without her black looks and sour mood.

Cecilia and I went to the cottage to finish making it just right for our wedding night. Beth was to stay with Freddie and would join Wilf and me tomorrow. It was a busy time of year and this was the only day Wilf could take off work. Cecilia clapped her hands in delight when she saw all the little touches we had put together to make our home just as we wanted. We both laughed at the depth of the bed and admired Wilf's carving on the headboard.

'Are you anxious, Esther?' she asked me, gently. 'I know the human body holds no surprises for you but are you prepared for what is to come?'

'No, I am not anxious about what happens between a man and his wife, but I am worried that I won't be attractive to Wilf, what with my leg,' I said. 'I know it is greatly improved since Dr. Grieve taught me how to work my muscles, but I can't lose the thought that it is ugly and weak. It's silly, really, as Wilf has never shown the slightest concern about my limpy leg except to help me if I am struggling - but the thought is there in my head and I can't get rid of it no matter how much I try.'

'Once you have wrapped yourselves in love you will lose that worry, Esther.' said Cecilia. 'If Wilf is as tender as I am sure he is, he will make you feel like a queen and all else will disappear.'

Clearly Cecilia had a wonderful relationship with her husband and I hoped that ours would be equally as passionate; being wrapped in love sounded heavenly to me.

We had brought some fresh food with us and stored it in the scullery. I was very pleased to have a good area for cooking and preparation, and the little outhouse which was under cover would be a godsend. Wilf was going to light the fire later in the day and hopefully it would hold for a good while before I needed to puff up the temperature for tomorrow's bread. It would serve to warm the cottage for when we returned to begin our married life in earnest. Though it was summer and warm, the cottage had a chill to it, probably because it had stood empty for a while.

'Did you think, Cecilia,' I said, 'when we went to St. Anne's church that time, and prayed for our heart's desire, and left our tokens, that everything we wanted would come about in such a short time? You have little Freddie and I have a wonderful young man who really wants to be with me and be a proper father to Beth.'

'We have been fortunate, indeed,' Cecilia agreed, 'and I give thanks daily. There is so much sadness and desperation in life and Lewes has its fair share of troubles, but we have been blessed, my friend. Anyway, enough of these deep thoughts! Today's your wedding day and we will be full of happiness, though I think I must get back now to make sure Mrs. Fisher has not lost her head over the numbers of people who are coming to celebrate with you.'

'Aye, I promised to help before I have my wash and get ready,' I said. 'I can't wait to put my dress on, it is so pretty.'

'I will come and help you dress your hair,' Cecilia said, as we prepared to leave. 'And I have a special gift from Mrs. Makepiece which will help you feel even more cherished.'

Try as I might to persuade her, she refused to tell me what my present was, and I had to be satisfied with being told to wait and see. Getting dressed in my finery was like being turned into a different person. My dress was simple in style with Cecilia's delicate lace at the neck and wrists. I had chosen a cream background with tiny sprigs of violets embroidered onto the bodice which was laced tightly and gave me a shape I was almost embarrassed to see. Cecilia was as good as her word and used all her skill to force my unruly hair upwards with tiny little curls cascading down the side and back. As she leaned back, satisfied with her creation, she produced a little box; nestled inside was a very beautiful hair clip, a wedding gift from Mrs. Makepiece. 'I believe this was a piece she wore at her own wedding and she wanted you to have it.'

I felt very humbled to have been given such a beautiful present.

We dressed Beth after me as we knew she would be unable to keep clean for very long. She wore a mint green dress which came to just above her ankles and was hemmed with yellow flowers which had been cut off one of Cecilia's old dresses. A yellow sash with a big bow completed the picture. I handed her posy to her and she settled into pretending to be grown up; she understood the flowers were fragile and became calm and steady as we both walked down the main staircase towards our new life. Those still at the house were gathered around the front door and Farmer Elwood came forward to take my hand and help me into his best carriage with Beth at my side and Cecilia, with Freddie on her lap, opposite.

The bells were ringing loudly as the horses stopped at the main door of the church and we climbed carefully down. We waited for Cecilia to take her seat in the family pew. Beth was clutching her bouquet to her chest and the three of us stood for a moment, collecting ourselves. My arm was linked with Farmer Elwood's as we, with Beth, walked slowly and steadily down the aisle towards Wilf. I saw him twisting his hat in his hands but as I reached him he raised a smile that was as happy as could be. He whispered, 'You look just beautiful, Esther. I am so proud to be your husband.'

The minister, a fussy little man with a rather sharp manner, stepped forward to begin the service. Beth didn't want to sit down; she wanted to be between us at the altar and I felt her little hand clutching my dress as we made our vows. I was so blissfully content and happy as I gazed into Wilf's eyes knowing that I had almost everything I wanted: a man who loved me, a child who brought me joy beyond anything I could imagine, and now my own home.

After the traditional marriage words were said and the replies made, a simple wedding ring (his mother's), was placed on my finger. At that very moment there came a loud scraping noise and I turned abruptly to identify it. I heard the church door slam shut, and in the silence that followed a voice rang out - cold, and full of malice. The entire congregation swivelled to see who shouted in this place of God. Three men were standing side by side at the far end of the aisle, facing us; they all carried weapons. The man in the centre was smaller than the other two and there was something familiar about him. I couldn't understand why they were there. I saw that their muskets were drawn and aimed at us but for what purpose? Were we all to be robbed?

Apart from the Elwoods, there was no-one present with great riches, we would make poor pickings. Then my confusion turned to horror as I recognised the man in the centre, a face I could never mistake anywhere. My Aunt Tilly saw the look on my face and roared with mocking laughter. Her hair was hacked short and she was dressed mannish. She made a good man, I'll say that for her. Then, with spite oozing out of her, she threatened everything that I held dear.

'Aye, it's me, good old Aunt Tilly,' she shouted. 'And now I am going to do to you what you did to me.' She raised her arm, a musket pointed from her shoulder directly at Wilf.

'No,' I screamed, unable to move, as she lowered the muzzle slowly towards Beth who was standing in a patch of sunlight, her arms wide and welcoming. She had clearly recognised Tilly, but not understanding the meaning of her words nor the threat of their weapons, she had started to totter towards her, a bright smile on her happy little face.

'Aye, niece, I'll take that girl from you in payment for what you took from me,' said Tilly. 'My sons, my two fine boys.'

I found my voice, though it cracked with fear as I yelled back at her, 'I didn't kill them, it was you, you and your wicked, evil ways, that's what killed them. It was your own fault for raising them in your mould.'

For a moment, I thought she was listening and I felt Wilf shift from my side, briefly blocking my vision, but then she fired the musket, leaving the stink of gunpowder and a great cloud of thick black smoke billowing through the air. As quickly as they came, they were gone. The door slammed shut again and all the candles flickered as my heart contracted in shock.

There was a brief moment of silence then panic ensued with people screaming and scrambling to leave.

'Beth, Beth!' I cried, but I couldn't see her anywhere. All I could see was the discarded posy of flowers and Wilf spread out before me on the stone floor. The door started slamming again and again as I cast about in a frenzy, thinking she might have run into the congregation, but the pews were emptying with people rushing to get away. Afterwards, when it was all over, I was to think how strange it was that people wanted to flee when my aunt and her companions had only just left and might still be outside, waiting.

I fell onto Wilf, trying to pull him up from the cold stone, screaming that he had to find Beth. He lifted his head and looked at me, his eyes unfocused, as he whispered, 'Is she shot?'

It was only then that I saw her, sprawled beneath his body and soaked in blood. As I reached for her, I realised the blood was not hers but his. He had lunged forward to throw himself in front of Beth as Tilly had fired and had taken a musket ball in his chest.

'Help me, help me,' I screamed, as I tore at his clothes trying to get to his bare skin. Hands lifted and pulled me away while Farmer Elwood and Billy saw to Wilf's wound. I remember catching sight of the minister backing away from us all, as if we were the devil come to life in his church.

Beth and I were carried out bodily and put in the carriage, which returned to South Farm at great speed with those of the remaining congregation who were on horseback surrounding us. Cecilia held me, trying to soothe, reassuring me that Wilf would be in good hands and a doctor had been sent for.

Beth was wailing loudly, unsure of what had happened, terrified by all the blackening sticky stuff spoiling her pretty dress, and crying out for Wilf, left lying on the cold floor of the church. The shock was too much. I collapsed, harrowed by the fact and speed of such violence on our happiest day. I fainted away, all the while hearing Cecilia's voice and Beth's cries as they receded into darkness.

Later, I rallied when someone burned a feather under my nose. I found myself surrounded by friends with Beth clinging desperately to me, sobbing piteously.

'Wilf?' I whispered, as I remembered.

'He lives,' said Farmer Elwood. 'His injuries are severe, but the doctor has hope. He is comfortable but unconscious.'

'Dr. Grieve?' I asked, my spirits suddenly leaping.

'We don't know where he is, Esther, but the new man seems to be capable.'

I wasn't reassured and started to cry.

'What are his injuries?' I asked, even though I had seen the mess that was his chest.

'One gunshot to the chest area. The ball has been taken out and every effort has been made to stop the bleeding. He is a strong man, Esther, he has every chance, and the doctor was soon there to stem the wound. Luckily Billy found the new man at Dr. Grieve's home.'

I remembered the wife's dirty cap and had no confidence in the man. Where was Dr. Grieve, just when I needed him most?

Chapter Eight

*A few weeks ago, a midwife stood in the pillory, at VIENNA
she having been convicted of drowning several new-born infants,
and Embezzling the money entrusted to her for procuring them
a reception at the Foundling Hospital of that city. She is to be
imprisoned for Life, and will receive 100 lashes annually.*
Sussex Weekly Advertiser and Lewes Journal 1750/1806

We were locked into a living nightmare. Wilf was carried from the church on a table found in the vestry and removed to Farmer Elwood's home. Men from the farm carried him with props slotted through the runners and it must have been a hard task, for he was a stocky man and it was a fair way to the farm on foot. I did what I could for him after pulling myself together. Gradually, he seemed to rally, and I asked that we be allowed to move to our new cottage where I could focus on bringing him back to health. Cecilia wanted Beth to remain with Freddie in his nursery, allowing us time to ourselves and not to be subjected to the privations of a sick room. I reluctantly agreed, despite not wanting to be separated after having so nearly lost her. Cecilia pointed out that my aunt had not been caught and would remain a threat to Beth.

'She will be safer with us than with you, Esther,' she said.

Once again Wilf was carried on his church table to our cottage. I made him comfortable downstairs by the fire. I was unable to bring our own bed down to him, so the table was used as a makeshift sickbed, and with help, I lifted him, unconscious, and slid a pallet and linen beneath him. I nursed him to the best of my ability, never leaving, constantly turning, cleaning, feeding, trying everything that might help bring him back to full consciousness. I used every herb and every skill I had ever learned: herbs to clot the blood, herbs to knit bone and herbs to restore vitality. I scoured my pa's notes for any scrap of knowledge that I might have forgotten.

Days passed and Wilf regained consciousness but never really engaged again with those of us who loved him. On one of the few occasions when he struggled to speak, he mumbled, 'They got me pa and now they've got me.' I tried to make him believe that he had every chance of regaining his health, but he had lost heart, while the pain and infections that set in and got control reduced him to skin and bone as his life ebbed away. I brought Beth to see him towards the end and he touched her briefly as he smiled at me. Wilf died four weeks after we were married. He fell asleep, his breath rasping in his chest and gradually slowing until he drew no more. I sat with his body for a long time; even in death I didn't want to share him. We had never been together as man and wife. How I regretted now that I had not loved him properly before our marriage.

After the funeral, which was attended by all the farming families and their workers, Farmer Elwood hosted a wake for Wilf. Hundreds of people came, many of them staring at me and Beth, probably wondering how much more trouble I could bring to this place. I was grateful to everyone who honoured my husband, but I just wanted to go home to our little cottage where we could have been happy. During the wake, I was approached by a constable from the town and told that my aunt had melted into the countryside and no one knew where she was. The town was in uproar at this further atrocity from her and I was reassured that it was only a matter of time before she was taken. An even larger reward was being offered for her capture which was probably the only hope of getting her back in court, this time for murder.

During the many lonely nights that were to follow I would cast my mind back to the time when Beth and I were in Southease Church for another wedding, albeit one forced upon me. Twice I had been taken to the altar, twice Beth and I had been the victims of violence, and twice men had died. My cousins shot down by the preventative men and soldiers, and now, my lovely Wilf, another victim of my accursed life. Would there never be an end to it?

Part Two

Chapter Nine

A kitchen, near the market house in this town (Lewes) was on Wednesday left open for the sale of cheap soup, and several hundred messes of a pint and a half each, at 1 penny per mess, were disposed of and gave general satisfaction. The above kitchen, we understand, is to be open for the sale of soup to all the inhabitants of the Borough, the Cliff and South Malling, on every Wednesday and Saturday,

Sussex Weekly Advertiser and Lewes Journal 1750/1806

Beth and I did our best to make a home in the cottage after Wilf died but I feared it could not last long. As his agent's tied cottage, the place was far too large and important to Farmer Elwood. No matter, I carried on as if it were our permanent home. What else could I do? I had no money coming in, just some small savings, though I had found some coins that Wilf had secreted away. Even with these, I knew it wouldn't last long. I asked Farmer Elwood if I was entitled to it, as I was Wilf's widow. He reassured me that there was no-one else who should benefit; he suggested I keep it and sell anything that might raise some funds for us. He offered to put any money that was over our daily needs into the farm safe, which I was glad to take advantage of. My spirits were low, and I thought my existence threadbare, but I tried to keep this to myself; it was only in the late evening when Beth had been put to bed that I indulged in the misery that followed our loss.

As the nights darkened and the season ground towards its autumn finale I often felt cold and desolate. At times, I laid my head upon the table instead of going to our bed to sleep. I was comforted knowing that Wilf's essence was there, embodying all that was left of him; and if it was what I needed to console me, then so be it. The table top was made up of three flat, broad planks, such as would have come from an oak tree. It was a rich mellow brown and scarred with chips and digs as well as tankard marks. The stretchers were worn with use and I wondered if it had come originally from a public house and - as it was clearly very old - what life it had seen before Wilf breathed his last on it. In a moment of weakness, I told Cecilia about the table and how I felt that it had something of Wilf in it and that it gave me comfort. She seemed shocked by my revelation and I could see she was concerned for my state of mind. I felt the same about the table as I did about Becca's comb.

I missed Dr. Grieve and the society of Mr. and Mrs. Jenkins. As I no longer needed Flossy for work, Farmer Elwood had put her back amongst his other horses and when I went to the stables at South Farm, she was often absent, so I missed her too. I missed the patients who made up Dr. Grieve's workload: some were healthy but thought themselves ill; others were poorly but thought themselves well. Even the fashionable ladies who came because they had little else to do and wanted a man like him to admire them, I missed them too. I couldn't see a future for myself and I sometimes wondered if I should try and contact Dr. Grieve and accept his offer of 'closest companion'. At least I would have security for me and Beth, housing and work, I thought bitterly. What good had my chastity and good name done me? I was beginning to know through my own painful situation that women sometimes need to tread many paths to feed and protect their children, maybe some not to their liking or choice. Why should I think I was different? The approval of society doesn't put food on the table and it was not my place to look down on those women who have been driven by circumstance to do what was necessary to survive. I could imagine that I might yet become one of them.

One late October day, I made my way, on foot, to Mrs. Makepiece's. I had heard that Mr. and Mrs. Jenkins were taking tea there and had asked me to join them all. I was feeling particularly low because Cecilia had told me that the letter Farmer Elwood had sent to an address in Venice for Dr. Grieve had been returned marked as 'unknown'. She thought that he had either not arrived or changed his mind about going there and assured me that the letter would be sent out again to the other addresses that he had given her husband. She looked a little crestfallen at giving me this news, but she had no idea that the doctor and I had parted so awkwardly, so I had to pretend a disappointment to match her own. It was only later that I realised how downcast it actually made me.

Mrs. Makepiece had made a lardy cake and we all took tea - I didn't ask where it had come from and the information wasn't volunteered. We talked about the town news before Mrs. Jenkins pulled me to one side and confided in a low voice that she had a parcel for me and that I wasn't to open it until I was at home. She told me that she had been approached by the new doctor's wife, Mrs. Crabbe, and that I was to take any parcels that she might send me by Mrs. Jenkins, read the content and return them as soon as possible. I was dumbfounded that this woman, whom I barely knew and had judged so harshly was prepared to help me in going against her husband's direct wishes, and such a husband at that, a bully and mean-spirited man if ever I saw one. The documents were all relating to health matters that I might have an interest in when I try and resume my nursing. I felt humbled that someone would put herself at risk for me, and that Mrs. Jenkins would agree to act as a go-between and thereby risk her own livelihood.

When I got home and had put Beth to bed I sat by the light of a precious candle and read every single word and, where I was unclear of meaning, I copied whole sentences for later study. I read a treatise on infection and how to minimise risk, as well as case studies of midwifery and reasoned arguments between physicians in the form of letters. Oh, how it lifted me up. I ventured to hope that my worst had come and gone, and I could climb out of this despondency and get on with a meaningful life, a life of nursing. All my ideas about establishing a cottage with accommodation for lying-in mothers who were medically unfit to have their babies alone in their own homes would have to wait; probably for years, if at all, but at least I could offer support in their homes. My care would be better care than the old women, those 'Mother Midnights', who still did their worst with their dirty manners, hands and clothes; these same old women who might have just returned from laying out a diseased body. There were two of them in our area and their ways filled me with horror. One woman I heard of regularly in Lewes drank heavily and encouraged her expectant mother to do so as well, almost to the point of insensibility. She was often seen to lay out the dead and then move straight on to pull an infant from its mother. She was rough in her handling and her fingers grimed with muck and human soil. Dr. Grieve, in his role as Coroner, had done his best to drive such women away from birthing. He regularly saw the results on his examination table when called upon to pass judgement on the death of mother or child or, tragically, both.

On that first night, after I had packaged up the papers and slipped a tiny tablet of pressed rosemary soap in amongst them, I went to my bed and slept soundly for the first time since Wilf had died. Mrs. Jenkins told me later that she had come to admire the little woman who was Mrs. Crabbe. She did not go into detail, but it appeared that the doctor's wife took every opportunity to counteract her husband's dictatorial ways; her nervous energy was turned to mending and healing relationships that suffered under his arch manner. He was courteous enough in attitude to his paying patients, so very few realised how objectionable he could be to his own household. I thanked heaven for Mrs. Crabbe and was pleased to think of her as my friend. When I returned the papers to Mrs. Jenkins, I always included a little unsigned note and, on occasions, a homemade gift of lip salve or more scented soap. Beth and I had often pressed flowers in the summer and it pleased me to pass on to her one of these tokens of happier days.

Another little incident occurred that very same week which, initially, frightened me badly but once I had thought it through, also lifted my spirits. I had been dusting Wilf's table when I happened to glance out of the open door. I thought I saw a movement where there were only low bushes. I was terrified for a moment but made myself go outside and look around. I was greatly relieved when I saw it was only a young lad, hiding behind a hawthorn.

'Hello,' I called, 'are you looking for me?'

The lad stepped out into the sunlight and I gasped as I realised it was the youngest Coad boy. Our paths had crossed twice in recent times and it had been down to him that I was rescued from the forced wedding to my cousin Sam: he had warned Wilf and Billy-alone what was happening. I hadn't seen him since but knew he wouldn't want any acknowledgement of his part in my escape; he would be too fearful of retribution from his father and brothers should his actions become known. We stood looking at each other and neither of us said a word. His clothing was stout and looked like it had been handed down from one much bigger than he. I could see that he was well nourished if on the small side. His eyes lifted from the ground and met mine directly as he finally spoke, 'The little gel, she be well, then?'

'Beth?' I said, thinking carefully for a moment before adding, 'Your sister. Yes, she is well and not too much troubled by what happened. Children forget easily. She never understood what was going on at the time, though she still asks when Wilf is coming back. She is visiting friends today.'

'Aye, I thought she weren't about, I ain't seen her awhile.'

I didn't ask where he would have seen her and wondered if he spied on us. Somehow, I couldn't see the same malice in him that his brothers had. I waited for him to say something else or leave.

'Best to take care o' little 'un. There be people about might want to do her harm, like.'

I felt a sharp stab of fear. 'My aunt, you mean. Do you know where she is, then? Is she still around here?'

His eyes slid away from me. 'I don' know nothink,' he said, 'but you should watch out, she might be about.'

He turned away and disappeared as quietly as he had come, leaving me bewildered but grateful; for whatever else I might think of his family, he had given me a clear warning and I would continue to ensure that Beth's safety was kept at the front of my mind. My aunt knew no mercy where I was concerned and hurting Beth would be her vengeful justice on me. She had tried once, who knew if she would again? Beth's little life had been saved by Wilf's actions on our wedding day and I didn't forget it.

Perhaps there was some good in the youngest boy and though I couldn't quite bring myself to name him, he seemed drawn to Beth and concerned for her as his half-sister. It was unlikely that either of the other two boys felt the same way; they were vicious if past memory was resurrected. I tried to recall the events at Coad Farm – who had done what, who led, who was the instigator of all the little cruelties. I couldn't remember the details, but I knew it was always the eldest two I was most afeared of, though Becca, Beth's mother, mocked their ways and belittled them. Their father encouraged her and it all created such a poisonous atmosphere at the farm that I still shuddered at the memory.

Chapter Ten

When Cecilia sent a message asking me to come and take tea with her at South Farm I sensed that there was something afoot. Beth had been with Freddie for the day and Mrs. Fisher was giving both children some bread and scrape when I arrived, so I ran up to Cecilia's sitting room where she was making our tea. Some tiny gooseberry pastries were waiting to be eaten and I suddenly realised how hungry I was. I hadn't really had a good appetite for months but today was different, I could eat. Perhaps, at last, I was coming out of my low mood.

'Is something wrong, Cecilia?' I asked. Her hand was trembling as she held the delicate teapot.

'Not wrong, Esther, but difficult.'

'Is it the cottage, you need the cottage back?'

'Yes, I am afraid so. We don't want to do this, but we need it for the new agent.' She looked up at me sadly. 'I am so sorry, Esther, but it goes with the job and John has employed a new man. He has a wife and children and that cottage is the only one big enough for them.'

I turned my face aside so she wouldn't see my tears. 'When will they be moving in, when do we have to leave?'

'I have a plan and if you will listen to me for a few minutes,' she said, 'we might be able to resolve the problem of your home, your work and some wages for you.'

Bleakly, I nodded, not seeing how anything good could come out of this news.

'John is quite happy for you to take one of the smaller cottages on the farm, but I think I have found a better solution. I would like you to come and live here, not as you did before but as our governess and nurse, a paid position,' she emphasised. 'We want you near us, Esther. You have such skills and kindness that we would like you to take on the task of helping me care for Freddie, and Beth, of course, and perhaps, if God is willing, another little one. We would find accommodation for you and pay you a wage as well as providing all your food and needs. I have had a good look round the house and there are quarters off the kitchen and still room that are barely used which could be turned into a home for you both. We could make a cosy sitting room, a separate bedroom for you and Beth, and there is even a small area where you could store all your herbs and books. You already use the kitchen and still room and Mrs. Fisher will not feel put out at your presence in her domain.'

Cecilia was younger than me by some years, yet she had the aura and the authority of her status that made her seem far my senior; yet I still remembered her as that desperate childlike woman who had contemplated ending her life when her first baby died. But, here we were together, friends and at times accomplices. I knew she had my needs at heart and it would be ungracious of me to feel bitter at this latest turn of events. The cottage was the last place that united me and Wilf and to lose it was a dreadful blow, even though I had known it was likely. Her little hand reached out to me and I gripped it in mine as tears fell, unbidden, onto my lap.

'I'm sorry, Cecilia, I don't mean to seem ungrateful...'

'I understand, Esther, it was to be your home with Wilf, of course you are sad,' she said, 'John and I realise how painful this must be for you, but we need to make changes and this little plan of mine has so many possibilities for you and Beth. There is your safety to think of, some wages, Flossy - I have asked John that you have Flossy returned to you - and you can still do some nursing outside our home when you have time, though Freddie must come first,' she went on, warming to her theme. 'We will make a schoolroom up in the nursery for them both to do some work and play. Freddie will need to know his letters and Beth can join in too with everything he does. In due course, he will have to go to school in Lewes before he is prepared for whatever role we think fit - that might be one of the great colleges, or medicine, or law, though I pray not the army. Let us go and explore the rooms that I have in mind for you and we can talk about furnishings as well as plans for your future.'

I nodded vigorously, determined to shake off this misery. I just needed to think but already there was a sense of relief that we would have a home, whatever else transpired.

'Shall we eat these tarts first?' I said. 'I'm getting my appetite back and we don't want to upset Mrs. Fisher.'

She laughed, and I managed a small smile as I took one of the little pastries.

'Before we look around, Cecilia,' I said, 'do you think we could talk about the other option, the possibility of me having one of the small farm cottages?'

'We will discuss every option available, Esther, but for the time being let's finish our tea and then go and explore this house.'

I had thought I was quite familiar with South Farm but had no idea that there were so many rooms, all beautifully furnished, and though many were not used daily, they could be opened at need. Clearly, Farmer Elwood's family had entertained a great deal and money had been available to create such fine furnishings. Cecilia told me a little of the history as we went from room to room. In fact, the place that I called South Farm was a manor, not a farmhouse as I had carelessly named it. It was rather old and quaint in places but had been added to in recent years, particularly to accommodate the growing farm into which Farmer Elwood poured his energies and passion. He was perhaps, according to Cecilia, a little unusual in being a gentleman farmer who was also involved with every aspect of the farm's daily working. He had shown that he was prepared to get his hands dirty, which earned him the respect of his employees and he was a practical man despite being a gentleman of the first order.

When we finally made our way to the servants' work quarters, we walked down a passage off the still room which I had always assumed led to a series of rooms for storage;

and, essentially, that is what they were, but with some finer features than you would expect. The first room we entered was quite large and would be well-lit if the windows were cleaned. There was a deep fireplace with a huge beam across that showed it to have been a kitchen at some point. On either side there were cupboards and inside the fireplace lots of hooks and old-fashioned utensils hanging amongst the soot and cobwebs. I couldn't help being excited at the sight of such a beautiful space where I could do so much drying and preserving of fruits and herbs. The floor was dirty, having been trod by many working men's boots, but underneath the mud and dust were flags, old and uneven in places, but whole and easily cleanable.

'I wonder how long ago this was used as a kitchen?' I spoke aloud.

'John says not in his lifetime and he wasn't even aware that it had been a kitchen – he would have had no reason to come down here at any time. Come, let's go through and see the adjoining room; I thought this would make a lovely bedroom for you and Beth,' Cecilia held out her hand to me as we pushed through a creaky old door into a similar room, but without the great fireplace.

'I think this might have been the upper servants' eating quarters in the past,' she reflected. 'We know there were a great many staff in the time of John's grandfather and they would all have had to be fed.'

I tried to open one of the windows; it was very small and had unusual glass between the leads.

'I think this must be very old, Cecilia.'

'Possibly - but the area doesn't feel disheartened or tired, does it? It is dry and would be warm if the fire were lit, and the room size is far bigger than you would have at any of our cottages. With some cleaning and your furnishings, why it would soon be homely, and you wouldn't be forced to remember the tragedy of Wilf, as I am sure you do every time you enter the cottage.' She looked questioningly at me before saying, 'Anyway, before you decide, look in here.' I followed her into another room and though it was quite small it had shelves all around the walls with a heavy wooden slab table in the centre on which were more bowls and utensils,

'Perhaps this was a scullery,' I mused, fascinated by the soft, worn texture of the wooden bowls which I couldn't resist sniffing. 'Oh, Cecy, these are wonderful, and the room is perfect.'

She laughed. 'Now you can see why I wanted you to consider our offer, Essie my dear. I think you would love it here and it is big enough for your wonderful carved bed and even the table, should you wish to keep it. The minister is very approachable, and I am sure he would be happy to take it back or let you have it - we are, as you know, parishioners of his church and have made some generous donations in recent years; samplers, plate, and so on - and recently John bestowed some candlesticks in memory of his parents. I don't think he would create any difficulties as to ownership, though you would have to go and see him.' Cecilia turned to me, gripping my hands, her enthusiasm lighting up her eyes before she said, 'Would you like to think it all over and then we can sort out the details, hours of work, tasks, wages - and if you want to consider one of the small cottages, we can do that too. However, I am concerned for your safety and most of the cottages are in isolated places. I know you will think of Beth when deciding.'

I nodded, knowing that the decision was already made, but I had to see what the arrangements would mean to me in terms of outside nursing; I couldn't give it up.

'Whatever would I do without you?' I said.

Chapter Eleven

Job Advert for Uckfield area

Wanted a housekeeper, properly qualified for A Gentleman's service, that can come well recommended, and not under 40 years of age. Wages ten pounds per year.

Sussex Weekly Advertiser and Lewes Journal 1750/1806

It was all decided. We would move into our new home as soon as it was clean. Cecilia told Billy-alone and one of the stable lads to scrub and freshen the walls and floor but not before the chimney had been swept. Years of soot tumbled onto the hearth, rising in a cloud of murky dust and causing a great spluttering and coughing. Once it had all settled, I went to poke around in the rubbish that had fallen. There were the remnants of nests, an old tiny shoe, insects, spiders and lots of small bones. I was thankful I wasn't doing the clean-up myself, but provided instead a steady supply of drinks and pies for the lads. I took all the old utensils into the still room to wash them thoroughly and see if any were still useful. Beth stood on a stool and helped me dry them before we re-hung them in Mrs. Fisher's kitchen to dry more thoroughly. It was all greatly enjoyable, particularly as the weather was still fine, and everyone in the household either joined in or offered their opinion.

I took it on myself to approach the minister to see whether he wanted Wilf's table back. After all, it had come from his church and was taken without even a by-your-leave. He didn't want it back; far from it, I think he felt it to be tainted and not clean enough for his fine church. He didn't commiserate with my loss or want to talk about the terrible ending to my wedding; he wanted me to leave as soon as possible. Clearly, Cecilia's patronage did not extend to me. I didn't care - I had the table and it made me happy as it connected me to Wilf. I wondered if his attitude to me was because of the troubles that always seemed to follow behind me or because I was too lowly to be welcomed in his well-endowed church. Neither situation seemed very Christian.

The day Beth and I moved in was exciting. We rose early and though the sky was leaden and sulky it didn't feel oppressive. We lit a great fire, and with Billy and Cilla to help, as well as some of the stable lads, we gathered all our bits and pieces: the curtains, the bed (which we had had to dismantle), the lovely spread I had made for it, the table and the contents of my bottom drawer – linens, some bits of china, my pa's apothecary books, my ma's receipts, my own nursing notes and pamphlets that Dr. Grieve had given me. I had kept Wilf's clothes and tools; they were so precious to me and I'd decided not to sell them unless I was desperate. There were also jars of herbs, dried and bottled, as well as fresh from the garden we were leaving. I had some sacks of grasses including lavender and ladies' bedstraw to keep things fresh. And finally, a jug of late daisies placed on the table to make it all look like home.

I had put by some apples for storing; they had a lovely smell which would develop more as the months crept by. I put them in a row on one of the shelves in the little scullery which was not too warm, but neither was it freezing: perfect conditions for storage. Wilf and I had enjoyed making a garden at the cottage for vegetables as well as my herbs and a few flowers, so I was planning to ask Cecilia if I could have a little corner of her kitchen garden for myself. The head gardener was very friendly and I was confident he wouldn't object, especially as our produce would be different from his. He was a curious man and we had many conversations about when and where to plant and how to fight the battle of the bugs that wanted our food for themselves. He was a mine of information on planting produce or flowers that worked together to discourage pests; I wanted to know more from him.

I spent a good deal of time cleaning the agent's cottage for the new family. They were to visit shortly to see their home and I wanted them to know that this place had been loved and wasn't just the aftermath of a tragic event. I left a small pitcher of dried flowers and a gift of sweet-smelling soap wrapped in brown paper with a tie of pink ribbon. Beth tucked one of her own dried roses from Cecilia's garden into the ribbon, crowing with delight at the pretty display. 'Oh, Beth, you are your mama's daughter. Becca so loved pretty things and you are as lovely as she was,' I murmured into her soft hair.

At long last the day was done. We had many visits from everyone who lived or worked on the farm coming along to help or just see how we were getting on. Cecilia and Freddie came down and applauded all our efforts and finally, exhausted, we went into Mrs. Fisher's kitchen to have a light meal before we fell thankfully into our lovely bed. Beth was snuggled tight into me and I lay for a long time just thinking. Though it was still a wrench to leave the cottage in which we had planned for so many of our hopes and dreams, I found I wasn't unhappy or cast down. This was a new beginning and my heart was lighter than it had been in an age; I would make the most of this opportunity and not allow the past to lower my spirits. It was with this thought that I finally managed to fall into a dreamless sleep.

The next day we woke to a newly-risen sun peeping through the rippled glass and picking out dust motes fluttering in a draught of cold air. Beth scampered out of bed looking for her woollen slippers and I flung a wrap around my shoulders. The day was crisp and had its own peculiar vitality as we scurried around lighting the great fire and laying the table for our breakfast. I had some oatcakes put by and though we could go into the house and have breakfast in the kitchens with Cilla and the housemaids, I wanted us to get into the habit of being alone together before the needs of the family took over.

Chapter Twelve

Christmas 1796

*Last week was the greatest snow in the East part of this County
that ever was known, it being in several places twelve feet deep but
in the West part was not shoe deep.*
Sussex Weekly Advertiser and Lewes Journal 1750/1806

Beth took to calling our new home the shoe house, after the shoe that fell down the chimney, and we settled in very quickly; so much so, that Bonfire Night and Christmas came and went without us noticing much. We spent Christmas as before, decorating the main house with evergreen plants and mistletoe. I had a store of old man's beard and wove it amongst the greenery. We also decorated the biggest of our own rooms, but not the other two. On Christmas Eve, we joined with all the servants as well as Cecilia, Freddie and Farmer Elwood to welcome the carol singers. I didn't want to go to the church on Christmas Day. There were too many painful memories and it might remind Beth of Wilf's shooting, which thankfully she seemed to have forgotten, or at least never mentioned. We stayed at home and watched over all the food being prepared for the Christmas festivities.

We spent most of our family time with Freddie and Cecilia who was expecting another baby in the coming year.

Her pregnancy was, as previously, full of nausea, and as well as looking after Freddie and Beth, I was able to help her endure the worst of it with some home-concocted drinks and herbal remedies. Occasionally I was able to help with women whose babies were due. It was all a case of managing time to meet everyone's needs, including my own.

Farmer Elwood was often from home now. He had many civic calls on his time as well as helping the new farm agent, Mr. Harvey, settle into his role - taking on the everyday tasks that Wilf had been so familiar with. I felt rather sorry for him at times as it was a big estate with lots of property as well as the animals and produce. Wilf and his father were both born into it which had helped them enormously.

Cecilia told me that they didn't expect the new family to be fully absorbed for at least a year, which put a lot of pressure on Farmer Elwood. Some good news was that Billy-alone had been taken on full-time and he was able to help things along with his wide knowledge of local families and who was likely to work hard if extra labour was required. Some families were shiftless and lazy and would put up a good act for the first day but then drop away. Billy knew all about them and would be able to guide Mr. Harvey. I was thrilled for him and hoped that this raising up from orphan parish lad who had run away from the workhouse, to farm labourer with special responsibility to help Mr. Harvey was what was needed to secure his future and perhaps, one day, make a marriage with Cilla. Their courtship was now official, as Billy had approached her father and secured his approval, though only after he got the job. Billy was such a good, kind boy and he still lived with and helped Miss Wardle with the piggies. Neither of us had forgotten how she took him in after being beaten by the Coad boys when he was searching the river for Becca's makeshift cradle. His help in clearing me of the charge of murder would never leave me and I regarded him as my dearest friend, alongside Cecilia, despite our difference in age.

There was still much unrest in the town and nearby villages as the price of grain was high, and though unscrupulous bakers had been discouraged from selling light bread by the threat of prosecution or violent reprisal, people still couldn't afford to feed their families. Starvation was a constant threat to many, particularly those from Cliffe. As had happened before, in times of need, a local solution was undertaken by families who had the means and the goodwill. A parish soup kitchen was a great success and both Mrs. Makepiece and the Elwoods supported it with work or produce.

I found myself too busy with the children, Cecilia's pregnancy and generally making myself useful, to help with the business of feeding the hungry of Lewes and Cliffe as well as Malling. I did hear of many women who trudged from the outlying hamlets to join the queue, and though they might not have been of the parish, some of the kindly townspeople didn't have the heart to turn them away. Messes of soup went to many districts, albeit unofficially, while those who were charged with overseeing the distribution had their backs turned.

Poaching was on the increase again and some landowners came down hard on anyone caught stealing rabbits, hare or bigger game; the local court was full of men who had succumbed to the wrong side of the law. There was very little sympathy on the part of the local magistrates - often whose land it was they had poached from.

★★★

Settling into my new role at South Farm proved harder than I expected, though I still had Mary-Jane to help me. Cecilia was fragile in her pregnancy and needed much care, especially as Farmer Elwood was constantly wanted on the farm or in Lewes and Brighthelmstone. His property didn't look after itself and he had to contend with some rascally tenants who treated his houses neglectfully before running away, leaving overdue rents unpaid. He was a good man but his patience was greatly tried by having to take on the burden of work that Wilf had done so easily.

Mr. Harvey, the new man, was a fine fellow but his wife caused some problems with her nagging demands. I tried to help and often mediated between the man and his wife which wasn't a pleasant thing. There were three youngsters who were all promising children but the atmosphere of resentful bitterness did not help to promote harmony in the family. I suggested to Mr. Harvey that it might be an idea to put the eldest out to be a kitchen maid at one of the neighbouring properties and remove her from her mother's influence. Mrs. Harvey clearly realised that this suggestion had been mine and I got the back end of her tongue when next I visited as she thought the daughter, Polly, ought to be her housemaid. Poor Polly, I thought, but with one thing and another then forgot all about it. Some months after they moved in, I met the unfortunate girl out in the fields when visiting the young lambs with Freddie and Beth.

She approached me shyly. 'Ma'am, can I 'ave a word?'

'Aye, but you may call me Esther.'

'Sorry, ma'am, Esther,' she said. 'I do wonder if you could try and get me ma to let me go? I will work anywhere you think best but not at 'ome. Me ma, she ain't reasonable and she takes out her anger at pa on me.'

'What about your brother and sister, Polly, how is she with they?' I asked.

'That's the strange thing, she be all cheery with they, but not me.'

'Why do you think that is? Is it because you are older?'

'I dunno, she never was cheery with me as far back as I can remember. I think she blames me for 'aving to marry pa all 'em years back.'

'I don't know if I can do anything, Polly. Your ma don't like me much and anything I suggest would probably go down badly on you.'

'Aye, but if you asked the master,' she persisted, 'he could make it 'appen and she won't be able to do nothink 'bout it, would she?'

I laughed. This girl had a head on her shoulders and a nice manner, despite her mother. 'I'll think on it, Polly, and if I can find a way, I'll speak up for you. But won't your pa miss you?'

'Aye, 'e will that, but it will remove another thorn from his side if ma weren't constantly moaning 'bout me and he wantin' to defend me.'

Freddie and Beth had had enough of the lambs and it wasn't warm enough to sit about outside, so we made our way back towards the house. The going was slow as Freddie's little legs were not ready for long walks. I picked him up and jogged him up and down on my back to screams of delight, with Beth racing around shrieking with laughter.

It was wonderful being able to play with little ones all day long and most of the time I was content.

Part of my duties were to get the children to bed at a reasonable hour. Cecilia wanted time to spend with her husband and the evenings were when she felt most capable, so I endeavoured to build a pattern into our lives that would work for her, but this left me with long evenings alone. I was still getting the periodicals from Mrs. Crabbe, but it didn't take long to read them and take notes if needed. As the evenings grew lighter, I could take Flossy to visit Mrs. Makepiece and it was to her that I told Polly's story, adding that I knew what it was like to work for someone who did nothing but find fault.

'I am surprised at you, Esther, for not thinking of Miss Wardle,' she said. 'Since Billy-alone spends most of his time at South Farm now, she is struggling, and she is not getting any younger. If this girl, Polly, is handy and can see to the piggies as well, then it would suit everyone.'

I thought on it before replying, 'Farmer Elwood has a lot on his plate, I'm not sure he will want to interfere with his agent's household arrangements. My earlier suggestion was not well received by the wife.

'Nonsense,' she scoffed, 'he is the master. He will have so many issues, one more won't make any difference, and this is such a little request. Get Cecilia to talk to him. Now, shall we take a drop of something in our tea, dear?'

I turned it all over and decided to talk to Cecilia when she was feeling brighter, which occurred the very next day. Once I had explained about the poor girl's predicament and her thoughts as to why she was put upon at home, Cecilia agreed that we might do something to help her and, indirectly, her pa.

Cecilia was dandling Freddie on her knee as Beth crawled under my chair. We were up in the nursery and as the bright sunshine filtered in I couldn't help thinking how easy and pleasant my life was nowadays despite the loss of Wilf and my work. But Polly's predicament had brought back memories of our troubles at Coad Farm and the spiteful bullying attitude of the farmer's wife. I really hoped Cecilia and Farmer Elwood could help her.

'I'll talk to John,' Cecilia said. 'I'll wait until after he has had his brandy and is comfortable. I know he likes Mr. Harvey, so he will probably agree to do anything that makes his home life more palatable. Anyway, we have nothing to lose. If the woman is that much of a tartar then nothing we do will make her worse.'

'She probably won't want Polly taken,' I warned, 'because then she will have to do her own housework - the other girl is too young.'

'Well, who does she think she is? Her husband is a working farm agent, isn't he, not a gentleman? He's just one step up from the labouring classes. She should be doing her own housework. I think she must be downright lazy.'

'Aye, you are probably right,' I said, and couldn't help smiling at Cecilia's emphatic definition of the labouring-class structure. 'She might think she is better than she is, because her husband has got on.'

'Well, we had better put her in her place before she gets too carried away with her self-regard and delusions. Leave it with me.'

When I snuggled into bed later, I found myself giggling that once Cecilia made up her mind, Farmer Elwood would do what she wanted - he would do anything for his young wife, even if he grumbled at being 'pushed around by women'.

Polly started working for Miss Wardle within a month and could live in, but Billy continued to visit his piggies, so she did not have so very much to do in that line. Mr. Harvey didn't look any happier when I saw him about the place but at least the poor girl was better off, and she had the occasional afternoon to visit her pa and the younger children. Every time I bumped into Mrs. Harvey, she would look at the ground and just mutter an acknowledgement. On occasion, I had to visit the cottage and it was a sorry looking place now. Gone were the bright clean windows and the pretty flowers; the whole place looked forlorn and dingy, as did the two youngest children. But they were not my problem; at least I had done my best by Polly.

Chapter Thirteen

1797

*Wednesday last as a woman was cleaning out an empty
uninhabitable house in Lewen's Mead*

*In a coalhouse, she found a basket filled with sawdust and sand
and in it the body of a female child, supposed to be about five or
six months old, with its head and right arm cut off. The arm under
it's back and the head upon its breast. The head was perished and
the toes rotted off.*

Sussex Weekly Advertiser and Lewes Journal 1750/1806

Mrs. Makepiece had asked me to call upon a young woman whom she knows, and I set out with Flossy as my companion. Beth and Freddie were both fast asleep in the nursery with Mary-Jane keeping an eye on them. Cecilia and Farmer Elwood were having a leisurely meal together and knew that I had gone out to see this woman, Eliza, who was of good family but in straitened circumstances. We made our way to Cliffe and beyond the bridge. It was a long time since I had been down there, and I looked round curiously to see if the area had come up at all. It stank as much as I remembered, but then so do most towns. I couldn't help thinking that if I had the management of this place I would do something about the muck in the road, particularly as there was a great tidal river full of water nearby to wash it all away!

Eliza was but seven months gone and after I examined her I could pronounce that the baby had a good heartbeat and was positioned right for her time. Her home was sparse of comfort, but it was clean and well-kept, so I gave her some general advice about preparing for the little one's arrival and what she might need. I rode away in good spirits, pleased that I had been able to help with settling her worries. She seemed very interested in my work, and I wondered if she might help me in the future. I think that was why Mrs. Makepiece wanted me to visit her.

Since I had begun working for Cecilia, I had been able to save some money and it warmed my heart to think of my little store and begin to dream again that one day I might be able to branch out and have a place of my own with one or two beds for women who needed medical help before their babies were due.

As usual, I constantly looked about me and though dusk hadn't yet fallen, I was wary of anyone on the road I didn't recognise. I could see there was a man yonder near a stand of trees which I usually trotted through as fast as I could. I slowed Flossy to a halt and wondered if I should turn back. I hadn't heard much or seen aught of my aunt since the wedding and I wondered just how long I was going to feel threatened like this. Suddenly, I heard the clatter of hooves behind me and was relieved to see one of Farmer Elwood's friends coming towards me. I pulled off the track to let him come alongside and greeting him loudly I asked to accompany him to the farm.

'Aye, Miss Esther, were you spooked?'

'Aye, it's just I thought I saw someone lurking in the trees yonder and what with the unrest and hunger about it seems better to travel with a companion.'

'Well, you'll be safe with me, girl,' he said, laughing.

As we trotted through the trees, I looked about me but saw no-one and wondered if I had imagined it.

On occasions, when Freddie was busy with Cecilia, I could take Beth to visit her grandpa. We always met at Mrs. Makepiece's and frequently Mrs. Jenkins and Miss Wardle would also be there; so it was when we called one warm day in the late spring. It was beautiful weather and some of the leaves still had that freshly minted look, a busy little breeze causing them to flutter happily. Beth was excited to be riding with me on Flossy who desperately wanted to drop her head and munch the tasty grass. I kicked her into a trot just to keep her from trying to manage me! Once we had taken our cloaks off, my friends resumed the conversation that our arrival had interrupted and, as it was about people I knew and feared, I listened open-mouthed to what they had to tell me.

Mrs. Coad, the farmer's wife, was dead - she who threw Becca out into the night to give birth to her husband's child - and there was some interest in how and why she had died. The man who had taken over Dr. Grieve's responsibilities as coroner had remarked to someone who knew Mrs. Jenkins that her death was due to falling down the stairs. His name escapes me, but he was not of the same ilk as Dr. Crabbe. He had become well-respected in the town and Mrs. Jenkins said that he was concerned that this was no accident but there was not enough evidence to prove otherwise. How people talk! According to Mrs. Jenkins, she was a healthy woman of no very great age, and the question she and others were asking was why would a healthy woman trip down the stairs that she used every day of her life when she had no obvious reason to fall?

I asked if the gossiping would have been so great if there hadn't already been one dreadful event relating to that family - Becca's suicide. They all looked at me and said nothing.

I also asked when the funeral was and where. Apparently, this 'accident' had occurred two days ago and once the coroner was satisfied with the cause, the funeral would take place very quickly as the spring temperatures were rising. I shuddered at the thought and lost my interest in the day. I didn't stay longer than was strictly polite, and gathering Beth, we made our way home as soon as we could without appearing rude. I hated it that anything relating to that horrible family could throw me instantly back into such a painful sequence of events.

I had no cause to care for Mrs. Coad. I had spent months in their house under her direction and some of that had been no worse than other skivvies experienced. She was always a strict woman but as soon as Farmer Coad became interested in Becca she had changed for the worse and we had all felt her bitterness and anger. I felt conflicted now because I had suffered from gossip myself, most of which was untrue, but I suppose the difference was that I was alive and could still be hurt by it. I resolved not to waste my sympathy on a woman who had treated Becca so very badly. She hadn't *caused* Becca's death, but neither had she shown mercy to a young girl - barely a child herself - who was made pregnant by her husband repeatedly forcing himself upon her.

When Becca's waters broke, Mrs. Coad had just shoved her out into a storm and locked me in our attic bedroom. It still chilled me to the core to think of Becca giving birth alone in Hamsey Church, knowing that she had to get rid of the child if she wanted to keep her position. She had nowhere else to go; her stepmother wouldn't take her in; if she stayed, she was likely to suffer further abuse at the hands of Farmer Coad and his two eldest sons whom I had overheard threatening her. It was in this terrible state of mind that she had given the baby up to the river, putting her in a cradle that she had made from reeds, and then, still weak from the birth, she had drowned herself. Becca had endured months of torment but towards the end she had been swayed in her actions by Farmer Coad reading from the Bible the story of baby Moses being found in the bulrushes. I found Becca's body; it still breaks my heart to think of it. But I had saved her child, Beth, whom I had discovered, still in the cradle, and caught in the reeds. When I look back now on that dreadful day, I wonder if those events determined the beginnings of my desire to become a midwife.

It was just a few days later, and Mrs. Coad must have been put into her coffin by then, that I found the youngest Coad boy hanging around the route that I took to Lewes. I pulled Flossy up and sat looking at him, waiting for him to address me. Once again, he asked, 'How be the little gel?'

'Beth, she is fine, and playing happily with Farmer Elwood's son.' I deliberately mentioned the Elwoods to remind the Coads that we were befriended and protected.

'Me ma is dead.'

'Aye, I heard. Is she buried?'

'Yesterday we put 'er in the ground.'

'I'm sorry,' I said. 'It must be hard for you.'

He nodded and twisted his cap in his hands.

'Did she suffer?' I asked.

'No, they made a tidy job of it.'

I gasped, wondering if he was telling me that she had been deliberately killed.

'I'm sorry,' I said again. After all, whether I liked her or not, she was his mother. 'How have your brothers taken it, and your pa?'

'They don' care, no one cares, 'cept me.' He turned and disappeared through the hedgerow leaving me wondering at what had just happened. Later, when Cecilia and I were alone in her sitting room and discussing the day, I told her about the boy's visits and his strange comment. She was as shocked as I was and thought that I had misunderstood.

'No, I don't think so,' I replied. 'And there is gossip in Lewes that it was an unnatural death. Mrs. Makepiece told me, and Mrs. Jenkins told her, and she got it from someone who knows the replacement coroner.'

'Well, if people were already speculating and the boy suggested that 'they made a good job of it,' it could be true, but who is he talking about?' she asked. 'Surely the brothers and father would not kill her?'

'My first thought was that Aunt Tilly might be involved,' I said with a tremor in my voice. 'We know she is in the neighbourhood and has changed her appearance. What if she has been living at Coad Farm?' I ventured. 'The boy came and warned me to watch out for Beth a while back - he implied she was around. Perhaps Tilly is trying to start up the smuggling here again, and we know that the Coad family was part of the network. Perhaps Mrs. Coad didn't want another woman in her house and made a fuss, then was got rid of?'

'We can't speculate, Esther,' said Cecilia, after a while. 'We don't know anything, really. As you say, we don't know whether Mrs. Coad's death was murder and you can't make a case based on the passing comment of a distressed young boy.'

I didn't sleep well that night.

Chapter Fourteen

Wednesday last a ship belonging to the French King of about 400 tons burthen, loaded with timber, called La Carpe, from Havre degrace to Brest was lost between Burton and Abbotsbury. The Country people, to the number of near 2000 came down with hatchets etc., and cut down all the masts, yards, rigging and sails, broke open the cabin, carried away 5 hogsheads of wine, took all the master's chests, clothes, some silks and linens, barrels of herring and everything they could remove. They are the same fellows that plundered the money ship that came on shore there about 5 months ago.

Sussex Weekly Advertiser and Lewes Journal 1750/1806

No move was made against anyone in relation to Mrs. Coad's untimely death and, as is usually the case, the gossip-mongers soon moved onto fresh fodder. I kept a close eye out for the youngest Coad boy, though; I felt some softening of heart towards him.

One evening, I was alone in our rooms. Beth was sleeping in the nursery with Freddie as he was a bit miserable and wanted her for comfort. Cecilia was well and taking dinner with her husband and several town dignitaries and their wives. I knew they were to discuss the continuing local unrest and I was looking forward to hearing what was likely to happen. There were many advantages to living in such an important household, not all of them obvious! It being a fair evening, I went out to my little patch of garden and settled down to some weed-pulling, and, as often happened, the head gardener appeared and we had some conversation. I felt that he had an interest in me and I was very careful not to give him any reason to think I returned that interest; I had wanted no-one since Wilf. It is difficult to be friendly and not have that friendship taken beyond the bounds of polite behaviour, but I had to tread that thin line, which I seemed to be managing. But who knows what others think within themselves; look at how I had misunderstood Dr. Grieve. I had to keep aloof. Once he had gone - rebuffed but not insulted, I hoped - I sat back, turning over in my mind how my life was developing.

Since Christmas I had been called in or involved in a number of the local women's births. Steadily, I was being entrusted with the most important event in their lives – the birth of their children. I did my utmost to increase their confidence and reduce anxiety and pain. I wasn't always successful but, in those cases, it wasn't an outcome that I could have influenced. Childbirth could be a terrifying process and many women and children died, either during or after. My ladies, and that is what I felt them to be in my heart, all benefited from my care, my knowledge and my efforts to instil cleanliness and reduce infection. Some women started their birthing at a point when I couldn't attend them; but if I was called in prior to the birth, I could ensure that they knew how to make the best of their chances until I could get there. It wasn't ideal, but it was better than putting their trust in a Mother Midnight. One of the ladies, Eliza, had the makings of a sensible helper for me. I had no money available to pay her, but she was a kindly young woman and interested in what I did. She had a supportive family and could leave her own baby with her mother if she was needed. It was good to have a friend with the same interests - I didn't feel quite so alone. I couldn't do what I did though without support at home from Cecilia, practical work from Mary-Jane, and from Cilla who often looked after Freddie and Beth during the evening, the only time I could leave South Farm unless Mary-Jane was there. Between us we never left the children alone; one or two of us were always with them.

Dr. Crabbe's wife continued to assist me with documents and little notes with snippets of information she overheard from her husband. I was under no illusion that she was at risk from the wrath of her odious husband. However, I suspected that she got quite a boost by thwarting him, so I didn't feel too guilty at taking her help. She gave me knowledge, I gave her revenge. I think the same applied to Mrs. Jenkins; they were both important cogs in our little group. It was satisfying to all of us.

My savings towards my own house and beds for mothers had not progressed far as very few of my ladies were able to pay me and I didn't ask. I was surrounded by goodwill in the Lewes area, though; something that I had never experienced before, having been thought an object of notoriety rather than someone who does something useful to help people. It wasn't only the women who valued me; their menfolk, the fathers of the babies, also acknowledged my part in helping their families and it was one such who warned me that I was again in danger. As I sat in the evening sun, a visitor suddenly appeared. It was May Higgins, the young woman who had called me to her ailing mother in North Street. Her ma had sent the girl to me again with a message asking me to visit as soon as I was able, but it wasn't an emergency as last time.

I couldn't go for a day or two, but eventually I made my way to their cottage wondering what the problem could be. I hoped the baby I had delivered was thriving and that the mother wasn't pregnant again. It is my belief that women and their babies thrive better if there is a gap of at least two years between each pregnancy. It was only my opinion.

I knocked at the door and was invited in. Mrs. Higgins was feeding her baby and the smaller children were preparing for bed which involved spreading straw pallets on the floor. The older ones, excepting May, were all doing chores and were preoccupied with their washing for the prisoners in Lewes lockup. They were clearly successful as there was a great deal of clean clothing draped around and over bushes nearby. Some of the washing had great holes in it and the third eldest girl was attempting to sew the rents together, explaining that they got more money if they could do some running repairs. What an industrious family - but again their father was absent.

Mrs. Higgins nodded to me to sit near her and spoke very quietly. 'My Sam is living away, but he sometimes hears things. Mayhap it would be helpful for you to know what he hears?'

Surprised, I answered, 'Aye, tell me?' I was curious how a stranger to me could have information that I would benefit from.

She patted the child's back, winding him. 'He be around, living near - but not with, you understand - a gang of smugglers,' she said, 'and he heard that a woman who is setting up some new routes has been living nearby to Lewes.

She be living with a family, where there be three sons.' She looked up at me to see if I had understood.

Instinctively, I grasped her arm as my stomach lurched at this confirmation of my worst suspicions. 'The Coads?' I whispered.

She nodded. 'This woman has moved in and the missus died, soon after, like. My man wanted you to know. He be grateful what you did for us, he says you should watch your back. It would be best if you was not to tell where you heard this.' There was fear in her eyes as she spoke, and I nodded, both grateful and anxious for this knowledge.

She changed the subject, nodding towards the baby. 'He is doing well, he be that greedy I have trouble keeping 'm fed.'

'Well, if you drink plenty you will have enough milk - the longer he feeds the better for you. Some people think that if you are feeding a baby, you are less likely to fall pregnant again.' I said. 'I don't know if that be true but maybe it is.'

'Aye, I've 'ad enough of babies for now and when my husband comes home from Kent, I does my best to avoid 'im.' She laughed at my look of understanding.

'Your girls be doing well, I see,' I said, getting to my feet. 'I am that glad they have found a way to earn some money.'

'They be good girls and puts all their earnings in the pot, so we can afford some meat on occasion. We get soup from the town and Mrs. Makepiece sometimes brings eggs. We are doing good,' she said with great satisfaction.

I patted her and said, as I took my leave, 'I am grateful to your husband, thank him for me - and I won't talk.'

Once again, I slept uneasily. I wondered whether I should tell people - Farmer Elwood or the constable - what I had heard. But I couldn't say where I had got the information from, so it would all sound a bit far-fetched. I resolved to keep an even closer guard on Beth and perhaps mention it later to Farmer Elwood. At times, I deliberately kept my worries to myself, anxious that if I was too much of a risk to his own family he might ask me to leave. Not many people would have put up with having me in their home.

Chapter Fifteen

On Wednesday last great part of the roof of St. Anne's Church in this town fell in and did great damage to the seats underneath, it was very providential it did not happen on Sunday in time of Divine Service, which if it had must inevitably have killed several people.
Sussex Weekly Advertiser and Lewes Journal 1750/1806

I had been so busy with Cecilia, Freddie and Beth, that I had neglected my herbs. I determined that I would spend the whole day outside in the kitchen garden with the children and try and get some learning into them about plant life and natural things. I wanted to teach them the names of some of my herbs and perhaps, with Beth, explain their uses and at the same time continue my thinning and weeding. Cecilia laughed at me and said that I was overly optimistic about their levels of attention, but I hoped that if I could make it interesting enough, I could combine work and play.

Freddie was a very contented child and would sit and observe much more than Beth who wanted to flutter around like a butterfly. It was a challenge, but we managed the morning this way before I put them both down for their afternoon nap. It was such a precious time and I made the most of it, except that people of the household would keep coming and talking to me. I wished them away as I pulled and replanted, keeping my head down. Finally, Beth came to tell me that Freddie was awake and squalling for me so that was the end of that for the rest of the afternoon. We retired to Cecilia's sitting-room where she could play with Freddie without taxing herself with lifting and carrying him. One of the games they liked best was making little camps with cushions under which they could play 'peep'. How we laughed at Freddie's enjoyment of this robust game. Cecilia told me that as a child she was never allowed to play games such as peep or hide-and-seek. She was expected to sit with her mama for about an hour a day and do needlework or listen to her mama read improving tracts that would instruct her in ladylike behaviour. The only time she played was when she escaped the confines of her mother's attention to accompany her brother to the stables.

'Surely you played with your nurse or your governess?' I asked.

'Everyone was too frightened of mama to misbehave and she had her own maids who would report any wrongdoing. My brother, however, could get away with anything and would never be told to sit and behave.' She sighed sadly. 'Anyway, that time is long gone, and Freddie and our new baby will play as well as learn.'

We sat reflectively watching the children before I said, 'Cecilia, I would like to take the children for a picnic down to the copse. It is in plain sight of the stables, but I think it would be better if we had someone with us. Do you think Billy could come? I don't think he is quite so busy now with lambing at an end?'

'Oh, I am sure they would enjoy that,' she replied. 'I'll ask John. When do you want to go?'

'The day after tomorrow, if the weather holds fine.'

I hadn't told Cecilia about my aunt likely putting up at Coad Farm. I wasn't sure what to do and thought I would ask Billy if he knew anyone who went there regularly. Aunt Tilly surely wouldn't be openly living there; she had a price on her head and she was too wily to put herself in danger from anyone outside the smuggling gang. If I told the local revenue men, I didn't think they would catch her. Perhaps it would be better just to know where she was - within the house or farm - so that any search would be unexpected and accurate. The other problem was that many people, including the law and magistrates, were in the pay of the smugglers. Once again, I wished Dr. Grieve was nearby to advise me and take charge; he would have caught her for sure. I didn't want to worry the Elwoods until I had thought of a plan. I needed to talk to Billy - he was still my best friend and I could talk freely to him.

The weather didn't fail us and Billy took charge of the blankets, the basket of food and a selection of Freddie's toys. We walked down to the copse, me carrying Freddie as Beth trotted alongside. She wanted to pick some of the daisies to make daisy-chains. It was a warm gentle day with puffballs of cloud sitting on the horizon but not interfering with the sun, just as I liked it. We settled down on our blanket and ate some of our picnic while Beth sat making her necklaces and Freddie played with his wooden toy horses.

'Billy,' I said, 'have you heard aught about my aunt living with the Coads?'

He looked at me in astonishment. 'Na, yer fibbing me.'

'I heard in secret that she was there before Mrs. Coad died and she is still there now.'

'How d'yer know?'

'I can't tell you, but it is likely true.'

'What yer thinking, then?'

I liked that about Billy, he came straight to the point.

'I need to know if it's true,' I said. 'I'm wondering if we can find out what's going on at Coad Farm, if she is hiding there, and whereabouts. There are barns and cellars as well as hayricks and all sorts of places where she could hang about and not be seen. She is not one to be in the house doing the washing and cleaning.'

'An' if we found out, what do we do?'

'I think I would have to tell Farmer Elwood and perhaps he would bring in the militia, like he did before. I don't trust the local people. Billy, do you know anyone who goes upriver to the Coads regular, like?' I asked.

'Only the man who delivers there who took me with him one time. He might take me again if I asked. He was a good sort and said I could work for 'm anytime.'

'Would they recognise you, do you think? You were at the trial and gave evidence.'

He looked thoughtful. 'I've grown some. I can make me look a bit different.'

'Billy, the youngest Coad, his name is Job, but they call him Jo, keeps coming around,' I said. 'I think he spies on me and Beth and sometimes he just asks how she is. He told me, sort of, that someone there had killed his ma.'

Billy looked troubled before saying, 'He could be spying on you for his old man, trying to get you on his side so you get to trust him.'

'He could be,' I replied, 'but it doesn't feel like that. He is sort of lonely and he seems to want to talk about Beth, so I don't know, or quite understand, where he fits in. And, don't forget, it was him that told on the smugglers when me and Beth were rescued from Southease.'

We talked around it for a while and once the children had finished the picnic we talked some more, but other than spying out the land at Coad Farm we couldn't think of what else to do. I left it to Billy to try and find out what he could, but I made him promise not to go up there himself.

'Don't put yourself into any danger, Billy. You never know who's working with the smugglers, and don't tell Cilla.'

The little puffball clouds were ganging up together and the sun, as it moved across the sky, was going to meet them, so we packed up the picnic and Billy carried Freddie as Beth and I trotted along beside him. It was true, he had grown some. He wasn't the scrawny little lad I first met outside the workhouse; he was a well-fed and seemingly sturdy boy despite his early misfortunes. I couldn't put him in any danger. I had no right.

'Perhaps I should just ask the Coad boy outright,' I said, 'and see what happens?'

'Let me see what I can find out first. I do know who the smugglers be,' said Billy. 'Everyone does.'

Chapter Sixteen

Early this morning, three prisoners, said to be smugglers, detained for debt due to the Government, found means to make their escape out of Newgate, breaking the double braced iron bars of the second window over the gateway facing St. Sepulchre's and by the convenience of ropes let themselves down from thence, and have not since been heard of.

Sussex Weekly Advertiser and Lewes Journal 1750/1806

A letter came for Cecilia containing the worst kind of news: her mother, Lady Harriet, intended to visit on her way to Brighthelmstone. Since the Prince of Wales had taken up residence, it had become quite the place to see and be seen, reported Cecilia as she perused the letter, adding that the militia were camped nearby and the officers were very much part of the social life.

Although Cecilia wasn't looking forward to this visit, at least, as she said to me, it wouldn't be for long, three days at most. Farmer Elwood looked very glum when she spoke of it. I think he worried that Cecilia would be whisked away again, and none of us wanted that as the pregnancy had settled down and she looked quite wonderful. The baby was due in September and it was now June, so we had a way to go, but no-one was taking any risks with her general health and well-being. The better she looked, the worse stood her mama's case for her removal to Hadgwick Hall.

I didn't have time to keep worrying about her mother. She wouldn't even be aware of me except as the governess of her grandson. I didn't expect that Cecilia would tell her that I was the same Esther that she refused to have in her house before, so I decided to keep out of the way and if I were to meet her I would keep my head down and my mouth shut. I didn't even know what you called someone from her station in life: Ma'am, your Ladyship, your Highness. Your Awfulness is what I would have liked to call her.

As the day of Lady Harriet's arrival drew near, the house was in complete uproar; all the rooms were being spring-cleaned and dust sheets removed. Mrs. Fisher was ordering food for the army of people who would accompany her. She travelled with no less than five servants as well as three friends, all nobility; in addition, each of these ladies had their own lady's maid to prepare their clothing, dress them and tease their hair into the most elaborate of shapes. Freddie was to be presented within minutes of their arrival and I had to keep him clean and prepared from morning until whenever their carriages arrived, which could have been as late as evening. Farmer Elwood was quite disgruntled with all the upheaval but mainly because he too was obliged to keep himself available and couldn't therefore be out on the farm where he was needed. Instead, he shut himself up in the farm study, with various workmen, his dairy manager and his agent all calling throughout the day; every time the door opened a cloud of smoke billowed out.

I had promised to help Mrs. Fisher with some of the preparation of food the day before they arrived, and I gave her some of my herbs to improve her stockpot which could be quite bland. Every time I ventured into the kitchen I saw red faces and heard strained voices. A messenger arrived to tell us that her Ladyship's cook, Monsieur Philippe, was accompanying the party and would require use of the kitchen for the duration of the visit. When Cecilia told Mrs. Fisher this, I thought she was going to collapse. I asked Cilla to prepare some restorative tea and a nip of brandy. The poor woman flopped into a chair and sat with her head in her hands, weeping.

Gradually Cilla and I jollied her up with promises of support and help so there would be plenty of food ready before the party arrived. Then, if Monsieur Philippe wanted more or different dishes, we would make sure that all the basic ingredients were to hand. Orders had been sent out far and wide to procure produce that wasn't available on the farm: fancy fruits, unlikely vegetables and even more meat than usual despite having our own fowl, coney, beef, and lamb. Fish from Brighthelmstone would be delivered on the morning of arrival, early, and kept ready for the fussiest of cooks. My room was commandeered for storage and I undertook to use the fire in our sitting room for anything that was needed that wouldn't fit in the main household ovens and, as the room was ideal for proving of bread, I undertook the baking of it, which was a good idea as I have a lighter hand.

Cecilia had given us menus for each day with the proviso that each might change according to the whim of her mother or her cook. It was a difficult situation for Mrs. Fisher, Cilla and the extra ladies brought in to help. The dishes would be far more elaborate than the family usually ate, even when entertaining.

On the morning of arrival all was ready. The house had been dusted, polished, and adorned with the best fresh flowers the local markets could supply and some produce came from family friends who had hothouses. There was enough food prepared or in the throes of preparation for the most exacting of households. Mrs. Fisher was dressed in her best clothes; a black dress I had never seen before, with a new and very clean apron tied about her, and one kept as spare. There was much the same for Cilla who would also help with service; she had two aprons as well, one to wear when preparing the meals and another lighter, frilly one for serving. Billy-alone was called on to become boot boy and general household helper. He also had to open the carriage doors and help the ladies down. He had been given new breeches and a clean shirt and waistcoat and could be found admiring himself in the silver he was polishing. The breeches were a mite long, so I tacked them up and pulled in the shirt; he was skinnier than I had thought.

Cecilia was in a state of anxiety and I had to force her to retire to her sitting room and trust in her staff and husband - if not for herself, then for the sake of her unborn child.

Her Ladyship arrived during the afternoon and, with her entourage, was welcomed with tea and sweetmeats, all served beautifully by Cilla and Polly (who was borrowed from Miss Wardle for the occasion). Both girls looked a picture in their black dresses with white frilled aprons and caps.

Freddie was produced and doted on by the ladies of the party and he rose to the occasion with winning smiles and cuddles. Grand-Mère was delighted with him and Cecilia flushed with pride at his good manners and behaviour.

Fortunately, I did not have to meet any of the party, just keep everyone in readiness should they be called for. They only stayed for two days in the end and happily the cook was a genial body who fitted in with Mrs. Fisher's plans and menus. He did make one or two changes to the presentation of the food and provided his own mix of seasonings for the game and fish; I must say his sauces were far superior to Mrs. Fisher's. By the time the first day was over they were collaborating and learning from each other; my bread was praised, and my special teas admired, so I felt quite pleased that I had been able to contribute. One thing I was surprised to learn was that the ladies of the party did not eat fresh fruits and the cook showed us how to prepare them so as not to spoil the texture or colour in cooking. He told us that fresh fruits were considered unhealthy for the digestion. What nonsense, I thought. All in all, it went off well and her Ladyship seemed satisfied with her daughter's style and standard of living after she had thrown open the doors of all the main rooms for inspection. She did suggest that Cecilia return home with her when the visit to Brighthelmstone was concluded, which could be in a week - or six weeks - depending on what company was to be had in that fashionable place. But she did not press the point when Cecilia declined, explaining that Farmer Elwood needed her at home to run his busy household. Farmer Elwood looked so much happier than he had of late and resumed his daily outings on the estate.

Billy-alone didn't want to give his smart clothing back but was slightly appeased when I explained that it would be kept in readiness, should he be required to join the indoor staff in the future. Young Polly returned to Miss Wardle with tales of fine food and wonderful colours and hairstyles that adorned the ladies' heads with feathers and ornaments and even bits of fruit pinned into great sweeps and curls of hair.

The ladies' maids were an uppish lot, and no-one was sorry to see the back of them after they scorned the household's facilities, its furnishings, its food and inhabitants. Excluding Cecilia and Freddie, nobody else was good enough.

My impression of Cecilia's mother softened and, even though I did not meet her, I got the feeling that she had her daughter's well-being at heart, and she loved little Freddie, which made me think better of her, but I was glad when she left and the household returned to normal.

After the visit, Cecilia called all her staff together to thank them for their help in making her mother's visit a success. As she had no need to do so, they were greatly appreciative, especially as there was a lot of food left over, some of which found its way into their own families' welcoming hands; everyone benefited from the Elwoods' entertaining. I had heard tell that other families would rather throw leftovers in the pig swill than give them to their servants.

Chapter Seventeen

Jugg's Road, Lewes, once part of the coach road to Brighton, named after the baskets, or jugs, of fish which used to be carried by fisherwomen from Brighthelmstone for sale in the market of Lewes.
The Coach Roads to Brighton by Geoffrey Hewlett 2014

I so often wished we knew where Dr. Grieve was. I had been in sore need of his advice and Dr. Crabbe did not fill me with confidence. Things had been going so well with Cecilia's pregnancy until she called me to her bedroom to say that there was some bleeding. The baby was not due for about two months, so I listened for the heartbeat which was easily heard and strong. I also examined her and could see no excitability of the tissue, so had no easy or immediate answer to her distress.

We called Dr. Crabbe in and he came promptly but his manner in general was not enough to make us think he knew what he was about. If the decision had been left to me, I would have advised immediate rest in the hope that things would settle down, but he wanted to bleed Cecilia to rid her of bad humours. I couldn't see how this would help and, knowing that Dr. Grieve was not keen on the practice, I set about dissuading Farmer Elwood from agreeing to it.

As it happened, Cecilia herself refused to submit to being bled, having been present when we had all discussed the merits, or otherwise, of bleeding one evening around the supper table before Dr. Grieve had left us. Dr. Crabbe was extremely offended at this turn of events and left saying that he could not be responsible for a patient who didn't heed his advice. I had stayed out of the way whilst he was in the house, not wishing to make him even angrier as, after all, we might need his services in the future. As soon as he had gone, I hastened to Cecilia's room and set about calming her. I removed her many pillows and bolsters, laying her flat before raising her knees and feet. I made a posset from my herbal store that would not harm her but might calm her nerves and sat by her side until she settled into a deep sleep. When she awoke I proposed that she stay in bed until the small amount of blood had stopped and thereafter take things a lot easier. I listened to the baby's heartbeat daily just to reassure us both and it never faltered so I hoped that the bleeding was just a temporary thing, maybe caused by the strain of her mother's visit.

I had no idea if this was so, but it seemed plausible enough to Cecilia so we both opted to believe it. In all, the loss of blood was probably less than a small measure and it was irregular of occurrence, but whilst it was happening we were not to know that, and I am thankful we took the least action. To my mind it was foolish to take blood when we were desperately trying to stop bleeding in another area of the body. I searched my pa's notes on childbirth, and other than what I had done already, I couldn't find anything else that would help; I felt angry again at Dr. Grieve for abandoning us to the mercies of a man that I thought a quack. I considered calling on one of the other physicians in the town but both Farmer Elwood and I remembered the doctor's disparaging remarks about all of them. The entire household waited with anxiety and after two weeks with no resumption of bleeding, Cecilia was able to leave her bed and return to her sitting room. She would rise late, and I would bring the children to her and remain to ensure they did not get too boisterous. After our midday meal, she would retire to her bed for a nap, often with Freddie tucked up beside her. Farmer Elwood went about his business but didn't leave the property at all, not even to go to Lewes, and we were always aware of where he was. Gradually we relaxed, and things went back to normal except that Cecilia rested more and didn't attempt to lift Freddie.

As I was occupied in the house continuously, I couldn't go to the aid of any of my ladies; but my friend Eliza, who had fulfilled her earlier promise, kept in touch to let me know how they fared. She was unable, as yet, to do much but she was a sensible young woman and had watched and listened to me as I had gone about my business. She knew my standards of cleanliness and it was there that she was able to make a difference, as well as in the preparation of more nourishing food and drink for expectant mothers who were often too poor or too discouraged to try. Wholesome food could be made with a little effort, and the town soup kitchen was a boon. On occasions, I had brought eggs and milk for some of my ladies and showed them how to make food that was appetising and nourishing and much better for mother and baby than gin.

Once I was sure that Cecilia was safe, and when the children were put to bed in the evening, I might venture out. I was so fortunate in having the maids to call on if I needed to, but I didn't feel I could do that during the daytime. This made me fret, but there was nothing to be done about it.

Chapter Eighteen

On Tuesday last died in childbed Mrs. Newnham, wife of John Newnham Esq., of Maresfield in this County eldest daughter of Dr. Russell of Malling near this town.
Sussex Weekly Advertiser and Lewes Journal. 1750/1806

At last a letter arrived from Dr. Grieve for Farmer Elwood and from the content it was clear that he was unaware of all that had been happening here in his absence. Apparently, he had been having an adventurous time on board a ship accompanying Horatio Nelson's Theseus.

Farmer Elwood was clearly captivated by the letter, as he kept reading excerpts of it to Cecilia. He glossed over why Dr. Grieve was on board a fighting ship, mentioning only that he was in company with the ship's surgeon. That he was called upon to dress the wounds of men who were badly injured during an assault on the island of Tenerife in July seemed to have sparked exhilaration in both himself as well as his friend Farmer Elwood, who could barely conceal his excitement at receiving this first-hand account of a battle against the Spanish.

This attempt to take the island for Britain was ultimately unsuccessful but it seemed of small matter compared to Dr. Grieve's admiration for many of the men who were involved, including the man who repelled Nelson's forces, a

Captain Gutierrez, despite having fewer soldiers and relying on the island's inhabitants and the contrary seas to withstand Nelson's superior forces. Nelson was wounded and lost part of his arm in the battle and once the poor man was rowed back to his own ship, it was amputated and the discarded part thrown into the sea for the fishes to eat. All this was related by Dr. Grieve in the most excitable language and he was clearly taken with this young fellow Nelson despite the loss of so many brave men: he wrote of 250 dead and over a hundred wounded. I wondered how surgeons dealt with so many men while on a vessel that rocked and pitched with the waves. It made me shudder.

The letter to Farmer Elwood was very long, and while it had found its way to us in a very short space of time, it was full of the sort of detail that neither Cecilia nor I wanted to listen to. I think he was very disappointed in us and took it off to share with someone who understood the ins and outs of battle strategy, even if the assault was a failure. I believe myself to be patriotic, but I also think of the lives lost, of the widows, sweethearts and orphans. Fighting the Spanish and the French was consuming our little island, with more and more boys and men sucked into the King's forces. I can't see war as glorious; and where a battle is fought to further Britain's empire rather than protect its citizens, I didn't feel I could applaud it.

However, perhaps it was better to keep my views to myself as the newspapers that circulate are full of the glory of our other naval skirmishes. The men in power are convinced that the French are about to invade us and they are building a lot of strange tower-like places all along the coast for defence. Perhaps, if the Frenchies were on the immediate horizon, I would be as frightened and as ready to do anything to repel them as my neighbours are. But, for the moment, I was more concerned with the womenfolk who are left picking up the pieces, with husbands, brothers and sons gone, and so many unlikely to return. Where is the glory in that? The papers and periodicals are full of the exploits of a young man, a Corsican, who leads the French armies into great battles, which he always seems to win. His name is Napoleon Bonaparte and parents invoke his name to frighten their children to bed. 'Go to sleep, or Boney will come and get you' is a thing I have heard said recently.

***

Cecilia went into labour and I hoped that I could deliver the baby for her as she was insistent that she didn't want Dr. Crabbe called. Once again Farmer Elwood was a bundle of nerves, but I asked him to have his horse ready, which would give him some purpose should I feel we needed help; I had sought another physician other than Dr. Crabbe if she should need one. There were two other men in the town that could be called upon even though Dr. Grieve had been disparaging of their skills. I knew that either would be pleased to attend on the Elwoods as a family of great patronage in the district but I hoped it would not be necessary.

The labour was longer than it had been with Freddie but there was no reason for alarm. The presentation seemed normal, the heartbeat strong and Cecilia was in good shape compared with many of the women I have helped. Every now and again the contractions slowed down and then presented again with renewed vigour. It was harder than I would have hoped, considering that this was Cecilia's third birth, but every baby is different. I had to keep reminding myself of that fact when I felt anxious for this very precious woman and her baby. Cecilia was as important to me as a member of my own family, and I sought to help her endure as little pain as necessary.

It was a long night and Farmer Elwood was beside himself with fear as I tried to reassure him that this was still in the normal range of labour. Cecilia was weakening but remained resolute that she and I could do this between us. I did what I could to help her, but my ministrations were purely in the realm of comfort for there was nothing physical I could do, short of pulling the baby out; nor would I have trusted even a physician to interfere at this point, though I knew that some do with the help of some outlandish contraption. This baby was coming - slowly - but coming and we were just waiting. I wished so much that Dr. Grieve were still here and teaching me; my competence was not enough for my own peace of mind.

I went down to the kitchens where Mrs. Fisher was throwing dough violently on to her work table and praying that all would be over soon; the whole of the household was on tenterhooks. The children were kept up in the nursery where they couldn't hear any noise and I flew up to see them for a few minutes whilst Cilla sat with Cecilia. I hadn't been up there for very long when she came pounding up the stairs,

'I think it's happening, Essie, come quickly,' she said.

And it was. Soon I saw the head, and then the shoulders, and Cecy was putting everything into getting this little mite out into the world. The baby was a girl, a beautiful, fragile, delicate little girl. Felicia; her name was to be Felicia.

Once I had cleaned both mother and baby and wrapped Cecilia in a beautiful shawl, sent by her mother for this very purpose, I invited Farmer Elwood in to meet his daughter. He was quite overcome and as he picked the baby up in his great big hands, I could see him trembling with emotion. I left the family together to enjoy their pride in Felicia, in the knowledge that all had been accomplished with no harm to either of them.

Much later, I found Farmer Elwood asleep at his desk. Billy-alone had been stood down from horse duty while Mrs. Fisher had retired to her room after sending up a light meal. Cecilia was asleep, and I sat beside her with Felicia in my arms. I couldn't bear to put her down, she was so perfect: her tiny hands and feet, her beautifully shaped mouth, all were exquisite. Silently I prayed that one day I might experience such happiness myself, but there seemed little hope of that.

Chapter Nineteen

We hear from Horsham, that one day last week Robert Clarke, Executioner, there hanged himself with a Bridle in the hayloft belonging to the Anchor Inn at Horsham. The cause of his committing this rash action was his being entrusted with half a guinea to pay for a pig, which money he lost at All-fours instead of paying for the pig. The place is vacant and will be conferred on others that can make the best ....

Sussex Weekly Advertiser and Lewes Journal 1750/1806

I knew that Billy-alone had been trying to catch me for days, but I had been so busy that I hadn't had time to seek him out. He spent most of his time on the farm with trips into Lewes to see Miss Wardle and the piggies. I knew he still lived in fear of the King's naval men who looked for likely lads to fill the warships, so he was happier out of the town. Cilla, his betrothed, was a contented young lass who asked for nothing more than his company.

I met Billy in the stables and we walked out to the orchard where no-one could overhear us. As we walked in the September sunshine, I kicked some windfalls aside, anxious to hear what Billy had discovered.

'I been up to Coad Farm three times,' he said, 'and I ain't seen no woman thereabouts but there be a mean-looking man oft' with Farmer Coad. Them boys is usually out in the fields, the two older ones together but the youngest seems always to be alone.'

'Are you sure it is a man and not a woman dressed different?' I asked. 'I know she did dress mannish when we were at Southease and you saw her at our wedding.'

'I weren't able to get that close, but it looked like a fella to me, and I didn't take a lot of notice of what she looked like at the church. I was too busy trying to get to you,' he replied.

'I didn't know that, Billy. I was so shocked, I didn't take in what everyone else was doing. I barely saw Wilf move to protect Beth.' We were both silent for a few moments as we remembered that horrific day. Billy look pensive and I shuddered as the memories flooded back.

'But back to Coad Farm; what was this man or woman doing?' I went on, trying to shake off the disturbing images and thoughts.

'Well, that were the strange thing he, or she, were doin' the ordering of things.'

'And the youngest boy?'

'He were skulking about, but never where anyone else was,' Billy replied. 'And one time I did hear his old man yelling for him but he was hiding in the barn and didn't come out until he was fetched, and then he got a beating. If that fella be your aunt, she got her feet well under the table and she is not likely to be recognised by anyone. What we gonna do, Esther?'

'I don't know Billy,' I said. 'It has been a while now since I heard she was there, but I am sure she will make a move on me soon. She is planning something, I know she is, I can sense it. She can't get to Beth, she is too well protected, so it will be me!'

But I was wrong, dreadfully wrong. The Coads along with Aunt Tilly were to make their move only days after Billy and I had talked.

I had taken Beth and Freddie out to the stables to see the horses. We did this most fine days, but this day was special because there was a new foal in the yard. The children were excited and dancing around my skirt as we made our way towards the stables. A warm soft light brought out a peach tone in the mellow walls as we turned the corner of the house. We were all laughing merrily at the excitement of naming the foal and there had been lots of suggestions from everyone in the household. I was looking around and taking pleasure in the day - and the children - when I heard Cilla calling me just as we reached the stable doors. I turned around and retraced my steps to see what she wanted.

Everything seemed normal but someone must have been hiding amongst the stalls because one minute Beth was there, and the next, she wasn't. By the time I heard one of the stable lads shouting, 'Stop! Stop!' it was too late. He'd seen a man grab and make off with her, then fly away on a big horse that was tethered out of sight behind the outer wall. I remember tearing through the gate to find Freddie screaming and the boy running after the kidnapper with a pitchfork.

Beth was gone, the place where she had been suddenly silent and empty of her laughter and chatter. I cursed myself for not varying the time of our activities outside; we always went to feed the ponies mid-morning after they had been mucked out. I shouted to a stable lad to saddle Flossy for me and flew indoors with Freddie under my arm, still screaming for all he was worth. I dropped him into Cilla's arms and told her to find Billy, Farmer Elwood and any men who were around. I would be going upriver to Hamsey and she was to tell them that and to bring anyone else they could muster. I didn't wait for anyone. It was hare-brained to rush off alone but I couldn't see any alternative, I had to get after her. I was but fifteen minutes behind them, but I knew where she would be – at Coad Farm.

Chapter Twenty

(List of local smugglers):

Samuel Brown, of the Cliffe, near Lewes - the County of Sussex,
Basket-Maker

Francis Bollard, otherwise Pollard, at or near Piddinghoe, in the
said County, Labourer

John Ashcraft, of Bishop-Town in the said County, Labourer

Richard Bollard otherwise Pollard, at or near Tarring in the said
County, Labourer

John Clare, of Rodmill in the said County, Labourer

John French, of Lewes, aforesaid, Labourer

William Strake, otherwise Strait, otherwise Stephens, of Rodmill,
aforesaid, Labourer

Benjamin otherwise James Burt of Tarring, in the said County,
Farmer

Sussex Weekly Advertiser and Lewes Journal 1750/1806

My heart was pounding, and I was sweating hard as I pulled Flossy up behind the farmhouse. I made some attempt at secrecy but could not disguise the noise of horse's hooves; and though all was quiet I knew they would be waiting for me somewhere close-by though they might not have expected me to get there so quickly. Coad Farm was a rambling place with lots of outhouses and barns - if they were not in the house I might be able to sneak up on them and find a way of snatching Beth back. With luck, Billy and Farmer Elwood were not far behind and, by now, the neighbourhood would have been alerted. I dropped Flossy's reigns and ran towards the kitchen. I tried hard not to breathe too loudly even though I knew I could be walking into a trap and, as I lifted the latch, I saw my friend Becca once again in my mind's eye, as she had been when last I saw her alive, being pushed out of this very door by Mrs. Coad, who was screaming abuse, her face contorted with rage. I pictured the fear in Becca's eyes, the whiteness of her skin as she fell on the cobblestones and crawled out of the rain-soaked yard towards the Church. As I remembered Becca's plight at this same godforsaken place, I imagined that Beth was already dead, back here at Coad Farm. I tried to ignore the torment of my thoughts as I pushed the door open.

The room was cold, the fire unlit and there appeared to be no-one there but, suddenly, just as I sensed movement behind me, a foul-smelling sack was thrown over my head. I was thrown over someone's shoulder and carried outside before being tossed onto a cart where sacks of rotting and putrid vegetables were dumped on top of me. I yelled at the top of my voice until I felt a sharp prick in my shoulder, almost certainly from a knife.

A gravelly voice said, 'Shudup, bitch.' The cart jolted into movement and I heard a horse whicker as we trundled out of the yard. I sobbed, quietly, not wanting to be stabbed. My mind was full of fear for Beth who, if she was still alive, must be terrified. I have no idea how long we trotted but when we did stop, I was dragged by my feet out of the cart and onto a grassy bank. Again, I was picked up bodily and carried into an indoor place. I could smell hay and horse shit but otherwise had no idea where we were, and worse still, neither would anyone else who might think to rescue me and Beth - if she was still alive - and here too.

I heard a sniffle, and in the distance, a young voice saying, 'Shush... there, there, shush,' and then another, saying, 'Shut 'er up.' It was my aunt speaking.

The sack was dragged off me and I blinked in the gloom of a barn. It was nowhere I had ever been, but it was large, and I heard rather than saw lots of horses. I could see sunlight lancing through wooden slats, the air was dry with the stuffiness of old hay. Her voice came from behind me: 'So, my dear niece, here we are together again. It's been a while.'

I turned in the direction of her voice. 'Where is she, what have you done with Beth?' I croaked.

'That milksop of a boy has her, outside, and unless you do as you are bid then I will personally drown her. Boy,' she shouted, 'bring her in so my niece can see she is really here.'

The youngest Coad stood silhouetted in a doorway. I blinked again, not quite sure whether the bundle he held was Beth, but then she wailed, and I knew it was her. I tugged at my captor's arms trying desperately to get to her, but his grip tightened viciously as I called out to Beth, 'I am here, lovey, no-one is going to hurt you.' She cried even louder as she recognised my voice and perhaps saw me in the gloom.

'Go on,' my aunt said to the boy, 'get the brat outside and keep her quiet.'

'What are you going to do with us?' I cried, but it didn't sound like me as my voice cracked in desperation. I had to pull myself together and bargain for our - or Beth's - life. It was no use me collapsing under the weight of terror, that wouldn't get us out of Tilly's clutches. At the very least I must play for time.

She smirked and took her cap off; her hair was cut such as a working man would wear. It was completely grey, and she didn't look at all like a woman. It was difficult to believe that this mannish, ugly creature was my pretty mother's sister.

'You wouldn't recognise me, would you, girl?' She laughed, relishing her power over me.

'Not to look at, no, but I know your voice and so will others,' I shouted defiantly, hoping that the men Billy would bring might track us down soon. I had to spin things out; we weren't dead yet, there was still hope of rescue.

It was as if she read my mind. 'No-one is going to find you, girl, and young Beth – why, she will be brought up by her father now. Milksop will look to her and you will never see her again after tonight nor will your fancy friends,' she gloated. 'Blood is thicker than water, girl, in the eyes of the law.'

I shook uncontrollably, my teeth chattering but not with cold. 'What happens tonight?' I quavered, dreading the reply, knowing that it would be something malicious.

'We are leaving the area, and you and I will be smuggled onto a transport ship. It's all arranged, niece, and when we get out to sea, no-one will know, or care, who you are. You'll join the hundreds of other old lags who all protest their innocence.'

Horrified, I cried: 'You can't do that, people will know. There'll be lists and documents, descriptions…,' I blustered, fearful that she could indeed do what she threatened.

'I have a long arm, girl, and I am telling you I *can* do that. Everyone can be bribed - I got out of Newgate with a bribe -

and two ladies of the night will oblige us by leaving the ship, with us put in their place.'

Terror at this monstrous plan all but robbed me of my wits but eventually I found a small voice. 'But why you?' I questioned, not understanding. 'What would possess you, why do you want to go on a transport?'

'Well, thanks to you, my girl, I have a price on my head, a big reward offered, and if I am taken it will be the gallows for me. Better a new life in another country where nobody knows me. But they *will*, once I've been there awhile; I will become someone who matters,' she declared vehemently, her arms raised in threat.

'But what about Beth? The boy can't bring her up, she is too young. Send her back to the Elwoods, please, I beg you.'

'Not a chance girl,' Tilly mocked and leaned in towards me. 'I want you to suffer thinking of her settled with the Coads. No-one can take her away - she is, after all, his daughter. With you gone and the Elwoods of no relation, why, she will fit nicely back into her papa's farm.'

I retched - from the smell of the place, the heat stealing up my body like a rash and the thought of Beth in such a wicked household, growing up into drudgery, or worse. Tilly was laughing at my humiliation and enjoying every last moment of her long-planned revenge.

'Please, I am begging you,' I said, 'do what you like with me but leave Beth with her grandad or anyone who knows how to care for a little one. She is still but a baby. You can't leave her with that family. They killed her mother, or as good as.'

'Aye, Farmer Coad 'as told me all about pretty Becca. She were a comely lass, he said, and he was much taken with her. Perhaps he will be too with her daughter.' She laughed as she flicked a look to someone behind me.

'Strip her,' she ordered a coarse-looking man who was clearly enjoying my discomfort. 'Put 'er in them clothes and get those boots off 'er. They're too fancy for a convict, she can go barefoot like the rest of 'em. She be nothing but a cripple without them boots,' she added, spitefully.

Again, I lost my voice, choking, as my throat seemed to swell with the fear that was overwhelming me.

'You gonna get a new outfit, niece, not quite as soft and ladylike as what you've got on but one that will mark you out as a proper convict on a transport ship.'

The indignity of her and others watching while I was stripped of my clothing and special boots then bundled forcibly into a coarse cloth petticoat and jacket was as nothing to when she took up some shears and hacked at my hair, cutting it all off and doing so with venom crafted onto her face.

I cried, I couldn't help myself, but my tears did nothing to erase the nub of dread that I had for Beth and her future. Could I hope for her rescue? My friends, I knew, would do everything to get her back to South Farm. But it was true that Farmer Coad was her natural father and his crimes of the past might not be enough to keep her out of his reach. Once again, I retched and was pushed into the hay, my hands and feet bound. My hopes were fading but for one: if they had me now, they might eventually let Beth be, once they got tired of trying to raise a child and when this malign woman was out of the way.

Part Three

Chapter Twenty-One

"From distant climes, o'er wide spread seas we come,
(Though not with much eclat, or beat of drum)
True patriots all, for be it understood,
We left our country for our country's good."
The Barrington Prologue by Henry Carter

I was force-fed a mess of broth which clearly had a sleeping draught in it as I remember nothing of the journey to the Thames, nor even what day it was; and thereafter only hazily do I recall my aunt whispering that if I didn't do as she directed, then word would be taken back to kill Beth. I was in no doubt that the men who accompanied us would do exactly as she ordered; and if that involved killing a child, it would be done.

As I regained consciousness, I sensed we were moving through water. I could hear and feel the sloppy lapping of waves as we pitched on the tide. The foul damp air had an underlying whiff of tar. Tilly yanked my head up by what was left of my hair and gleefully pointed out a lumbering shape wallowing deep in the water that was, she said, the hulk - where most prisoners were kept until the transport ship was ready. We went frighteningly near this monstrous vessel from where I could hear ragged cries of despair carried on the wind. I tried to shut my ears to the sounds. My blindfold had slipped down completely, so I could see it was full dark as we ploughed on through the water which was becoming fretful and turbulent, darker than the sky, with licks of yellowing foam on the crests. I felt sick but fought to keep the bitter taste down as we pulled alongside a great ship with a rope ladder hanging down.

Somehow, I was pushed up the ladder with her behind me, prodding whenever I stopped to recover myself. I remember swinging outwards as a sharp wind caught the treads before slamming back against tar pitched wood, my skin catching against razor-sharp shells and the dripping slimy weed that clung to them, their salty tang caught in my throat. I was too frightened to let go and fall into the dirty drowning water of the Thames but equally afraid to go on climbing. Eventually, I was dragged on deck, gagged, and a coarse blanket thrown over my head and shoulders as my aunt clambered up alongside me. In the darkness, I heard muttering and scuffles. The blanket slipped and I caught sight of the white faces of the two women who were being exchanged for us as they were hoisted over the edge, quickly disappearing. I didn't hear any great splashes, so they must have been safely received in the little wherry that had carried us to the transport ship. All hope of discovery was now gone; we were exchanged for two street walkers. That was my identity now, a prostitute on a transport ship. How would I bear it, and what would happen to my Beth?

My aunt abandoned me almost immediately after our arrival, to set about taking control of the unhappy women convicts, I suspected. Clearly, she knew people aboard, but I was friendless and terrified of what was to come. A sailor, or I took him to be such but later found out he was a guard, an entirely different breed, pushed me into a cavernous and foul space that had no opening onto the outside. He prodded me forward to a stretched bit of material hung from hooks in which he indicated by means of grunts that I was to sleep. Climbing up into this swaying rope-like contraption took me some effort and time. I was still feeling sick and dazed and no-one offered to help me, so when I finally managed it, I felt some relief at my achievement.

As I lay listening to the whimpering sobs of my unknown companions, I tried to find within myself the means of survival. I thought of Wilf and his last moments as he died in my arms; I remembered the time he had lifted me out of the cart when we were trying to rescue Billy-alone from the King's press gang. I had never had a man touch me and when his big strong hands went around my waist, I experienced the most delicious sensation of pleasure and want. Our marriage had never quickened to the joys and experiences that a loving man and woman enjoy, and I ached with sorrow as I took myself back to that time. I thought too, of Beth, my lovely Beth, who was held by those godforsaken Coads; of the Elwoods, whom I trusted would move heaven and earth to bring us back into their household; and Flossy, would they find her? None of this could I influence. My only hope was to survive for as long as possible; I had to find a way to get back home to Lewes. It was, I decided, no use fretting about what had happened. I just had to get on with my changed circumstance by getting by as best as I could and look for any opportunity to get off this ship. I knew nothing about boats, ports, or even the geography of the world, but I believed my aunt to be right when she said that my story would not be believed, that I was just one of many on board who would protest their innocence. In short, I had to somehow make the best of it.

So many hours passed in that uncomfortable swinging bed, not knowing if it were daybreak nor anywhere near. The ship rocked and rolled as I listened to groaning timbers and a distant rattle which I couldn't identify. I thought I heard a cock crow, which seemed ridiculous. I supposed sailors got used to such lurching but I would rather have had my feet on firm ground. I wondered if there might be opportunity to jump overboard before the ship sailed and it was with that thought in mind that I must have fallen asleep; but it was restless sleep with a sullen expanse of water haunting my dreams.

★★★

We, the inhabitants of what is called the 'tween deck, were numbered at 39 female convicts. We were rudely woken by coarse language and brutality and were then tipped out of our hammocks if we were tardy in reacting, as I was. This manner of being woke was so violent, my whole body quivered in fright. I hadn't known what to expect, but it wasn't this. Everyone was converging near the hatch to an upper deck. I was behind most of my companions and the air was shrill with cursing and shrieking. As I tried to get my bearings, I was pushed and pummelled as women kept surging round me. Dishes were handed down from a hatch above us and a bowl from which food was ladled. It was everyone for themselves as hands grabbed for the ladle and those who couldn't get it just scooped slop out of the bowl with their bare fingers. I was too slow and by the time I had got through the crush there was nothing left; I would go hungry. Orders were shouted to unhitch the hammocks and hand them up through the hatch where they were counted, as were the returned dishes. I wondered why; perhaps it was to prevent attempts at self-slaying or just to keep people moving. If all the hammocks had been left in place there would be even less room.

I looked for somewhere to sit where I could watch what was going on. Clearly some of the women were known to each other as they had mostly come from the hulk moored out on the river, and once the food had disappeared they all shifted about as if they were gossiping in a market place. I could see that some were in poor health and others were more at ease with the circumstance, but I did notice that I was not the only quiet and frightened woman. A young girl near me was trembling and her unhealthy pallor looked alarming. My aunt and I were the only healthy-looking people there, which was not surprising, I suppose, as all the others had likely been in the hulk or a gaol for some time. My skin was pock-marked but clear, no boils or eruptions. My hair was messed but clean unlike the matted locks that most of the women bore. My teeth were still my own and mostly complete, but these women barely had a tooth between them and those they had were blackened and broken thanks to hard living and probably alcohol. The woman next to me saw me looking and chuckled. How anyone could chuckle when they were in such a dire condition was beyond me.

'You's not one of us, then?' she said.

'I suppose I am, now, but I wasn't yesterday,' I replied shortly.

'What yer in for?'

'Revenge. I was kidnapped and substituted for another last night. I can't see how to get off, so I am one of you now. My name is Esther. What about you?'

She sighed. 'I got caught stealing a pocket watch. I were going to sell it and buy some food, but I got picked up afore I could get rid of it. Who got put off in your place then?'

'A night walker. I didn't see clearly, there were two of them.'

'Blimey, them's the lucky ones, ain't they!' she said. 'Bad luck for you, though.'

I stared around me, my eyes becoming accustomed to the gloom. 'Is this what it was like on the hulk?' I asked.

'Aye, much the same, but it was more crowded and smelled rank,' she replied. 'We hope we will have a better time of it here. We was told we would be fed proper and allowed outside at times once the ship sails.' She looked me up and down. 'If I were you, lovey, I would mess yerself up a bit. You don't look the part for all yer convict clothing and you will get picked on. You better watch out for one or two as have nothing better to do than pick fights.'

'Thank you,' I said, before asking the question that was at the front of my mind. 'When do you think we will sail?'

'Oh, it'll be today. The sailors were all about making everything ready yesterday and the guards are really twitched, keepin' us away from the upper deck. They won't want anyone up there in case they jump. None of us women would do that but there are some fellas who might try it.'

'There are men here?' I was surprised, I don't know why.

'Aye, not many, but they is all ironed, just in case. This ain't a regular transport ship so they be extra watchful.'

I was still looking at what was going on around me when

I saw my aunt in close talk with a red-headed woman. They were as far away from me as it was possible to be, but I could hear them getting louder by the second. Suddenly, I saw my aunt land a blow on the other woman's face and not to be outdone the red-head kicked out and pushed Tilly down where she proceeded to kick her repeatedly. I started to get up and then sank back. It was nothing to do with me and I owed her naught. Within a very short space of time, a whole crowd of them were fighting.

'See what I mean,' muttered the woman next to me. 'You wanna stay clear of some of they. Don't recognise that old bird, though.'

'She was put on with me last night. I know her well. She is my aunt, my mother's sister, and I intend to stay as far from her as I can. She murdered my husband and kidnapped me and my child.'

She looked at me curiously. 'Oh, aye, that's a lot of bad blood between you. Stay near me, Esther. My name is Lucy and I'll tip you the wink if I can.'

'I am glad to know you, Lucy. It is good to put a name to a friendly face.' I was so appreciative at this gesture of friendship, I nearly cried.

'The more people you know, the better it will be for you. We look out for each other against the cranky ones, like her, the red-head. She be as mean as a pack of dogs chasing a rabbit.'

She can't be any worse than Aunt Tilly, I thought gloomily.

The anchor was lifted some hours later with a tremendous screeching noise of metal dragging on metal, and even down in the hell-hole that was our home for the foreseeable future, we could hear the racket of sailors running about and shouting. The ship pitched alarmingly and we all flopped this way and that as we tried to stay upright. There was no attempt to give us any fresh air and I felt sick and dizzy in the foetid atmosphere.

We were kept on the 'tween deck for three whole days, by which time the air had become foul and hot with so many bodies crammed together. There was no privacy, with everyone compelled to eat and perform their bodily functions in general view. I despaired and began to think I would be better off dead. The slop buckets became so full, they overflowed and then tipped over, so our feet were in the excrement. On the second day, the women seemed to sort themselves into groups and gradually some order came about. Food was distributed more fairly thanks to some who forced others to share; there clearly was some sort of hierarchy. I made no attempt to join in anything that would push me to the fore and by this method I was ignored and discounted. Lucy introduced me to one other, an older woman who was suffering badly in the heat, her breathing shallow and laboured. I quietly showed her how to slow her breathing to harvest the benefit of every gasp. For a few minutes she did as I suggested but then panic set in and she ended up gasping and fighting for breath once more. I tried again and again until she understood and mastered herself. She smiled and thanked me, and said her name was Alice. Now I had two friends.

Our lives were controlled by the guards. They delivered food and water, counted bowls and utensils down and up again, the same with hammocks, and a blanket for each, though it was often so hot that we didn't need it on top of us, but it did make the hammock more comfortable if you lay on it. Occasionally, I saw women taken above and two at least didn't return. Lucy reckoned they had been selected for the use of the guards or sailors who saw the women on board as one of the benefits. One came back with a black eye and bruising all around her face. Clearly, she had not submitted willingly.

One morning, about four days after we set sail, we were allowed to go up to another deck, which was wonderful: fresh air, blue sky and seabirds following closely in the wake of the ship. A group of women were given scrapers, brushes and sea water to get rid of the soil we left behind, the buckets not being adequate for our needs. While we enjoyed the freedom of the upper deck, we were being closely watched by the ship's company and I huddled amid my fellow prisoners so I wasn't picked out for 'wife duty'. Others however did choose to mix and saw this as an opportunity - they flaunted themselves openly to the guards and sailors in the hope of better treatment and more food. I saw some women bare their breasts to a ragged cheer from the watching men.

After a while I became used to the smell and the itch of lice and dirt that now clung to me. We had been at sea for many days, though some of those were spent on the top deck whilst the 'tween deck was scraped clean. I never saw the male convicts, but I am sure there was some method of contact between us all as the currency of the groups was gossip and there was much of it. I volunteered to do some of the cleaning, even though my leg was hurting, because it allowed me to get my hands washed in the rinsing sea water. The lack of cleanliness was distressing to me but very few others seemed to care. Our whole day revolved around food;

not much of it compared to what I was used to, but Lucy said it was better than they had on the hulk. Mostly it was a mess of soup with bits of tough meat and some vegetables bobbing about in it. You had to be careful not to spill it as the ship rose and dipped in the waves.

One morning, whilst we were up above, we were permitted to wash our clothing. Blankets were draped round to give some privacy but there were a great many men up in the rigging, more than usual, who would watch every move we made, throwing coarse comments down to their mates. None of us cared, we were past caring, we just wanted some clean dry clothing. It was on one of those occasions that I saw some other women on the ship. It seemed that some of the officers' wives accompanied them on journeys and there were also women aboard who were clearly maids and servants. One woman in particular drew my attention. She had long hair and was well turned out compared to our sorry selves. She looked familiar somehow, but I couldn't place her. She saw me looking and turned fully to study me before suddenly shrieking out loud, 'Esther, why it's Esther!' I had no idea who she was and as I was being hustled away to return to our quarters, I lost sight of her. After that, I always looked out for her but when I didn't see her, I came to think that it must have been a strange delusion born of despair.

Chapter Twenty-Two

Many convicts, having already spent some months in the insanitary, fever-ridden gaols or in the noisome hulks, were sent aboard the transports in a sickly and emaciated state and, often enough, suffering from an infectious or contagious complaint.

The Convict Ships by Charles Bateson

The following day the weather was dreadful, and we were all pitching and groaning in our quarters. Nearly everyone was sick and the pails were full and overflowing. I prayed for good weather days and a visit to the upper deck. It was difficult to tell who was being sick because of the violent seas or who were ill from other complaints, and many were. We had people amongst us who should have been isolated and treated by a doctor; I tried to help where I could. Somehow it had become known that I was a nurse though I had told only Lucy, but in truth there was not much that could be done without medicaments or even clean water.

One morning, I got up the courage to approach one of the friendlier guards and ask if there were any medical supplies on board to help with an outbreak of sickness and runs. He told me to mind my own business but came back later with another man, an officer who thrust his way through the women towards me. He was a tall, thin man with a hard stare and as he looked down on me, I felt a quiver of apprehension. Was it wise to have stepped forward, away from the safety of the shadows? They pushed me roughly over to one side but even so some of the ladies gathered around us, ready and able to hear what was going on.

'Your name is Esther Coad, is that correct?' said the officer.

Deeply shocked that my real name was known to this man, rather than that of the night-walker I had replaced, I replied, 'It is the name I was born with. I was only married for one month, so I don't use my husband's name – nobody knows me by that.'

'Well, the thing is, Miss or Mrs., whichever you are, there is no-one supposed to be on this ship with that name.'

'Oh,' I muttered. Was this my chance?

'How do you account for yourself?' His tone was icy and insistent. 'I want you to explain how you come to be here.' I trembled, not sure what to do or say, but say something I must, and quickly.

'I was forced here, against my will,' I blurted out. 'I am not a convict but a woman who has suffered a monstrous wrong at the hands of others, one of whom is on this boat masquerading as a convict.'

The women nearby all gasped and began repeating my comments back through the throng.

'You will forgive me if I say that your story defies belief,' he sneered, 'but I have been given reason to question you. You will accompany me to the upper deck. Come.'

I was wedged between them as the guard forced his way back through the women who moved aside reluctantly. I clambered up the ladder after him and as I was about to leave the ghastly conditions behind me, I looked back at my fellow prisoners. Every eye was on me, every emotion on the faces that followed me - curiosity, jealousy, envy - and from my aunt, something else, perhaps even fear, as our eyes locked. I clutched at my threadbare clothing as I hurried behind the lanky, stern man. I was ashamed of how I looked - my shorn hair, how I smelled, how my skin crawled with lice - and it came home to me how much like a convict I had become.

We stood out on the deck and I gulped fresh air into my lungs, rejoicing in the feel of a gentle sun on my back.

'How do you know my name?' I asked, before he had a chance to speak.

'We will come to that,' he said, 'once I have established who was involved in putting you here.'

I was shocked and disappointed that he wasn't interested in the wrong done to me but rather who, on this ship, had been bribed and who else knew about it.

'I have no idea who knows about me,' I said. 'My aunt, a woman called Tilly Kempe, who is also aboard, is wanted for crimes that would see her executed should she be caught. She is a notorious smuggler and recently escaped from Newgate prison,' I went on. 'Her arm is long. It was she that bribed us onto this ship. We came aboard the night before we sailed, and two night-walkers were taken off. It was a simple substitution, but I was forced into it by her use of drugs and blackmail. She threatened my child with death. She is the very devil,' I swore vehemently, as I sought to convince the officer of my terrible predicament.

'So, you know the names of these night-walkers that you and she are supposed to have replaced?' he asked, sarcastically. Clearly, he didn't believe me.

'No, I do not. My aunt didn't tell me their names and I am not sure she knew them herself. Possibly she hadn't thought further than getting on the ship - for her it was an escape from certain execution. But I can't be expected to answer for her.'

He looked out towards the great ocean, wrinkling his brow and pursing his lips before going on, 'And what were you going to do when we get to Australia?'

His voice had changed slightly, his tone less hectoring; perhaps I was getting through to him.

'I don't know. My only thought has been to find a way off this ship and get back to my life in Lewes. Please, I have a child. She was stolen by my aunt and is in great danger,' I started to break down as I said this, tears stinging my eyes. 'Please, can you help me, please?'

'It is not as easy as that, Miss. We are contracted to take 39 women convicts to Australia and just because you *tell* me you are not a convict doesn't mean that I should believe you and set you free,' he said, impatiently. 'You could be selling me a cock and bull story, for all I know. Until I have proof otherwise, you remain a convict.'

Tears spilled from my eyes. Brushing them away, I heard myself begging him, 'Please help me. My baby - her name is Beth - her life is in great danger from my aunt's smuggling gang.'

I could see he was getting exasperated at my emotion and for a moment he seemed perplexed.

Then he said, abruptly, 'Even if I had proof, I couldn't just release you against the judgement of a court of law. Either way, you would have to be delivered, as a convict, to the Governor at our destination. It would be for him to establish who you are and whether you can be returned to England and the courts.'

I crumpled to the floor, defeated. My limpy leg was trapped under me at an awkward angle and I couldn't help gasping as a stab of pain shot up into my hip. He saw me wince and this time I saw real doubt in his eyes.

His voice softened slightly as he told me to rise. I did so, pressing my hands to the deck to get some leverage in lifting myself up. I looked downwards, not wanting to be further exposed in my misery and struggling to suppress my anguish.

'There is a woman on board,' he went on, 'who says she knows you and has given us an account of your history. She declares you to be Esther Coad, of Lewes in the county of Sussex, and that you are not a convict.'

'Who is this woman? What is she to me?' I asked, taken aback at such a likelihood, but then I remembered the woman on deck whom I thought had shouted out my name – but later discounted it as too unlikely to be true.

'Her name is Sarah. She is the doxy of one of our crew members - not an officer but a senior crewman. She is a convict like you and has found an easy billet in hitching up with our man. Such women get certain privileges,' he said, with contempt in his voice. 'It is not a legal or acknowledged situation, but the captain takes a pragmatic view of it so that his crew are kept happy on a long and difficult voyage. She has been on this ship for a while, and as long as the crewman wants her, then she keeps her freedom from delivery to Australia. A lot of convicts die on these journeys and numbers get blurred.' He shrugged.

'You say a 'convict' like me, except I am not a convict,'

143

I insisted. 'But, Sarah – yes, I briefly met a Sarah in Lewes! She was tried and sentenced to be transported. I visited her in the cells and gave her a small gift. I felt sorry for her.'

It was strange to know that I had friends on board and one that was above deck as well as Lucy and Alice below. I struggled to believe that my short acquaintance with Sarah could have such a direct effect on my life. I hoped to meet and thank her, and my thanks would come from the bottom of my heart.

'Well,' he said, dryly, 'your kindness seems to have been reciprocated in testimony from this woman that you are not who we thought you to be. But, you must understand, we cannot just undo a court order. You need to go through official channels to get yourself declared a victim of mistaken identity, kidnap, or whatever. Now,' he said, in a brisker tone, 'I must take steps to locate the crewman or men who enabled this situation. If they support your story, it will help your case. If they don't, and that is far more likely, then you will have to find some other way of establishing who you are. Sarah's testimony will not be enough, as she is a convict.'

I clutched his arm. 'Do I have to go back down below?' I pleaded. 'I am afraid of my aunt. She will not like this turn of events. She is a truly wicked woman, she murdered my husband and kidnapped and threatened to kill my little girl.'

'I don't know, Miss, this is a very unusual occurrence, in fact it is almost unbelievable. I will have to consult with the captain, who prides himself on running a tight ship. Many don't, but he is a man of principle and won't like this situation on his watch.' He paused. I could see him turning things over in his mind as I waited. 'Until I have some answers, I will put you in the care of one of the crew and you may remain up on this deck for the time being. As a matter of interest, I understand from my guard that you were asking for medicines?'

'Yes, I have some experience in nursing and midwifery.' I said quickly. 'There are many women who are very sick, as well as some in general ill-health. I hoped you might have some medicines to hand which would help.' As I still had his attention, I enlarged briefly on my experience. 'I was a pupil midwife before I became embroiled in my aunt's schemes. Is there not a medical man on board?'

'Unfortunately, no. The agent decides on the facilities necessary and though there is talk of putting a physician regularly on all the transports, it has not yet come about. We are not a usual transport ship which is why there is but a small number of you. We are carrying more cargo than convicts, though some might say that convicts are cargo! I will leave you now, Miss Coad, and Jones, here, will escort you to a place where you will wait.'

He turned to a sailor who had been loitering nearby and said, 'Jones, keep this woman under lock. She can be given food and drink when the guards take theirs.'

'Aye, Sir,' said a small but wiry sailor.

I was taken to a small cabin, which was clearly used for stowing goods. Seaman Jones moved some items out of the way and offered me a seat on a crate while he remained standing on guard, though he went to great lengths to assure me that he was a seaman and not a guard. Sometime later I was given a meal and biscuit but still no solution to my predicament. Jones turned out to be a chippy character and would talk to me out of the corner of his mouth. If someone were watching from the other side of his face, they would not realise he was speaking at all. He was very droll and before long we were chatting freely.

'Some old bint has been dragged up afore His Prickship to answer questions as to how someone as old as her can be listed as a night-walker aged 23.'

'Who is His Prickship?' I asked in bewilderment.

'Him as put you 'ere,' Jones replied, with a grimace.

'Has he got her true name out of her?'

'Na, she's keeping quiet about herself but swears you are her companion on the streets. He wants to know if the others will say she and you 'as been on the hulk with them.'

'Well, she wasn't, nor was I,' I said bluntly.

'Na, but they won't grass. It's their code.'

My spirits slumped again.

The food I was given was better than what we got below; while I ate, Jones locked me in the little cabin before going off to get his own rations. He returned later with a mug of ale and continued his blow-by-blow account of what was happening with His Prickship.

'He's 'eard from Carrot-Top that the old bint is not one of them of't hulk.'

'I thought you said they would all stick together?'

'Seems they don't get on. Carrot-Top don't take kindly to someone muscling in on her patch.'

I allowed myself to hope, just a little.

Later, there were voices outside. The door was opened as a woman slid cautiously in, quietly shutting the door behind her. It was Sarah, but I barely recognised her as the prisoner from the Lewes lockup.

'Esther, I knew it were you, lovey!' she said, excitedly. 'I told my fella all about you when I first got transported – and when I saw you up on deck, I knowed it were you.'

I clasped her hand. 'Sarah, I can't thank you enough for helping me. My aunt kidnapped me and my little Beth. She threatened to kill her, and she murdered my husband at the church. Sarah, can you believe it? And then I was drugged and forced onto this ship.' I gabbled my sorry tale to her and could see the bafflement in her face, but she believed me without question.

'Bitch, and her pretending to be a tart! She must be all of 60.' Sarah laughed. 'I'm just sorry I can't say as who she is but I did say what happened to yer afore and you lived in that stew of a place, Lewes, and you was not a street walker, and that you got friends in 'igh places, like,'

'Oh, Sarah,' I said, weeping again, 'I am that grateful to you.'

'I must be off now. If 'is Prickship catches me, I'll be for it.' She turned for the door. 'I'll look out for thee, Esther, don't you worry none.'

She disappeared, leaving me to contemplate in amazement all that had happened and to work out how I could help myself. Perhaps if I asked to see the captain, he would be merciful and not send me back down to the 'tween deck. As I waited, as patiently as possible, I wondered why Sarah and Jones called the officer 'His Prickship.'

Chapter Twenty-Three

Conditions aboard the convict ships, more particularly in the early years, were not such as were calculated to prevent or check disease. The prisons in the 'tween decks were gloomy, dank and insanitary, and frequently the prisoners, generally handcuffed and leg-ironed, were confined in them for long periods. As gross over-crowding was common, it is not surprising that the prisons were fertile breeding-places for diseases of all kinds.

The Convict Ships by Charles Bateson

I was to be quartered in a cabin on the upper deck, far away from the convicts! In return, I had agreed to help the ship's company with their medical needs and try to improve the health of those convicts who are suffering from the effects of close confinement. I was also to be given access to the ship's medical supplies under supervision. I was still regarded as a convict but His Prickship said again that the captain was a pragmatic man and that he wanted to make the best of a bad situation. My story was helped by two of the ship's company who were found to have accepted a bribe; perhaps, Jones says, their admission was made with a view to being sent home. They were to be flogged and probably further punished once we made landfall. My aunt was now to be kept under close guard and she had lost the right to go up on to the exercise deck with the others. She had been threatened with irons if she caused any more trouble and her actions laid before the Governor. She had even more reason to hate me now.

I was taken to a cabin where there was basic medical equipment and a locked chest containing supplies. I was to be shut in the room in the morning, given my meals there and the key to the chest which I must return at night. I would have to account for everything I used with detailed notes of who I treated, with what and the outcome.

I had discovered from Jones that the boat was fully laden with cargo as well as the convicts, and with space so limited, I asked if it would be possible for me to string up a hammock in the cabin. I hoped so because there was a lock on the door. Though I had no freedom, I was so much better off, I could hardly believe my turn of luck. Sarah had visited me again and was going to try and find me something to wear over my convict garments. Seaman Jones seemed to have taken me under his wing and was my source of all knowledge. A great deal of turning a blind eye appeared to go on aboard the ship and I hoped I would be able to give a good account of myself whenever we got to land when I would have to beg the Governor to return to Britain. I was so indebted to Sarah and I thanked God for her presence on this ship and her stout defence of me.

It was as I had hoped. I was permitted to sleep in the cabin and lock the door. How I rejoiced at the privacy.

His Prickship was stern, but fair. He had stipulated that I could attend any of the ship's company that he permitted but always in the company of another, either a senior sailor or officer; for this I was to be available at all times. As to the convicts, I would be allowed to treat them in my new room but if I needed to go down below, I was to do so with a guard, who would be armed. Any treatment that I deemed necessary would have to be talked through with him first and noted in writing. This was all to be for a trial period until the boat docked for fresh supplies and to unload some of the cargo in a place called Gibraltar.

My spirits soared, and though I was separated from Beth and my friends, I already had much to be thankful for. I'd found four friends - my two convict colleagues, Lucy and Alice; Sarah and Seaman Jones and perhaps also an ally in Prickship whose real name I had discovered to be Mason. I'd heard that the ordinary sailors thought him too high and mighty and rigid in attitude which was how he got his name. Jones said to me, 'He's a prick, what else should we call him?'

My greatest worry was that I would be unable to deal with the medical matters that occurred, another concern that kept me awake at night.

I had opened the chest and found detailed records of treatments needed on other voyages. Some or part of the entries were in Latin and covered areas of medicine beyond my knowledge. Oh God, I muttered to myself, as it came home to me in painful detail how limited was my learning. I didn't even recognise the contents of the chest: all the creams, ointments and bottles of different coloured liquids that might be poison, for all I knew - there was certainly quite a number of blue bottles. The previous surgeon, his name was Brooks, had been capable of amputating, setting bones and dealing with diseases way beyond my skills and, furthermore, I had always had my herbs to fall back on. There were no herbs here. I was sickened and terrified that these people would expect more of me than I could give. I sat back on my heels and burst into tears. I felt that I just couldn't do this.

Later that day, Sarah visited me again and I told her why I had been crying after she commented on the streaky face I was presenting to the world.

'I am a fraud, Sarah.' I wept. 'I have no knowledge of most of the conditions that Surgeon Brooks refers to. I don't even recognise the terms he uses. I can't pretend that I do - I will be discovered immediately and then sent back to the 'tween deck.' I started to cry again at the thought of that and the retribution of Aunt Tilly and what she might do to me.

Sarah joined me on the floor and started pulling everything out of the chest, saying, 'Let's just have a gander before we give up, Esther. You are better than nothing in their eyes, and if you just use your noddle, you can get by and give a good account of yerself. There is no-one else on this ship that can do better than you so they, and you, have naught to lose and you are not costing them a penny piece. Use your common sense, lovey.'

'But I have, Sarah,' I went on. 'I jumped at this chance, yet, if I don't succeed, at least in part, I will be returned to the convict deck.'

'No, you won't,' she scoffed. 'I heard that they believe your story, especially as those two sailors admitted to swapping you for them hussies. They are gonna be flogged tomorrow and handed over to the soldiers in Gibraltar when we get there, so there is no likelihood of you being treated as a convict - on this ship, at least.'

Her straightforward reasoning cheered me a little and we did as she suggested, removing everything from the chest and putting it in piles. There were charts and medical diagrams and tucked away in the bottom of the chest a list of all the medicants and, wonder of wonders, what they were used for, with likely quantities. Jones told me later that cargo ships didn't always carry a surgeon, so an officer had to be roped in to do basic doctoring if needed. Serious cases involved sailors taking their chances until they put into port, which sounded unfortunate for them.

Sarah and I sorted everything into likely need and I undertook to sterilise, with alcohol, any instruments that might be useful.

I pinned up some medical diagrams to inspire confidence, mine as much as anyone else's, and by the time we had finished there was an air of professionalism in the cabin. I resolved to read Surgeon Brooks's journal, except the Latin bits, and hoped I would be able to understand some of the simple cases. If I could decipher his writing and treatments, then I would be halfway towards making a sensible diagnosis of my own.

Chapter Twenty-Four

Prohibited from selling the convicts' services, the contractors derived
no financial benefit from landing them in a physically sound and
healthy state. Indeed, dead convicts were more profitable than the
living, since every prisoner who died on the passage represented a
saving in the expenditure on provisions
The Convict Ships by Charles Bateson

The men of the ship's company began seeking me out straightaway with problems ranging from sores, blisters on the eyes, boils, and a stab wound after a fight between some of the guards. After a couple of days some of the women were allowed to come to my cabin and I was more than capable of dealing with their problems, including the sickness and runs. Luckily the sickness had abated slightly with better weather and perhaps we women were all getting used to the peculiar motion of the seas. Everyone I saw would have benefited from my herbal preparations, but it was not to be - I had to make do with what I had. The quarters of the female convicts were damp and unhealthy, as I knew only too well, and I was sure they bred sores and fungal conditions. Fortunately, I now knew that there were medicines available for most common ailments, but fresh air and simple cleanliness would improve everyone's lot and I resolved to try and bring this about.

I thought some of the seamen and guards were more interested in avoiding work than in getting better and several of them hadn't got anything wrong with them at all; they just wanted to see me! More seriously, I treated two cases of fever among the women convicts and I asked Jones if there was anywhere I could put people in quarantine. He thought I was joking! Most of my work involved simple dressings, healing ointments and offering basic advice. I breathed a sigh of relief after my first day, though I'd been greatly alarmed by the stab wound. Fortunately, it wasn't as bad as it looked, more of a deep scratch than a serious opening, and I was able to sew it up neatly. I confided in Sarah, who visited me regularly, that I was still very nervous every time a new patient appeared at my door. I worried that they might have a dread disease that could wipe out most of the crew and passengers. Sarah was always such a tonic though, so buoyant and happy with her man and new status; and she still treasured my gift to her, a tiny bar of soap with a coin buried inside it. Whenever I felt overwhelmed with sadness at my loss or terrified by the responsibility thrust upon me, I sought a visit from her, with Jones acting as our go-between. I was so glad of his presence, particularly to protect me from the uncouth guards who sought me out in the guise of ill-health.

The officer called Prickship started to take quite an interest in my work and when I suggested that the prisoners' quarters be cleaned more often to prevent disease, he was open to the idea, once I pointed out the considerable benefits. To my mind, if the convicts were held more on the upper deck, the floors could be cleaned more thoroughly, and they would dry before everyone was sent back below again.

The captain had agreed that access to the upper deck could be more frequent and long enough to allow the 'tween deck to dry after it had been scraped and swilled down. The convicts did the work themselves; they had made a rota. Even the male convicts were allowed up for longer, but the guard was then a lot more vigilant and the men and women were never mixed. I felt really pleased to have been able to manage all this by letting Prickship think that it was his idea that cleaner quarters, as well as better air, would keep everyone in a much healthier state. Sometimes the weather was much too rough for the convicts to come up from below, but then the hatches are left open for fresh air to ventilate their quarters. Even when the wind was blowing and the sea rising with turbulent waves, I found I was enjoying the exhilaration of it – I thought I might make a sailor yet!

Every night when Prickship heard my report of who was sick, who was better, and who was malingering, I found his gaze fixed on me, and Jones commented that he visits me even when he is off duty.

'Got a soft spot for you, he has, Miss. He was never interested in the prisoners' welfare before you took it up. You wanna watch out,' This was said with a lot of winking and grimacing.

I laughed. 'Has he got a woman on board?'

'Why, you interested?'

'No, of course not, I still have my husband in my heart.'

'Well, I don' expect he wants to be in your 'eart, Miss, 'e'll be more interested in bein' in other places.'

'Mr. Jones!' I protested. 'Don't dare say such things to me, even in jest.'

155

He roared with laughter as I locked him out of my little room.

Every day I had been feeling a bit more comfortable in my role and Jones took the opportunity to slide off on his own business and when he returned I become his confidante. He seemed to know some scurrilous detail about everyone on board and, by the end of the day, so did I. I enjoyed his company and his tales were so very wicked, I couldn't help but laugh. I had never known how enjoyable gossiping could be!

One day - an important day, though I didn't realise it at the time - I heard a great deal of whistling and jumping to attention before there came a sharp rap on my door. I was stitching up a deep cut on the arm of one of the surliest guards, the cause of which was unclear and unlikely to be divulged to me. My friend Jones was attending, and he leapt to salute as the door was flung open and the captain swept in. I had never seen Jones move so fast and I stared, with my needle poised mid-air, at this smartly dressed and very attractive man who filled the whole room with his authority.

'At ease,' he said. 'Carry on, Miss.'

I continued to stitch, though I wobbled a bit under his scrutiny. Once I'd finished I gave the guard some advice as to why he should try and keep the wound dry and clean, but he wasn't listening - he couldn't get out of the room quick enough.

I wiped my work surface clean and put the needle into a solution of alcohol and some liquid recommended in Surgeon Brooks's diary.

'You are comfortable, Miss?' asked the captain. 'Not too put upon by all the malingerers?'

'No, Sir, but there are a lot of them.'

'The convicts, they are better purposed now we have implemented your suggestions?'

'Two have a worrying fever, but it doesn't seem to be progressing to anything more serious. I am keeping a close watch on them, though.'

'I understand you want to know if there is isolation space available?'

'As a precaution, yes. It might be necessary if any of the conditions that Surgeon Brooks came across should appear, which is why I am concerned about the two women.'

'We will make space available, if necessary, but I don't want the men spread thin in guarding half a dozen different areas.'

'There are only two who give concern and they can be kept together as they have the same symptoms.'

'Argh, well, we will wait and see how they do.'

'Thank you, Sir.' I looked enquiringly at the captain, wondering what he was thinking. He seemed hesitant about leaving even though we had come to the end of our conversation. There was a long and uncomfortable pause before he changed the subject completely.

'Mason tells me you are trained to help women give birth?'

I couldn't think who Mason was, having got used to thinking of him as 'Prickship', but recollecting, I replied, 'I have attended many women in Lewes where I am of the household of Mr. and Mrs. Elwood. She is the daughter of an earl and is my patron. I was in attendance for both her live births.' As the captain was nodding encouragingly at me, I took the opportunity to elaborate on my circumstances.

I went on, 'The Elwoods are frequently part of the Prince of Wales's circle. Because of their influence I was taught midwifery by Dr. Grieve, the coroner for Lewes. Unfortunately, the doctor went on an extended tour, so my pupillage wasn't completed. After he left, the local women came to me for help, particularly as most of them couldn't afford to pay any of the other physicians in the town. I learned quickly, by deed and result.'

'The Prince of Wales, you say?'

He was clearly impressed, so I continued in the same vein.

'Yes, Captain. Lewes is very near the village of Brighthelmstone where the Prince bought land near the sea - he plans to build a fantastical palace there. He attends the races at Lewes and the Elwoods dine with him on occasion.' This was an exaggeration, but I had to make myself seem important to people of standing if I was ever to get off this ship.

'Argh,' he said and turned on his heel and stalked off.

I collapsed onto the chair, gasping at my own cheek.

'Well, that told him,' said Jones, laughing.

'Yes, Jones, that told him. Do you think he believed me?'

'He'd have balled you out if 'e didn't. He probably wanted to check you out before letting you near 'is wife.'

I gasped. 'His wife is on board?'

'Aye, an' expecting a nipper she be, and woe betide anyone who gets on the cross side of her.'

'What do you mean?'

'She's a bit of a tartar and keeps him on his toes.'

'No! He looks so full of authority, he quite made me tremble.'

'Not where 'is missus is concerned, Miss, she is holding all the cards and don't suffer other women around her husband.'

'Does she always sail with him, then?'

'Where he goes,' he smirked, 'she goes.'

Chapter Twenty-Five

*A history of the convict ships, of the officials and merchants
who despatched them, of the men of the navy, the army and the
mercantile marine who manned them, and of the hapless convicts
who peopled their dank and gloomy prisons below decks. It
is a history which has many dark and sombre hues – a story of
hardship and human suffering, of disease and callous brutality, of
mutiny and shipwreck, of cowardice and courage.*

The Convict Ships by Charles Bateson:
(Preface to first edition)

When Jones was not keeping me amused with his salty tales and ripe language, I sank into a depth of despair and worry about Beth's fate. I was certain that Cecilia would have tracked her down and taken her back into her care but always there was the worry that Farmer Coad might go to law and claim his daughter. Though he did not cover himself in glory at my trial, he was still her father and had greater rights than I did. If he claimed her back, she would become a servant to the family and not require paying, which would be an incentive for the Coads.

I resolved to speak to Prickship and ask him if there was any hope of getting a letter back to Britain. There were other ships on this great sea and sometimes they came within hailing distance, with news exchanged and occasionally a visitor rowing over to speak to the captain privately. It looked hazardous, but I saw it happen on at least one occasion.

I approached him as soon as I could.

'If I write a letter,' I asked, 'is it possible that it could be handed to another ship, one returning to Britain?'

'Well, it's possible,' he replied, 'but you would be more sensible waiting until we dock in Gibraltar. Then you will be certain that the letter will go with some chance of it being received.'

'But how long will that be?'

'Not too long, the weather looks set fair and we are making good sail.'

'But you can't say?'

'Winds are unpredictable - we are not yet through the Bay of Biscay, and there is the added risk that we run into enemy vessels. We have been fortunate so far but as we get nearer Gibraltar we remain on high alert. Write your letter and we will find someone reliable when we dock and speak to the authorities,' he went on. 'Gibraltar is a British fort and although small it has enormous strategic importance for London. Some of our cargo is urgently needed by the military so the Commander there might be amenable, and he is well known to the captain. There will be a lot of official post to-ing and fro-ing and if you can get your letter included that will be the quickest route.'

I went back to my cabin and sat with my head in my hands. An opportunity: I would write, all night if need be. Maybe, in as little time as a few weeks they would get my letter; they would know I was safe and they would know where Beth was being held, if they didn't already have her. Perhaps they could help to get me home by explaining matters to the people who count and help have my convict status dropped, or, perhaps I could persuade the captain to declare me dead and slip back that way. That would however force me to remain until we got to Australia and remain on board for the return trip. I didn't think it likely that the captain or Prickship would agree.

I didn't take all night, it turned out. I made several attempts to put it all down but became overwhelmed. The fear, the panic and the hurt all came back again when it came to retelling it all, as well as conveying my worries that my skills in my current situation were so limited but that my freedom might depend on them. In the end, I just stated the bald facts and begged my friends to help me and Beth. I was sure Prickship would help me get my letter into the right hands.

Having got this all off my chest, I settled down to wait the time out. I realised that I had become quite familiar with the ship and its complicated sails and the great hubbub of noise made by the sailors as they sought the wind; I truly enjoyed the excitement. We have had good sailing weather, according to Jones, and were making headway. The women convicts were cleaner and better fed than when we joined the ship and, as many of them had been sent to me for treatment, particularly the sickness and belly-ache, I had got to know their stories as well as their hopes and dreams. Lucy had been allowed up to my little cabin as she was experiencing some belly-pain, and once I had gotten to the bottom of that, we were able to exchange some gossip.

My aunt was still causing trouble but was so closely confined, she wasn't enjoying the power she had hoped for. The red-head was completely in charge of the women and

Lucy said that was unlikely to change. Clearly Aunt Tilly had met her match. The older woman, Alice, had continued with her breathing exercise and was much calmer in general; I was touched to hear that she asked Lucy to tell me that I had made such a difference to her.

My understanding of transportation changed when I realised that although it was a punishment for their crimes, almost all the women wanted to go just to get away from their past and start afresh. There were some women, like my aunt and the red-head, who would always find trouble because it was their nature, but others were just ordinary women who had got caught on a slippery slope of need, hunger and lack of work to earn enough to feed themselves and their families. I felt such pity for some of them and knew that there but for the grace of God and my friends, would I be too. When they got to their destination, they would all have jobs found for them in what would truly be a land of opportunity once their prison term expired. I wanted to help them in any way I could. I made notes in a diary of my own that might be seen by the Governor of the place they were going to and tried to give positive reference about those that I treated and how I found them.

Jones told me in no uncertain words that I was wrong in the head and if I had seen as many convict women as he, I would change my opinion. He seemed to think they were all of the same stamp and deserved every punishment man can devise. He talked of ships where the women migrate nightly to the sailor's quarters by getting through the bulkheads and, if caught, mete out the vilest abuse it is possible to know, more than even he knows! Some ships, he said, have ended up putting irons on the entire convict population, they were so badly behaved. I knew there were only a small number of convicts on board the *Lady Charlotte*, compared to other ships, but I didn't see any sign of such wanton behaviour; he informed me sourly that I didn't know where to look. The men, however, he said, were much more straightforward and apart from looking for an opportunity to escape, they were a lot less awkward and troublesome. It was his firm belief that the officers on board most transport ships do not want to carry women because they were just too much trouble and set all the men - sailors, guards, and convicts - at each other, sometimes with frightening results.

My interest in Surgeon Brooks's diary grew daily as I better understood his spidery writing and, as there was less Latin than English, I have been able to interpret some of the complaints he dealt with. I studied the treatments he prescribed and related the area of problem to the anatomical drawings and gradually extended my knowledge, particularly in understanding the medicants that we found in the chest, though I still wished I had my bag of herbs as many of them would have sufficed for the common complaints and I would have felt more confident.

Unfortunately, the diary did not help me diagnose what was wrong with Martha and Jane, the two feverish ladies. I managed to get them into isolation and spent as much time with them as I could, but they were sinking; each day they seemed less able to speak or show interest; and other than giving them cold ale (the water had deteriorated), and providing nourishment in the form of wet messes, I was at a complete loss. If only I had my herbs, I would at least have had other things to try. I was quite distraught as I watched them lower before my very eyes, but they knew I was there and trying my best. Martha, who was less sickly, smiled wanly as I sponged her wasted body down. The fever was not violent, but it was getting control in the steady progression of their illness, whatever it was.

A worrying time came after the two men who had accepted bribes from my aunt were sent to me to treat the lash wounds. Both had become infected and I wondered how much muck there was on the implement of this horrible punishment. I asked Jones to make sure that it was washed thoroughly between occasions of punishment, at the very least soaked in sea water. I held no grudge against these men even though they had caused me such trouble. It was all down to my aunt and I wished she could see the horrible sores they bore because of her actions; though one of them had clearly been flogged in the past as well. Neither of them seemed to realise that I was the person that had been substituted; I suppose I had just been a bundle with a sack over my head to them. I didn't enlighten them but I heard Jones giving them a dressing-down when they left my cabin. I couldn't make out half of what he said, using an excess of language that was foreign to me, but I did understand that they were to be handed over to the authorities when we got to port for even greater punishment. I also understood that Jones told them who I was and they didn't deserve what he called my 'tender care.'

One dreadful morning, I was greatly upset and saddened to find both Martha and Jane dead. They had succumbed during the night. Whatever had claimed them took them together even though I had thought Martha the stronger. I'd done everything I could think of to abate their fever, even requesting and receiving isolation for them, but to no avail, and the worst of it was I had no idea why they had died. I wept with frustration at my own lack of knowledge and sorrowfully attended the moment when their bodies were to be cast from the ship. No-one mourned them, and I was the only person who showed any respect as they were plunged into the deep. I wondered if their families would ever find out what had happened to them. I would ask Prickship and perhaps, if and when I got back home, I might be able to let them know myself of their end. I knew Martha had children and a man who loved her. She had told me that he had promised to wait for her.

As I made my way back to my cabin, Jones tried to cheer me with tales of previous voyages on ships carrying hundreds of convicts when many had died, which was no comfort to me at all. He said that this voyage was one of the best he had been on, with no bad weather and consequent sickness, no mutiny or fights between sailors and guards. In fact, he said it was a bit dreary and he was looking forward to a bit more interest once we got going on the next leg when the weather heated up which, he seemed to think, would liven things up.

'How can you say this is one of the best voyages you have been on and then say it is dreary?' I asked.

'Well, the weather is good for a start,' he said, 'and the cook is not all bad - the fella has judged the grub all right with animals kept alive until cook-up time so nothing 'as gone bad. The ship's biscuit is passable if you dip it in ale first to soften.'

Even as he answered, he jumped to attention as the captain bore down on us.

'Miss Coad, you will attend my wife this evening,' he said. 'Jones, here, will bring you to my cabin and mind you behave respectfully.'

'Aye sir,' we both replied together, and I had to stop myself from saluting.

'Well, well,' said Jones, and immediately resumed our conversation as the captain strode off.

'Course, this is a dry ship compared to some as I've been on - captain don't approve of drink. We don't get anything other than our rum ration, no more, no less, which is maybe why there's been no trouble. One brig I was on, there was more grog than you could believe and the convicts, the women that is, got hold of it in return for favours. That were a voyage, that were.' He chuckled at his memories.

We had arrived back at my cabin where Prickship was waiting, impatiently. He had a young boy with him who was doubled up in pain and groaning pitifully.

'A malingerer for you, Miss Coad. Please deal with him and let me know the outcome.'

He swiped the boy around the head as he walked off. The lad, not more than twelve years of age, grunted and made an obscene gesture at Prickship's back, before he entered my cabin and I began an exploration of his symptoms. While he was with me, he vomited, and I was able to see the results of a very unsatisfactory meal recently taken. I dosed him with a purge as used by Surgeon Brooks and told him to come back if he wasn't improved by evening.

Later, Prickship returned to ask about the lad; he also wanted to know where I had been. I was a bit irritated that he kept such a close eye on me. I had a feeling it was nothing to do with the ship's security but more likely his personal interest in me, so I answered shortly, 'I went to see the burial of Martha and Jane, the two women who died. I was upset and wanted to pay my respects.'

He snorted. 'You waste your sentiment on such as they. They probably had the fever before we even started this voyage, so you cannot be held to account.'

'I know I did nothing wrong, but I didn't help them get better and I am sorry for it.'

'If we get to our destination without losing half of the convicts, we will have done well. As only two have died so far, you should be pleased that your care and the changes you suggested have made a difference. Now,' his tone changed. 'More importantly, the captain wants you to attend on his wife and I have some advice. Remember to keep your place and don't try to get friendly – she can be a difficult woman and you need to keep on your mettle for the captain's sake. If he is happy, then everyone else gets an easy ride. If you upset her, then we will all suffer.'

I was quite astonished to be given this advice and thankful too as I showed him details of the boy's sickness.

'Argh, let's hope this is a single case. I wouldn't want everyone to go down with the shits. I will inform the captain and speak to cook.'

Later, I discovered that the galley area had been smoked and tarred and that a resident rat's nest was destroyed as were other nests all over the ship. In fact, there was a great clean-up by the sailors and the 'tween decks were inspected by the captain himself before he gave orders for them to be smoked as well. I wondered if we were nearing port.

Later I had time to reflect on the burial. Both bodies were sewn into a shroud-like garment and a short verse from the Bible was read. I was too far away, and it was windy, so I didn't hear all that was said over the deceased, but I could see that it was lacking in care. I felt they were just dumped as quickly as possible into the deep waters. Prickship was probably right in supposing that the women had the illness before they were put on board. Everyone was supposed to have been given a clean bill of health before departure, but I was told that many convicts hid their condition or symptoms, reasoning that they were more likely to recover once away from the noisome hulk or prison.

Chapter Twenty-Six

The number of prisoners embarked aboard the convict ships was substantially greater than the number landed at their destination. Disease took by far the heaviest toll. Scurvy, dysentery, typhoid fever, smallpox and other diseases were commonplace, especially in the earliest years of transportation, and effective measures to combat them were introduced but tardily.

The Convict Ships by Charles Bateson

My visit to the captain's quarters put me in an uncomfortable situation. As Jones and I approached the door, I could hear a shrill voice, shouting: 'I don't want some scabby convict invited into my rooms to examine me. God, what were you thinking, man? These trollops are filthy and contaminated with God knows what. And here you are bringing one to peer into my privates.'

'Dearest,' I heard the captain say, his tone conciliatory, 'Miss Coad is not a convict, she is a perfectly respectable young woman whose patron dines with the Prince of Wales.'

'I don't believe it!' came the reply. 'She's just another of your fancy women who has fed you a story. Get away from me, you fool.'

I looked at Jones and we both pulled a face as an object was thrown and smashed.

Jones knocked smartly on the door and it was wrenched open by a red-faced and sorry-looking captain who didn't look at all like the man I had seen earlier, being quite diminished in stature.

'Miss Coad, do come in, my wife is expecting you.'

I edged into the cabin expecting some china to hit me at any moment. She just glared at me coldly, so I plunged into an explanation of who I was.

'Ma'am, I am Esther Coad, a midwife from Lewes, in Sussex.' I looked at her, lying on a couch in a commodious cabin. 'May I come in?'

Her eyes raked over me before giving the slightest of nods.

'Where did you say you were from?' she demanded.

'Lewes, a small town, near Brighthelmstone in Sussex, Ma'am. My patron, Cecilia Elwood, is the daughter of an earl and a friend of the Prince of Wales. I have attended both her live births. She is also a close friend of Dr. Grieve, the coroner - I have been working as a pupil midwife in order to assist him in his practice.' I paused for breath, 'Mr. and Mrs. Elwood attended the prince's wedding and on occasion dine with his party. I am telling you this because I do not want you to think I come here on false pretences. I am only on this ship because I was forced, as an act of revenge, by my aunt who is down in the 'tween deck where she is ironed because of her dreadful deeds.' I gulped at the end of what felt like a speech.

I saw the tension leave her shoulders but there was no other sign of acceptance. I waited.

'Well, I suppose we might talk for a while about my condition. Leave us', she barked at the poor man who was captain of the ship.

Very carefully and respectfully I asked a few questions and nodded encouragingly as she began to warm to the theme of herself and her predicament - which I got the impression wasn't entirely welcome.

We established that the pregnancy was of approximately seven months in duration and she was feeling well but uncomfortable. I didn't dare suggest that I examine her but hoped she would invite me back when she was more accepting of my role. Once we were on cool but polite speaking terms, I suggested that I call back tomorrow when she was feeling more up to it and that is how we left things. I was very glad to escape and breathed a sigh of relief once outside the door. Jones was waiting and raised his eyebrows questioningly. I just nodded, and we returned to my room where I collapsed into my chair.

Later, I thought about the visit and wondered why on earth a woman would undertake a voyage of this nature when she was already very pregnant. I thought of asking Prickship but decided discretion was the way to proceed and not to discuss anything to do with the lady with anyone other than herself, and that included her husband! I hadn't examined her, but my instincts told me she was further on in her pregnancy than the seven months she claimed.

That night a mighty wind blew up and we were plunged deep into great troughs of water before rising, it seemed *vertically*, then falling so fast I thought my stomach was left behind. I kept to my room, on my knees and praying, as I heard the chaos on deck with men running frantically trying to keep the ship safe while confronting the great waves that broke over her, their voices lost in a battle between water and wind. I was terrified and sick until my insides were drained and aching. When I thought that the boat could surely take no more, it got even worse, a deal of crashing

172

and splintering wood as the timbers quarrelled with the sea and a vengeful wind. The roaring and howling were as if we were in Bedlam with everyone running riot together and screaming at the top of their voices.

Several times I heard a great shuddering boom and I felt certain that the masts were broken, and we would all be lost to a watery grave. Eventually, I pulled my blanket round my head, shut my eyes and stuffed my ears, trying not to pay heed to our peril. I must have fallen asleep at my desk because the next thing I heard was Jones banging on the door.

'Is it over, are we safe?' I asked as he entered.

'Just about, Miss. Quite a bit of damage but the carpenters and sailmakers are putting things to rights.'

'Did the masts come down?'

'I am going to have to teach you some nautical terms,' he laughed. 'But no, they didn't. We lost some rigging and sail, that's all. This is a tight ship and it will take a lot to cripple her. There will be a delay in the grub today, though, as the galley is awash and cook be drunk.'

'I thought you said this was a dry ship?'

'Well, 'e has access to brandy not given to us working men,' he grimaced. 'And he has been at it all night.'

'Was anyone hurt?'

'Some bumps and bruises and the 'tween decks are awash with stuff you wouldn't want mentioned in polite company. The fellas, too, seems their stomachs ain't up to a good blow.'

'Will we be able to get everyone up on deck,' I asked, thinking of the women cooped up below, 'or is it still too rough? It feels very pitchy to me.'

He chuckled. 'Pitchy, indeed. Captain will decide. Until then I suggest you prepare yourself for a lot of seasick folk.'

I didn't visit the captain's wife that day nor the next. As Jones had predicted, there were a lot of sickly convicts, both male and female, and some of the crew were suffering rope burns, cuts and bruises. The wind abated over the next 24 hours, allowing repairs and cleaning of the 'tween decks which were in a terrible mess. Gradually, everyone returned to their normal selves and were even become quite elated that we had survived the storm relatively unscathed.

On the third day after the storm, I received a visit from Prickship instructing me to call on Mrs. Campbell during the afternoon. We were quite becalmed, and I had no difficulty in making my way to the captain's cabin. It was a beautiful day and I hoped that the lady would be in a receptive mood.

I began by asking her if she had weathered the storm comfortably.

'Of course not!' she snapped. 'Just because I am used to this way of life doesn't mean I don't feel the tumult. However, I have some useful remedies for sickness and this cabin is well placed.'

I started to tell her that the convicts had suffered badly but she wasn't in the slightest bit interested so I gave up that line of conversation and contented myself with asking after her health. Eventually, after several brittle stops and starts, she dropped her shoulders. It was a mannerism I had noticed in our first encounter and clearly indicated when she was in a more relaxed state of mind and we were able to proceed with a mutually acceptable exchange of knowledge. She was not a young woman, I would hazard an age of 37, which is rather old for a first baby. She had intimated that she was not yet 30 but I didn't believe her and decided to keep my own counsel on that point. After we had conversed for a good time, I broached the subject of examining her which she was initially reluctant to allow, but when I pointed out that I could offer her little help unless I knew the position of the babe and how strong the heartbeat was, she agreed.

Fortunately for us both, all seemed quite normal, and I could reassure her on that point even though my belief was confirmed that this was more likely to be an eighth month child. However, the head was not yet positioned, so once again I kept my own counsel. Once she had restored her clothing, she became more amenable towards me and I plucked up courage to ask her where she intended to have her baby.'

'Well, I don't know. I was hoping that we would be in the Australias by the time it is due.'

'Perhaps,' I suggested tentatively, 'it would be possible to stay in Gibraltar where I believe we are headed, as I understand it is a British port and there are sure to be physicians of repute.'

She looked aghast. 'They'll all be military sawbones and anyway I don't believe it is necessary.'

'You might become uncomfortable nearer the time and wish you were far from the high seas where no-one can attend if your baby comes before the ship can dock. You would be at the mercy of the inexperienced sailors, like Pr... Mason.'

I saw her look at me, speculating.

'But *you* will be on board, Miss. As I understand it, you are listed as a convict and no-one can change that except the courts in Britain or the Governor in Australia. Or were you hoping to jump ship in Gibraltar?'

I flushed, as that was exactly what I was hoping to do, but it would be better to keep that to myself. What a secretive person I was becoming.

Chapter Twenty-Seven

It is stipulated that each ship should carry not less than three proper boats, that wholesome provisions and a sufficiency of water should be furnished to the seamen, and that two windsails for ventilation purposes and an Osbridge's machine for sweetening water should be in each vessel. This machine consisted of a hand pump which is inserted in a scuttle made at the top of a cask, and by means of it the water, being raised a few feet, falls through several sheets of tin pierced-like cullenders and placed in a half cylinder of the same metal. The purpose of it is to reduce the water into numberless drops, which being exposed in this form to the open air is deprived of its offensive quality.

The Convict Ships by Charles Bateson

One evening, having evaded my guard, as the light faded and a slight moon appeared, I found a quiet place on the deck to sit and think. I spent so much time in my little cabin that the air thinned and left me feeling quite wrung out. It was difficult to get away from the men who worked all hours to keep us moving towards a tiny corner of land in what seemed an endless sea. Despite Jones' attempts to educate me in seafaring, I still found it unbelievable that the captain and first mate could locate a lump of rock that rose out of the vast and ever-shifting ocean with no guide-points other than the stars and a few charts. I had to admit to being very ignorant of geography.

I sat myself on a reel of crusty rope and hidden from prying eyes turned my gaze to the darkening skies. Gradually pinpricks of light brightened into stars and a sliver of moon emerged through ragged clouds. The clamour of the boat receded as I managed to focus on my own thoughts; and as I watched the night deepen, I knew that those I had left behind could see the same moon as me, which was comforting. I had been through so much, yet I was still alive, still functioning and, surprisingly, still capable of normal behaviour: I laughed, cried, chatted and gossiped with Jones, Prickship and Sarah. Nevertheless, I wished so much to be at home in Lewes with my lovely Beth. I constantly prayed that she was back in Cecilia's care. Every hour, every day, she was in the foreground of my mind, yet, in order to function, I had to suppress these images.

But it was an altogether different type of vision that haunted my nightly dreams: I saw her as she might be - in the Coad household - and then I woke with a terrible sense of dread, my face wet with tears and my heart thudding at what might be. Sometimes, I let these visions play out in my head during the daytime, as if to punish myself for all the mistakes I had made. During those moments I looked inside myself and lost all hope.

As I keened for Beth, rocking back and forward on my rope seat, I caught sight of a small face peering in at me. Tears obscured my vision until some moments later, I was lifted out of my hiding place by Seaman Jones who carried me back to the cabin and placed me gently into the chair before producing a rag to dry my tears. The young lad who had fetched Jones slipped his fingers into my hand whilst patting my arm with the other, trying his best to console me. I swallowed down my sobs and tried to smile.

'There, there, Miss, don't fret yourself,' said Jones. 'Young Sam here thought you was a ghost when he caught sight of you in amongst the tackle. He said you was wailing like a banshee.'

Wiping my eyes with the heel of my other hand, I squeezed his fingers. 'I'm sorry, Sam, if I frightened you,' I said. 'I was just a bit unhappy, but I am alright now.'

They both looked greatly relieved and once Jones was satisfied that I wasn't going to break down again, they left me to return to their own quarters and I climbed up into my hammock. My pain had not gone away but, yet again, I needed to suppress it.

***

The following day, once my mood was restored, and despite the misery I had succumbed to, I had to admit there was something small within me that was relishing this adventure on the high seas and the people I shared it with. I was so lucky to be of value, whether it be to the crew, the guards or the convicts, and fortunate not to be cast down on the 'tween deck with the other women. They really never knew how they would get through each day: whether taken with illness - another woman convict was dropped into the sea this very morning, having died of the mysterious fever-like condition; tormented by the likes of the red-head and my aunt in their endless struggles for control (Aunt Tilly was still causing havoc, even though she was ironed); or, worse still, ravished or beaten by some sailor or guard who took a fancy to them.

Prickship told me we were likely to dock in the next day

or two and I was filled with anxiety as to what to do. Should I run and cast myself on the mercy of the authorities, or jump ship and hide until the ship went without me? Should I just accept my lot and travel on to Australia, hoping against hope that my letter would find its way to Cecilia and Farmer Elwood who might be able to influence the course of my life from afar?

I clutched a shawl around my shoulders as a fitful wind ruffled my hair and it occurred to me that I could at least try and improve my appearance so that I didn't still look so much like a convict. Sarah had supplied me with a comb and a clip for the mess that my aunt's shears had created. I had the means to improve myself and perhaps bring back the person I was, rather than the drab I had become. It was with this thought that I hurried back to my cabin. I had no mirror but there were some shiny bowls and with a bit of alcohol and buffing I would be able to see how dreadful I looked and how I could improve. This plan of action cheered my spirits and I set about my preparation.

Chapter Twenty-Eight

Whooping Cough......Bleeding is indispensable. The alimentary canal to be evacuated with Calomel which I find answers better for children than any other medicines. Emetics are also to be given and a nausea kept up with small doses of tartaric.... Antimony and lastly blisters which I have found decidedly advantageous. Treatment was used with occasional variations in 22 cases which occurred amongst emigrant children. Many improved once the ship met warmer weather but two of the youngest, still at the breast, appeared to succumb with further complications.

Diary of a Ship's Surgeon

The first thing to do was ask Jones to fetch Sarah so that together we could find the real me, and that is exactly what we did. I washed my hair as well as scrubbed my body to remove the grime and she wielded the scissors. Salt water was not the best thing to use but it sufficed; we had a happy time before my first patient appeared. Sarah promised to give me something pretty to wear which had been bought by her man. Eventually, she returned with a dress that had obviously had a few owners but with a bit of sewing here and there, I would have a colourful and pretty dress. It was clearly a dress chosen by a man and not really suitable or proper for someone plain like me but I thought to borrow it until I could repay her. She also brought a mirror, so I could see how attractively she had dressed my hair. I was shocked by how short it was but curls framed my face nicely, and with a bit of pinching and some grease I anointed my cheeks and lips.

'You looks the part, Essie!' said Sarah, standing back to admire her work. 'You'll just 'ave to watch out for those horny sailors who'll pretend to be ill just to get a moment alone wiv yer.'

I heard Jones coming down the corridor and hastily threw the hessian sack that I used as a work apron over my new dress.

'Wha's thee up to, then, ladies? You look like a pair of cats 'as got the cream?'

Sarah giggled and sidled past him before giving me a wink.

I enjoyed what was left of the morning, with stolen glances at the borrowed mirror to glimpse my new self but came rapidly down to earth when the captain appeared at my door looking quite dreadful, his face pinched and drawn.

'Miss Coad, my wife requires your attendance. Now. I will escort you.'

He gave me no time to question what was wrong, so I scurried after him. As we approached their cabin, I could hear a deep, anguished moaning and though the noise prepared me I was still shocked by what I saw. Mrs. Campbell was on all fours with her hair hanging lank and unkempt about her face. She saw me and bared her teeth, a trace of blood on her lips. The cabin looked like it had been ransacked and I dreaded to think what she and the captain had endured before she'd agreed for me to be called. Together we tried to lift her onto the bed, but she was too heavy and not co-operative.

'Fetch Prickship,' I ordered the captain.

'Who?' he asked, bewildered.

'Mason, I mean Mason. Fetch him quick.'

He was gone only a minute, but during that time she collapsed, all the fight gone out of her. The three of us managed to hoist her onto the bed before I pushed them out of the door, saying to Prickship, 'Go back to my cabin. I need water, scissors, a sharp knife and a needle and thread. You will find most of them in some sterile solution in a container near the desk. Also, clean cloths, and ask cook to boil plenty of water and keep it boiling until I say otherwise - and stay nearby in case I need you.' I looked at the captain and saw that he was not going to be of any use or comfort to his wife.

'I am not having this brat now, it is too early,' cried Mrs. Campbell. 'Stop it, will you! Please.' The last word was squeezed out of her pursed mouth with as much reluctance as you can imagine.

'I need to examine you again, I can't do anything until I know what is happening. Let me *help* you,' I begged, fearful for her and the child's safety.

'What happened?' I asked. 'When I last saw you, the baby's head was not fully in position. Did you fall?'

She didn't answer as at that moment we both looked down at her heavy gown which showed a creeping stain.

'Your water's have broken, Ma'am,' I said firmly. 'Your baby is coming, and it is best that we get you into a comfortable position for the birth. Let me help you undress.'

I struggled to remove her clothing, leaving just her shift. Someone knocked on the door and I rushed to prevent anyone entering. Gathering all the essentials that Prickship had brought, I said, 'I will call if I need you but don't go far.

Perhaps a tot of brandy in hot water with some sugar would be welcome to Mrs. Campbell.'

He nodded and strode rapidly to where I could see the captain slumped against the door of another cabin. I believed it to be their sitting room. They muttered a few words and within minutes Prickship reappeared with a bottle of brandy, then went away again. The captain picked himself up and disappeared in the direction of the galley and I hoped he was off to get a flagon of boiled drinking water. I tried to prepare Mrs. Campbell for what was to come but she just moaned and swore at me as if I was one of the sailors.

Prickship was back again promptly, knocking at the door. 'Miss Coad,' he said, 'cook has made up some refreshments and sent some sugar for the brandy, also some biscuits that Mrs. Campbell is partial to. And something for yourself.' Prickship was most definitely a useful man in a crisis and I was grateful for his thoughtfulness. I was sure cook wouldn't have thought of this on his own.

'Thank you,' I said, taking the tray, and then shut the door firmly. We toiled relentlessly through the afternoon and the night, and as the contractions wandered, I doled out the brandy as I thought fit. It might not have been what Dr. Grieve would do but the poor woman was suffering, and I had nothing else to ease her. I tried not to compare my actions with those dreadful Mother Midnights that I was so fond of denouncing. I didn't dare give her much of the laudanum from the medicine chest as it might have affected the delivery. Her screams were painful to my ears and the language of abuse can have left no-one on board that ship unaware of what was going on and whose fault it was. Once again, I longed for my herbs and teas; they might not have the strength of brandy or opium, but they were natural and some were pacifying. When she wasn't shrieking, the boat was still and deathly quiet as if everyone was willing the child to come, and as time dragged on and the force of the contractions waned again, Mrs. Campbell fell into a fitful and drunken sleep. I laid my head on my arms and prayed.

I awoke to the sunrise poking its rays through the porthole and before Mrs. Campbell awakened fully, I took the opportunity to examine her again and was much relieved to see that she was further on in her labour. Gently I bathed her face and neck before giving her a fresh rolled cloth to bite down on. I could have given her a piece of leather, but her mouth was already sore and bleeding.

I opened the door looking for Prickship who was slumped outside on the floor under a blanket, with a pillow at his head. He was fast asleep, so I prodded him gently with my foot before asking for some coffee and breakfast for us both as there was a way to go and Mrs. Campbell needed her strength for the final push. He told me that the captain had passed out in their stateroom; normally an abstemious man, he had taken to the bottle and was now unconscious.

While I waited, I watched her face. She looked so much older. I had thought she was about 37 but in the harsh morning light I could see she must be at least 39 and possibly 40. She was not in a good state to have a first baby.

Prickship returned with dishes cook had prepared for us both and by the time Mrs. Campbell's contractions became more forceful, we were ready for the final throes of labour. I was greatly relieved to find that she seemed to have had a change of attitude and, instead of screaming her outrage, had determined on her part to put everything she had into birthing, with me doing everything I could to ease the safe passage of the child, rather than having to confine myself to the well-being of a resentful, angry mother.

Eventually, after what seemed like hours of torment and pain, a tiny scrap of a girl struggled into the world amidst a great deal of baying and cussing from her mother. I was so thankful that the child was small; any bigger would have been even more brutal. I couldn't help noticing how bruised my hands and arms were, as Mrs. Campbell had clamped on them like a vice. I cleaned the baby who was alert and wailing before I put her into her mother's arms while waiting for the final delivery, the afterbirth. Once I had cleaned us all, refreshed the bedding and selected a wrap for Mrs. Campbell from the trunk at the bottom of the bed, I thought it time to welcome the captain back into the cabin to meet his daughter. I had seen him in the passageway, looking dazed and quite unlike himself. I thrust an armful of stained linen out to Prickship before the captain arrived, and just as I was about to open the door fully to him, she called me.

'Esther,' she whispered, 'be sure to remember that this is an early birth.'

I nodded and hoped that the question would never be asked; it was not for me to judge and I didn't wish to speculate.

My last job of the day before I retired exhausted to my cabin, was to ask Prickship, who was as proud as if he were the child's father himself (and I am sure he was not), to take the baby down to see cook and thank him for his help with the demands made on his resources. He had kept me constantly supplied with tasty bites for Mrs. Campbell and myself. The ship's carpenter had also produced a pretty cradle for the baby. Prickship took a very long time to return, stopping to show the little mite to everyone on route.

Her name was to be Charlotte. It was a fitting name for a little girl born on the *Lady Charlotte*.

Chapter Twenty-Nine

The Juliana sailed from the Downs and met with a series of storms.
The emigrants were very terrified, sea sick and unable to take care
of their children". The deck leaked and the bedding was wet and
the circumstances meant that cleanliness was not observed as it
should have been. Because the Surgeon Superintendent had no
power to enforce his regulations regarding cleanliness, it was very
difficult to clean the decks berths and bedding. It was necessary to
drive the emigrants on to deck by closing the hatches and smoking
them out with fumes of sulphur or cayenne pepper.
On entering the tropics, remittent fever became prevalent among
the emigrants, generally starting with heaviness and pain in the
head and pain down the spine.
Diary of a Ship's Surgeon

We put into Gibraltar the day after Charlotte was born and during the morning, before the ship was secured, I returned to Captain and Mrs. Campbell's cabin to check that all was well with both mother and daughter. I met the captain in the passageway and was sorry to have my bruised hands gripped tightly in his. The soreness would take a day or two to abate, but I didn't want to show him that I was hurting.

'My dear, I am so grateful to you, my wife is too, of course. I don't know what we would have done if you weren't with us. Such a shock for Charlotte to come early, but never mind, she seems hale and hearty and is feeding well. I would be grateful if you would keep an eye on my dear wife for the next few days. It is our first child and we are not experienced in what to expect. I hope you will advise her and perhaps take the child for a few hours while she rests.'

'Is Mrs. Campbell of a good frame of mind?' I asked. 'It was a long and difficult birth for her to endure and it would not be untoward if she were a bit low of spirit for a few days. It sometimes takes women that way. She needs to rest and take a nourishing meal regularly. Perhaps you would like me to speak to cook and make sure she gets the right food for herself and to create milk for Charlotte?'

'Thank you, my dear. Mason or Jones will escort you to the galley,' he replied, with a smile. 'We will take on stores here so there will be an abundance of fresh food available.'

I realised suddenly that I had to speak now while I had the captain's attention and gratitude. This might be my only chance.

'Captain, can I ask how long we are likely to be in Gibraltar and if it will be possible for me to speak to the Commander about my situation?' I asked, trying to keep my voice even. 'I have a letter for my patron, Cecilia Elwood, which Mason said might be taken in the military box on the next ship going to Britain.'

For a moment, the captain looked horrified and I truly think that he had forgotten my dreadful situation, so used had he become to my presence and usefulness. But then he sighed and answered me in an uncharacteristically gentle tone.

'Esther, I can't deny you your chance, you have been such a help to me, my wife and my crew. Yes, I will be seeing the Commander later today and I will bring your troubles to his attention. Ask Mason to give me the letter, but I feel bound to warn you that he is unlikely to want to intervene,' he said, a little sadly. 'I will do my best, though, to put your case before him as one of wrongful identity rather than being listed as the convict you replaced. The two men who were complicit in your being on this ship are being off-loaded here and returned to Britain for further punishment.'

I pressed him, saying, 'Surely, Captain Campbell, if they are being returned, then I could be too? It would be so unjust to send me on to Australia when they are being sent back. I did nothing wrong but am being punished, yet they who committed a dreadful crime are being returned. And, what about my aunt? Is she being returned to stand trial and be hanged?'

'It doesn't do, Esther, to tell the Commander what he should or should not do,' he said firmly. 'That would be a grave mistake. I believe Mason told me that you have a child back home and I promise I will make a case for you as best as I am able. I now understand how desperate you must be to return to your little girl. Please ask Jones to fetch Mason and we will do what we can.' With this he turned and walked away.

I felt sick with apprehension. I knew that the good captain had my interests at heart and I knew he would do his best, but the unknown Commander who had my future in his hands might be the worst example of mankind: bumped up with his own importance, annoyed by a matter that could present legal problems for him.

Though I had no experience of great men honoured by high office, I did have experience of men who didn't want to be bothered by women's concerns, who were irritated by emotion and who would rather just sweep us aside. But, this man alone had the power here, he was the Commander; he could make decisions that lawyers would quibble over and eventually accept. Of course, I well understood that England was at war and that he had weighty matters to deal with from this important military outpost. Even so, I had to make him regard me and my repatriation as a worthwhile cause.

Chapter Thirty

Treatment for Pneumonia included bloodletting with one patient having 3.5 pints of blood let in 3 hours with the patient "rapidly proceeding to a fatal termination"
Diary of a Ship's Surgeon

Everything was a-bustle at the quayside, with men shouting and running up and down the gangplank, from one end of the ship to the other, and up and down the rigging as the sails were dropped. Men in military uniform were very much in charge and there was a sharp exchange of words between the first mate and a man who seemed to be in control of mooring. Jones sidled up alongside me and we watched the unloading of barrels, boxes and crates. Captain Campbell followed, carrying a document box and accompanied by Prickship. I suppose I should call him Mason, as he didn't seem like a 'Prickship' any more after his heroics with Mrs. Campbell. Clearly this was an important moment as they were both dressed in full naval uniform and there were whistles piping everywhere.

'How long are we likely to be here, Jones?'

'About five or so days,' he said. 'Long enough to take on supplies for the next leg. Food will be good here and when we get underway there'll be better grub for a few weeks at least. After that it'll go downhill fast on account of the heat.'

I continued watching the busy scene below me and was able to take in the beauty of this strange place with its great rock looming above us. There were military buildings everywhere but behind them I could also see white painted houses of low build. Many people were on the quayside, some clearly connected to the military even though they were not in uniform. They stood straight and tall with what I would call a military bearing. Some were clean-shaven, which was surprising to me, and others wore powdered wigs. There was a great deal of saluting, stamping and more whistle-blowing. I also saw some women who watched from the sides of buildings, as if they were reluctant to step into plain sight. They were darker of skin and all had black hair. I suppose women plied their favours here as much as they did back at home. Some of them were brightly dressed though I could also see some much older women who were dressed from head to toe in black.

The smell here was so refreshingly clean and every now and again I caught a drift of an aroma which I took to be that of plant life. Even the sea smelled good here within this port. I hoped the ship would be thoroughly cleaned before it embarked again but the greatest delight to me was the warmth: a blue sky with no clouds and strong sunlight that warmed the air as well as the ground. It was so invigorating, despite all the hectic bustle and activity.

'Miss, Miss, excuse me, Miss,' a young voice called. 'Mrs. Campbell is asking for you to go to her cabin, Miss. She says to hurry.' It was the young cabin boy who had found me crying that time up on deck and whom I had treated recently.

'What sort of mood she in, boy?' queried Jones.

'Bad.'

We both groaned before making our way to the captain's cabin. I knocked on the door.

It was yanked open and I was pulled into the cabin, the door flung shut in Jones's face by an irritable Mrs. Campbell.

'I have told the captain that you cannot be allowed to leave this ship,' she shrilled, hysterically. 'You are listed as a convict and no matter what anyone says you will have to go on to Australia with us.'

'I am no convict, Ma'am,' I replied, 'and I will get off this ship, one way or another.' I looked at her, furious that she would try to keep me from my child because she did not care to look after her own. She looked a mess, her hair bedraggled, milk stains at her breast, and hollow-eyed. Charlotte was in the cradle and she was mewling insistently but her mother made no attempt to tend her. Instead she crumpled onto her bed and burst into tears.

I went over to the baby and picked her up, her tiny lips puckering. 'She needs feeding,' I said and pushed her into her mother's arms.

'I'm so tired, I can't do it anymore,' she wailed in return, dumping Charlotte beside her on the bed.

I didn't like Mrs. Campbell, but at that moment I did feel some sympathy. She didn't know how to be anything other than selfish. Charlotte was less than two days old, yet her mother looked as though she had a brood of children at her feet, not just the one new-born. I picked the baby up and suggested that she go and have a wash and do her hair; that once she was feeling more herself she might relax, and the milk would come more easily as the baby suckled.

She did as I suggested while I nursed the little mite who was sucking on my finger. After a good while, we both sat quietly as I put Charlotte to her breast again. She latched on immediately and Mrs. Campbell dropped deeper into her chair.

'Please don't leave me,' she said, her voice quavering as she spoke.

'Have you considered returning to London? Have you family who can help?'

'I have, but we haven't got a home. I would have to lodge somewhere,' she sniffed.

'Your husband must be able to provide for you both,' I said. 'You could hire a maid until you get back on your feet.'

'I don't like him travelling without me. Other women, you know,' Mrs Campbell trailed off. 'They are everywhere, and sailors – well, I am sure you have heard the phrase: a wife in every port.'

'Has the captain ever given you reason to think like that? He seems such an honest and kind man.'

'All men are like that, and more fool you if you think otherwise.'

As I watched her, I had the ghost of an idea. Tentatively, I broached a suggestion that I thought would benefit both of us, as well as the child.

'Why don't we try and help each other?' I went on. 'I need to return home, and if I were to agree to act as your nursery maid and take care of Charlotte while you recover, we could go back together to London. Such a solution might give the Commander reason to be generous and I think the captain would be happy with that idea too. You would be better off in my care – going on to Australia with a baby sounds extremely hazardous to me and I don't think you will cope alone.'

She sat in silence. I waited for her to agree or disagree, but she said nothing. Eventually I rose and left the cabin. A wave of despondency washed over me.

Prickship knocked on my cabin door later that evening and I invited him in, wondering if he had some news.

'The captain has raised your situation with the Commander and I am sorry to say it is not very encouraging.' He sounded angry. 'The Commander says he hasn't got the authority to act as judge and jury and feels it would create a hornet's nest. What's more to the point, he is angling for promotion and doesn't want to create a reason to be turned down. The man is damned lily-livered and needs some backbone. I am sorry to bear this news, Esther. I know how badly you need to return.'

I broke down in front of him, and as tears streamed down my cheeks, it was but a moment before he was putting his arm around me. I felt so weak and wrung out that I couldn't help leaning on him for support.

Gradually, I pulled myself together and dried my eyes, realising that it wasn't right for me to be entertaining a man in my cabin unchaperoned, particularly as I was still termed a 'convict'. It wouldn't hurt his reputation – in fact, it would probably improve it - but it could seriously damage me, trying as I was to be seen as a respectable professional midwife, not a convict or a loose woman.

I thanked him for his kindness and as I reached to open the door, Jones was 'standing guard' and I caught a leer as he peered in and construed the situation in his own way.

'Goodnight, Sir,' I said, 'and thank you for your kindness.' (I'm sure I heard Jones splutter.) 'I will think on what you have told me and speak to the captain in the morning. Perhaps I could accompany him onshore to meet the Commander?'

'What are you doing here, Jones?' Prickship snapped. 'Haven't you got work to do?'

'Just checking the young lady is safe from bother, Sir.'

'Well, get back to work.'

'Aye, Sir. As you say, Sir.'

I was alone at last and collapsed into my chair to dwell on the setback.

Captain Campbell finally agreed that I could accompany him into the garrison's headquarters the next day. It had taken a bit of persuasion on my part, but I felt he owed me this, at least - and his wife is not the only persuasive woman in his life.

I prepared carefully, wearing the borrowed dress and doing my hair like Sarah showed me. She had taken her mirror back but I could see myself in the shiny bowls. All dressed up, I sat and waited to be called. Jones and some of the sailors had gone into the small town; they were intent on finding a bar to make up for being on a dry ship. I had not seen any patients for two days from either the crew or convicts; the worry about fever had receded with no new cases coming forward. I was thankful but still ill at ease as to how it had developed in the first place.

Prickship had not visited me again but I expected he would accompany the captain and me when the time came. I had not heard any more from Mrs. Campbell and didn't feel like approaching her again about my idea. I wondered how Charlotte was faring, though. I went up on deck a few hours after sunrise, without my chaperone. I was surprised to find so much ado but as I looked to the horizon, I saw sails approaching: clearly another vessel was coming into the port. They were making good headway with a fresh wind plumping their sails. I laughed to myself as I knew Jones would not approve of that term. I might tease him about plump sails when next I saw him.

I returned to my cabin, waiting anxiously for the summons, but it was a long time coming and I fretted continuously as to how I would persuade the Commander to step out on a limb for me. I resolved to behave as a lady would and let the captain take the lead. If, however, he was failing to make an impression, then I would interrupt and call on the Commander's better nature, if indeed he had one. I practised phrases and reworked my thoughts repeatedly but only managed to reduce myself to a nervous wreck.

Finally, a knock came and Prickship was there. He said that the captain was waiting on the dock for me and asked me to follow him.

The captain took my arm and put it in the crook of his. I hoped his wife wasn't watching.

'Miss Coad, I trust you are well?'

'Indeed, I am Captain Campbell, and how are Charlotte and Mrs. Campbell?'

He paused, searching for words, 'my wife is learning to become a mother and it is not a natural situation for her, but she progresses. Charlotte is quite beautiful, and I am smitten with her,' he smiled down at me. 'I feel so proud to be the father of such a beautiful child.'

I smiled back but watched his face change from great happiness to that of someone about to impart bad news. I prepared myself to hear whatever worrying words he had to say.

'Now, Miss Coad, if I might offer you some advice, I would tell you to behave as your patroness would do, with quiet dignity and no harsh words if it can be helped. The Commander would like to think of himself as magnanimous, so it would be better for us to lead him to a decision rather than tell him what it should be. Do you understand me?'

'I do, indeed, Captain,' I said. 'I will try to keep my emotions in check.'

'Good, then let us proceed - in hope, my dear, in hope.'

It was lovely to stand on firm ground once more though I suddenly felt a little wobbly. I stopped and stood still for a moment as I got used to the sensation before saying, 'I'm sorry Captain, I feel a bit unsteady. I won't take a moment. We mustn't be late.'

Captain Campbell laughed and squeezed my arm within his. 'Don't worry my dear, everyone has to get their sea or land legs back. After the trip to Australia, it takes quite some time, but here you will acclimatise in a few minutes.'

I took a few deep breaths and felt uplifted by the lovely floral scent drifting on the breeze. 'Right, I am ready,' I said, walking on.

The garrison headquarters were well-appointed, with regimental tapestries adorning the walls as well as swords and other war-like paraphernalia on display, reminding me forcefully that we were at war. I also noticed a rude caricature of the man who was such a threat to the British Isles, Napoleon Bonaparte. We were shown into a large room where there was a magnificent desk as well as trestles with charts stretched out. A young man, with a quill at the ready, stood beside the Commander who was of upright bearing and sprouting a fine set of whiskers.

I searched his face and my heart sank for I could find no empathy in his demeanour. In fact, I saw myself through his eyes as a deranged woman who was daring to intrude into his important world and take up his precious time. He welcomed the captain and Prickship with a handshake but ignored me.

To his credit, Captain Campbell took me by the hand and introduced me as a woman of great skill who had saved the lives of many on his ship and who deserved to be heard in her justifiable request of being returned to London at the earliest opportunity. He continued explaining that I had been subjected to horrendous wrongdoing and had proved myself to be a victim of mistaken identity and not a convict.

'And how did this proof come about?' The Commander's tone was brusque. 'Speak up, Miss, tell me how you think you have proved your case?'

This was my moment – I stepped forward and steadied my voice. 'There is a woman on board, Sarah, who knew me from before as midwife to my patrons, Cecilia and John Elwood. She had seen them in court and heard details of my case when I was found not guilty of the murder of a work colleague whose child I am now responsible for. The Elwoods paid for my defence and I now live in their home and care for their children. I am their governess and nurse,' I continued, worrying that my mention of a murder charge would destroy my case. 'The charge of murder was deemed a malicious act by my ex-employer.'

He was fiddling with bits of paper on his desk and I felt he was not listening, so I spoke in a louder voice as I told him that there were two men in his lockup who had admitted smuggling me on board at the behest of my aunt, at the same time removing two street walkers.

'Is that the sum of your proof?'

'My skills show that I am not a street woman,' I said, proudly.

'I understand that your supposed patrons are familiar with his Highness, the Prince of Wales?' The Commander asked, after a pause.

'Yes, they attended his marriage,' I said, 'and are, on occasion, of his party at the races in Lewes.' He seemed more interested in this trivial point, so I carried on. 'Cecilia Elwood is the daughter of an earl. Her parents are close to the Court, her mother, Lady Harriet, a confidante of the Queen.' This was a lie, but I didn't care.

I broke off as a young man came into the room. He approached the clerk and whispered in his ear, who then whispered into the Commander's ear. There was a buzz of noise behind me.

'Silence,' he ordered. 'I have pressing business to attend to. Captain Campbell, I have no time to address this at present. You will kindly wait in the room next door with this young woman.'

I couldn't bear any further delay and pushed myself towards this self-important man. I would beg if I had to. 'Please, Sir,' I said, tearfully, 'my child might even now be in danger of corruption or death at the hand of my aunt's smuggling gang. Please let me go back to London. Please…' I broke off at a disturbance behind me as I felt, as well as heard, many hurrying feet enter the room.

A voice, a commanding voice, suddenly rang out: 'Esther, Esther Coad, it is you! My God, I was shocked beyond belief to hear that you might be here. I had to come and see for myself.'

I turned in the direction of the voice, a voice I knew and revered. Flushing with disbelief and pleasure, I saw Dr. Grieve striding toward me. For a moment everyone else stood stock still, and I felt like we were the only two people in the world. Was I in a dream, about to wake up at any minute?

'Dr. Grieve,' I gasped, as I felt the room sliding away from me. Prickship, always nearby, pushed a chair under me and stood with his hand firmly and possessively on my shoulder. I had no eyes for anyone but Dr. Grieve; the whole room might have been empty for all I cared. I stared at him, he was so very different in his manner and looks. His skin was brown and attractively weathered; there were gold lights in his hair and beard intermingled with the grey I remembered; his eyes seemed clearer and bluer than they were before. He looked so very different, his body lean and elegant in a uniform that must be part of the naval command he was serving with. He had lost that tired and peevish look he usually wore.

The cold voice of the Commander intruded through the fog that had taken over my brain.

'I take it you know this woman?'

'I do indeed, Sir. I apologise for my interruption,' said Dr. Grieve, 'and once I have divulged the message I am entrusted with, I am sure I will be able to clear up any problems that face Miss Coad. I am Dr. Bartholomew Grieve, Coroner and Surgeon from Lewes, temporarily on secondment to His Majesty's Royal Navy'.

As if to emphasise the point, he continued: 'My message is for the Prime Minister himself as representative of the

202

King.' The point was made and greeted with silence as the Commander took the measure of this confident emissary to his Majesty's Government. He rapidly adjusted his manner, the process clearly reflected in his face.

Dr. Grieve spun on the spot and knelt before me, his hand seeking mine and bestowing a light kiss on it.

'Esther, my dear, when I heard from sailors' talk about a young woman kidnapped and dumped onto a transport in the company of a notorious smuggler, a young woman who could heal and aided the birth of a child on board an English ship, and finally that this young woman was named Esther, I had to come and see if it was you,' he paused and dropped his voice. 'And, my dear, it *is* you! I will be honoured to be of service to you in any difficulties you might have in establishing your rights as a citizen of his Royal Highness. I will attend you shortly. Go back to your ship now and wait for me.' He had glanced at the Commander when he mentioned me being a citizen of his Royal Highness.

Stupefied, I sought his eyes and saw nothing but joy in them. I just nodded my agreement, unable to speak. I was led from the Commander's room, aware of the curious stares of the many people who seemed to have appeared in Dr. Grieve's wake.

We returned to the boat in silence, Captain Campbell supporting me on his arm and Prickship bringing up the rear with a stony look on his face. I was overjoyed and had no time for male jealousies. I wanted to be by myself to think about this miraculous twist of fate and recall the feeling of acute pleasure I had experienced when Dr. Grieve had appeared.

The captain personally escorted me to my cabin before saying, 'I am sure you will be granted your wish now,

Esther. The Commander will almost certainly be swayed by the good doctor's presence, particularly if he confirms the status of your patrons. The man is nothing if not aware of an opportunity, especially to be seen as saviour to one connected to the royal household, however loosely. Before the doctor appeared, I was preparing to ask that you be returned to London as my wife's nursemaid. I think that might have swayed the argument, but we will see how this new situation develops before making plans.'

I was surprised at this, having thought my idea had fallen on deaf ears, so I simply smiled and sank into my chair. I wished them both away. I needed just to think - and feel.

Dr. Grieve came to me later that day and we sat for a long time, unchaperoned, but with Jones never far away (I could hear him knocking about, whistling, and generally letting me know that he was nearby). We had so much to talk about. He seemed far less pompous than before and the outdoor life clearly suited him: it was like being in the presence of a younger and more vibrant version of the man I had known before. At first, I tried to explain why I had rejected him as I did.

He heard me out before saying. 'But Esther, you were right. I was so wrong to treat you as little better than a whore when you deserved someone more honest, like Wilf, who loved you unconditionally.' His voice dropped before he continued, his tone humble. 'I am ashamed now of how I behaved, though it has taken me a long while to come to that state. At the time, I felt only profound disappointment and anger that you couldn't see that I was offering you love and support. It came to me slowly to see things through your eyes, but once I did, I was mortified at my own behaviour. I must beg your forgiveness, Esther.'

I replied, 'When you went away I missed you dreadfully - but it was as a friend. I loved Wilf, I wanted to be his wife.'

'I know, and that is why I had to leave.'

I struggled to tell him how bereft I had been and that I now felt myself to have been very foolish in the way I had reacted. I acknowledged that I should have discussed my concerns in a rational manner rather than running away and behaving like a woman violated when, clearly, he had meant me no harm.

'No physical harm, Esther, but what I was proposing was very wrong in the kind of society we live in. It would never have done, and I am filled with remorse.'

We carried on talking. I had so much to tell - about Wilf and the terrible way he had died, Cecilia's new baby, the horrible replacement doctor and his kindly wife, Beth's and then my kidnap, my hope and belief that Beth was back with the Elwoods; and, finally, Aunt Tilly's venomous revenge in putting me on the transport ship, with little or no hope of getting off again.

He frowned before saying, 'Why are you so certain that Beth will be with the Elwoods?'

'Because the Coads would not want the bother of a child. There are no women on that farm and once my aunt left, there would be no purpose in keeping her. I don't believe they would kill her. She is their immediate family, when all is said and done. I believe they would have dumped her back at South Farm and no one would have been any the wiser as to who kidnapped her.'

It was getting late and I could hear Jones stamping about outside. He obviously thought it time for our interview to be at an end, so that he could slip away to his bunk. There was no need for him to be chaperoning me now, but clearly in his mind there was, or he was just being inquisitive.

Hurriedly, I asked Dr. Grieve if he would speak to the Commander on my behalf and ensure his assistance.

'Consider it done, my dear, and perhaps we can continue our conversation tomorrow.' He rose to his feet and went on, 'There is a little garden nearby. I would like to take you there while we plan how best to get you back to Lewes. I have much to tell you of my adventures and I really want to know more about how this bizarre sequence of events occurred.'

He left me and returned to his own ship. I made ready for my hammock and for the first time in weeks I felt happy.

Chapter Thirty-One

Drunkenness nowadays in the Navy kills more men than the sword and that with most diseases and accidents "you may trace grog as the principle cause of it"
Diary of a Ship's Surgeon

My personal problems were put in perspective as the *Lady Charlotte* continued to prepare for her long voyage. The following morning, I watched the loading of dry goods, biscuit, grain and barrels of fresh water. I heard livestock squealing and clucking and cook shouting at everyone to have a care for his provisions. Prickship and Captain Campbell were everywhere at once as the repairs to the boat continued. I could smell tar and sawn timber as the ship's carpenter worked to repair split and damaged wood. The convicts were allowed up on deck as the weather was fine and their quarters needed cleaning. I saw my aunt, who was brought up separately. She had irons around her ankles and looked unkempt. Sensing my eyes on her, she cast a vengeful look in my direction before drawing a finger across her throat. I met her gaze for a split second and turned away; I wanted none of her. I had no sympathy. I hoped she would die; better people than she had already died on this voyage.

Again, I asked Jones when the boat would leave, and if he had any idea yet of what would happen to me. He was usually a mine of information but on this occasion was unable to tell me what was going on. I went back down to my cabin, still with him on guard, and prepared to put everything in order just in case I was taken off the ship. As I cleaned and tidied, another patient came to my door. It was one of the male convicts and, unfortunately, he was displaying signs of fever. I immediately asked for him to be quarantined, even though it was a nuisance to the crew and guards who couldn't care less whether he lived or died. The previous cases had all been women and they had died. I knew Jones had said that there were ways that the male and female convicts got into each other's quarters when the ship was dark. It didn't matter to me if this was true, but it was worrying that this man was now displaying the same symptoms.

I saw the captain briefly and asked after Charlotte and Mrs. Campbell. He said that they were in good shape and that he would talk to me later about them and about my situation. I had to be content with that but was very happy to receive a message that Dr. Grieve would call for me in the afternoon and that I was to be allowed to walk with him unguarded!

It was wonderful to step off the *Lady Charlotte* again, I almost felt like a free woman. Dr. Grieve waited for me in the shadow of the ship and produced a feminine parasol to shade me from the sun; heaven knows where he had got it from. We walked into the little village where the street names reflected the nature of a military garrison. We soon found a small rocky garden where strange, colourful plants spread between the paving and rocks. They had thickened leaves which looked like they were full of moisture; I would have liked to know what they were. There was a bench in the shade and we both settled there to enjoy the warm wind which swirled around us. I was wearing Sarah's dress again and delighted in seeing the pretty pattern in such strong light. I felt elated with myself, with my companion and, best of all, that I was likely to be going home.

We sat side by side, close but not touching, as I recounted again all that had happened to everyone in Lewes. Dr. Grieve's face was in shadow but I knew he was scowling as I told him about his locum, Dr. Crabbe. He was, however, full of admiration for the man's wife. It was difficult to describe the pain of Wilf's shooting and the conflict of fear I had suffered when I thought it was Beth who had been shot. I even tried to explain why I had so desperately wanted to keep the table on which Wilf lay for the month or so that it took him to die and on which he finally took his last breath. I described how the youngest Coad boy had sought me out; and, when Beth was taken, how he had been given the charge of her by Aunt Tilly. I had to keep going back on myself as I forgot this or that fact.

He asked a few questions about Mrs. Coad's unexplained death and I told him that it was my belief that she had been usurped in the household and deliberately pushed down the stairs; I repeated what the boy had said about his mother being got rid of. When I got to the part about my kidnap, I wept as I described how Beth was kept from me and threatened with death if I didn't comply; my only comfort being that young Coad seemed to have become genuinely protective of his little sister and my instinct that he would take the chance to return her to Cecilia as soon as an opportunity arose. I had little basis for this belief other than that he had been the means of rescuing us before, and that I was convinced his visits to spy on her and me were not occasioned by malice. I even told the doctor that I had left Flossy at Coad Farm and worried for her safety as well.

My story took a while to recount and as the sun began to dip, I had only got as far as my being forced onto the boat. Dr. Grieve had already been given an account of my presence by both Captain Campbell and Prickship, so I didn't have to elaborate. We spent a few minutes talking about the medical conditions on board and how I had had to learn very fast to treat men as well as women whilst not knowing what all the medicants I had found in the locked chest were for. Finally, I described the symptoms of the fever-ridden women who had died, despite my best efforts, and I concluded my story by asking him to look at the man who was now in quarantine with the same symptoms.

Unfortunately, there was no time to talk about why he was in Gibraltar or what plans he might be able to make for me to return to London. He told me to be patient and that once he had got to the bottom of everything, he would ensure that I would be returned on the next available ship with no stain on my character and no charge of transportation linked to my name. I didn't doubt it as he radiated power and strength which I must declare was physically exciting to me.

We hurried back to the ship where Jones was waiting for me on deck. As we parted, Dr. Grieve took both my hands in his, saying, 'You have been very brave, Esther, and I ask you to trust in me for the next day or two.'

'Yes, I do trust you, of course I do, but the *Lady Charlotte* is preparing for departure and I am sure they won't want to wait on me.' I couldn't help allowing a note of anxiety creep into my voice, despite my assurances of trust in him.

He smiled and said, 'As soon as she is ready to leave, you will be taken off and billeted here on the island, possibly with Mrs. Campbell and her baby. I understand she is desirous of returning to Britain with you as her helpmeet or nursemaid - or whatever title she thinks you should have. The details still need to be worked out, but the plan is there.'

He was still holding my hands and I could see Jones taking it all in and his mouth dropping open as my rescuer pulled me towards him and kissed me warmly on both cheeks. How my heart raced, and I could feel a flush creeping up my neck as all the onlookers stopped still to observe this moment of intimacy.

As Jones and I walked back to my cabin, we passed Prickship. After Jones had made a rather lazy salute in his direction, he muttered to me that there was one on this ship with his nose put out of joint! He gave me a sidelong look, but I ignored his insinuations.

Chapter Thirty-Two

Venereal disease was a common occurrence on board. One surgeon conducts an experiment on a young woman with venereal disease, with both her keeper and an officer having "connexion" with her to see how gonorrhoea and syphilis are spread.

Diary of a Ship's Surgeon

All was arranged. The *Lady Charlotte* was to embark on the next leg of her voyage the following day and I was to be billeted onshore with Mrs. Campbell and baby Charlotte until a suitable vessel heading for home came along. I spent my last night on the ship cleaning the little cabin that had been my home and wishing my dear friend Sarah everything that she would wish for herself. Jones looked very down in the mouth; I believe he had enjoyed his work looking out for me just as I had enjoyed his salty tales and rough and ready manner, even his crude view of everyone. Everything was ready, and I had just one more night in my bunk before taking my leave of the captain and some of the crew at sunrise.

It was frightening, then, to be woken by a loud banging on my door late at night. I clutched my hessian pinny to me as I opened the door to a terrible sight: Prickship being half- dragged, half-carried, into my little room and pushed into the chair. He was bleeding profusely from his lower leg and I could see through a tear in his trousers that his leg was broken, the bone protruded alarmingly, and momentarily

I felt sick. He grimaced at me and clutched my hand in a forceful grip. I firmly removed it and cut his breeches from him to attempt to clean the edges of the wound, fearful, as always, of infection creeping in.

I told one of the guards to run to Dr. Grieves' quarters in the garrison and tell him what had happened. He was bound to have better equipment and medicines; besides, I had not the faintest idea of how to set the bone back into place and ensure that tissue was not lost. I knew that bone-setting was a specialised occupation for men who passed down their knowledge through the generations, men who were not necessarily physicians. There was one such near Lewes. I knew nothing of his craft but had heard of him by repute. Dr. Grieve would have set many bones in his time and I thought Prickship was lucky to have him nearby.

The following day, Prickship was moved off the *Lady Charlotte* and taken into the garrison headquarters. Jones told me that he had been deliberately attacked and beaten before being flung down to the lower deck. Unfortunately, he had landed awkwardly, resulting in his leg being broken. Jones swore that it was two guards who had objected to Prickship's methods of discipline and had taken it into their heads to assault him.

I knew he was not popular, but such an act was cowardly. I asked if Jones knew what had triggered it.

'He took a whip to them when they refused to take orders from him.'

'He whipped them!' I said, in disbelief.

'Aye, Miss, he can get a bit violent if the men don't jump to his bidding, like. They'll be sent home now, on a charge of mutiny.'

Dr. Grieve did all he could for the poor man but his sailing on to Australia was now out of the question. It had taken two strong men to hold Prickship down and pull whilst the bone and muscle were forced back into their proper place. A wooden splint had been fitted to his leg which was bound into place with wet leather strapping and, over that, linen strips which could be unwound and washed to try and keep infection away from the wound. Fortunately, it was not a bad break, but the strapping extended to his upper thigh and looked uncomfortably tight. The break in his skin and muscle where the bone protruded was sewn up and everyone hoped for a clean repair. I must admit I was fascinated by the method used to repair the break; probably such things were a common injury on a warship.

I felt very sorry for Captain Campbell as he was now short of an officer whom he relied on, as well as four guards, not to mention his wife, the child and me. Travelling with even such a small number of convicts had to be a worry for the captain, though I was told later that the two who had been involved with my kidnap had been replaced by men from Gibraltar, and of course several of the convicts had died. But already I was beginning to feel distant from these matters.

The morning of departure came and Mrs. Campbell, Charlotte and I readied ourselves to leave the ship. The men who were responsible for Prickship's injury were already in the lockup, along with the other two. A good many of the company lined the deck to wave goodbye before she was cast off. I saw the captain blow his nose forcefully as he looked down on his wife and baby. Sarah waved frantically at me and yelled that she would never forget me and not to forget that

I owed her for the dress. I laughed up at her sharp little face but felt very emotional; so much had happened to both of us. I cried a tear as I waved heartily to Jones. I would miss him.

A soldier waited to escort us to our new billet, a small, square, white house some way from the garrison. Mrs. Campbell and I would have separate rooms, so of course she took the largest. There was a tiny walled garden and I felt sure we would be comfortable while we waited for transport. I did my best to be a friend to her but she didn't want friendship. What she wanted was someone to take responsibility for Charlotte and went to great pains to indicate to all and sundry that I was her 'maid'.

I did not feel beholden to her, however, and though Captain Campbell had pressed some coin into my hand, I had no intention of being bought. I would do my best for Charlotte because I wanted to give the little mite a good start in life, not because the captain had paid me. Once I had settled into my room, I concluded that I had got the best of the deal, as my room benefited from early morning light while Mrs. Campbell's had to endure the heat of the afternoon sun, and it was hot on the day we disembarked.

It seemed strange to walk about unguarded, and it wasn't long before I headed to the garrison to see how Prickship was. He was billeted with garrison soldiers but his wound gained him privileges that the soldiers did not share. Without his uniform, he looked a lesser figure of a man but although he was in some considerable pain, he had shed the air of authority that he had carried on the ship.

'How are you, Pr… Mr. Mason?' I greeted him. 'I am so sorry you have ended up like this. If there is anything I can do to assist you, then please send for me.'

His voice no longer carried the stern tones he had generally used.

'I am as well as can be expected, Esther.' I noticed he was no longer calling me Miss Coad, or even Miss Esther. 'However, this is not a place I want to be. The doctor says I will recover should I rest and do as you tell me. He has given me a letter to a physician in London who he hopes will direct my treatment when I get back home.'

'Do as *I* tell you?' I repeated in surprise.

'Yes,' he replied. 'Dr. Grieve is not returning with us and I am to be put into your gracious care.'

I was bitterly disappointed to hear this as I had thought that the doctor would travel back to England with us.

Prickship must have noticed my downcast look. 'Clearly the doctor is an important emissary of His Majesty's Government,' he said. 'Why else would he have brought secret messages to the Commander?'

I had forgotten that it was in the doctor's official capacity that we had been fortunate enough to meet again and that his duties could not be just put aside at will; if indeed they were to be put aside at all!

We sat together for a while and talked of generalities, but I confess my heart wasn't in it, and I was rather relieved when a guard appeared with a message from Mrs. Campbell telling me - not asking, but telling me - to return at once. I stood, and Prickship reached for my hand before thanking me again for my part in his rescue. I hurried away, dropping his hand as quickly as he had taken it.

I returned to our cottage and went in with a determined air about me. I was not going to be treated like a lowly servant girl and it was time to set Mrs. Campbell right.

I went to my room to remove my shawl and was astonished to find little Charlotte in her crib, alongside my bed. She was fast asleep and looked just like an angel. I traced my fingers along her unblemished skin and sighed. How I would love a child of my own, a brother or sister for Beth. I went to her mother's room and was further surprised to find her abed with a hectic rash all over her face and what I could see of her body.

'Esther, where have you been?' she demanded. 'I felt so unwell and I can't have Charlotte with me like this. I have put her in your room.'

'So I see,' I replied. 'And what do you think has caused this? Have you a temperature?' I put my hand to her forehead and though it was warm it didn't seem to be anything to worry about. 'When did the rash come on?'

'This morning, after I washed and dressed. Do you think Charlotte is alright? I couldn't bear anything to disfigure her.' She was looking at my pox-damaged face as she spoke.

'Did you wash her?' I asked.

'Well, no, she was wriggling such a lot, I thought I would wait for you to do it.'

'What did you use to wash yourself with?'

'A soap that I bought at the market. It smells very pretty, of lemons and sweet stuff.'

'What do you usually use for your toilet? Have you still got any?'

'Well yes,'

'Then I suggest you rewash yourself with lots of cool water and your usual preparation and see if that makes a difference. You have no temperature and it might well be simply something that disagrees with your skin. It is a good job you didn't wash the child. We must be very careful of local produce until we have got used to things. I will keep Charlotte with me tonight but you will need to feed her when she wakes, and as soon as you are better, then she must come back to you. I am not your servant, Madam, and I would prefer that you notice that distinction.' I nodded coldly to her and swept out of the room. I knew all too well that I had suggested on board ship that I could be her nursemaid but that was when I had no other option and she hadn't actually accepted the suggestion. Things had changed now.

Chapter Thirty-Three

The surgeon recounts the medical benefits of tobacco smoke as he recounts the case of a man who had fallen overboard and been under water for 12 minutes. Brought on board with the appearance of a corpse, he was taken to the galley, where he was stripped and dried and put in a warm bed with bottles of hot water. Tobacco smoke was conveyed to his lungs through the tube of a common pipe. After a further 45 minutes the surgeon observed an obscure palpitation of the heart", the tobacco smoke was continued and after a further 10 minutes "he sighed faintly and closed his mouth".

Shortly afterwards a pulse was detected at the wrist and the tobacco smoke was discontinued.

The treatment was hailed a success however in the next journal he is discharged to Haslar Hospital with pneumonia.

Diary of a Ship's Surgeon

D r. Grieve called at the house later in the evening to introduce a young woman who was to clean and prepare meals for us. This domestic arrangement was of little interest to me as I only wanted to know about how things stood for him, and after the young woman had gone we sat down together, alone, in the little sitting room.

'I am sorry to hear you are not returning to London with us,' I ventured.

'Mm, yes, I suppose Mason told you,' he replied. 'I have some business to attend to, on behalf of His Majesty, and it is unlikely it will be completed for some time to come. However, as soon as I am able, I will be returning to Lewes and we can discuss future plans, for myself, and for you, if you so choose. I would like nothing better, Esther, my dear, than to return with you but I have obligations that could put our men in jeopardy if I renege on them.'

I felt so selfish at that moment and hastened to assure the Doctor that I was content to await his return, but I was cast down. So much can happen to upset even the smallest of objectives, particularly as we were in a fortified garrison which was clearly on a war footing.

Carefully, I composed myself to present a more cheerful face, as he continued, 'One of the reasons I came to see you tonight is to tell you that I have to leave tomorrow on an important mission and that I hope, for your sake, that you will be gone when I return in a few weeks.' He paused, seeing me struggle to maintain my spirits. When I had recovered myself, he went on, 'Also, that you will find passage on a comfortable vessel. I have received assurances from the Commander that everything will be done to ensure your safe passage and comfort. With luck your journey will be quicker than the one out. I know you will do everything you can to help Mrs. Campbell and Mason, but I have letters here that should ease your passage and, importantly, your status.'

He took my hand and looked directly into my eyes before lifting a thumb to wipe away a tear that had escaped and was finding its way down my cheek.

'The Commander has guaranteed that you will be under his protection no matter which vessel you are on, Esther,' he said gently as he offered me his handkerchief. 'I also want to give you some guineas to help if you are stuck here for any length of time and to help you travel once you get back to England. I know you have pride, Esther, but you must remember who your patrons are, and perhaps a good seamstress would help remind others of your position. Sadly, nowadays, people look at the outer person before noticing the inner, if indeed they ever do. One of the letters is to my tailor in London who will ensure you are comfortably dressed - you will find his direction on the reverse.'

I was so relieved, I hadn't wanted to return looking like a convict or an unsuitably dressed servant, and I had been intending to write to Cecilia to ask if I could borrow some money to enable me to get home to Lewes. I smiled thankfully, blinking my tears away before blowing my nose. 'Thank you, you have thought of everything. I am so grateful,' I cried.

We sat closely together in comfortable silence. Fortunately, Mrs. Campbell had gone to bed, and as my spirits lifted, I said, 'I can't wait to get home, but though the past few weeks have been terrifying at times, they have also opened my mind to different ways of life. Perhaps, what I am trying to say is that the way I used to think is not quite how I see things now.' I blushed at my awkward and obvious way of telling him that I might be open to his attentions.

'Let us not talk about such emotional things now, my dear. We have both learned much about ourselves, and I know you loved Wilf very much. It distresses me greatly to know how much you have suffered. When I return, and we are both settled back into the gentler environs of Lewes, we will look at ourselves and see what has changed.'

I nodded, smiling happily at him. He was looking at my feet which were protruding from under my skirt. I drew them in, ashamed of the grime.

'I notice that you don't wear your boots anymore, my dear, but you walk upright and with good muscle strength. Are you more comfortable now?'

'My aunt took them from me on the night of the kidnap. I have learned to walk barefoot, and I think I am stronger for it, particularly as I still do the exercises you gave me.'

'Stronger, indeed, but not so comfortable. We will address that problem when I return but, in the meantime, there is a shop nearby where you could fit yourself with some leather shoes made in the local style. They are perfectly serviceable, and the leather is good. You won't want to return home unshod.'

He had indeed thought of everything and I was touched by his practical care. I took his letters and guineas and put them next to my bed as I prepared for sleep. Charlotte woke with an insistent cry, so I carried her to Mrs. Campbell to be fed, returning for her sometime later. Mrs. Campbell had dozed off with the baby tucked into the crook of her arm but she had clearly been fed, if not changed. As I lifted her, I noticed that the angry rash on her mother's face was lessening.

'You will be back with your mama tomorrow, sweeting,' I whispered, 'but for tonight we will enjoy each other's company.'

I rose before sunrise the next morning and, as Charlotte needed her mama, I took her back and wakened Mrs. Campbell who grumbled that it was too early. Taking no notice, I left the cottage intending to wave Dr. Grieve off.

As I walked, I thought again how wonderful it was to be able to move freely with no guards, no fear or restrictions on what to do or who to speak to. I resolved never to take these everyday pleasures for granted again.

The doctor was already on board his ship when I arrived and standing at the rail; he was surprised to see me at such an early hour. I waved joyfully and was reassured to see him watching me for as long as I stood there. I wished heartily for his safe passage before wandering back to an early breakfast of coffee and warm bread with some sliced cheese. The young woman who was to cook for us spoke no English but we managed to converse by other means: lots of smiles and sign language, though she didn't look quite so happy when summoned to Mrs. Campbell's room.

Rather than be drawn into Mrs. Campbell's domestic tyranny, I went out again. The sun was fully risen and a delicious warmth lightened my step as I explored the narrow streets and alleys that were nearest the garrison. I quickly found the cobbler that Dr. Grieve had suggested and approached an elderly man who was working on the repair of some workman's boots. It was but a matter of moments to get myself seated on a box he had for the purpose and I was soon surrounded by dainty leather shoes. I eventually chose some that were rather more serviceable but very comfortable, with a lovely soft brown leather to encase my weathered and not very pretty feet. I paid the man and with many smiles of thanks from me and bowing on his part, I walked away but couldn't resist hitching my dress up every now and again to admire my newly-shod feet. Unfortunately, my limpy leg meant that one shoe did not quite fit as well as I would have liked, but I looked forward to the time when Dr.

Grieve would make me another insert to ease the pressure. Until then, I would stuff some material into the shoe to compensate. I also bought myself a light woollen shawl which was dyed a vibrant blue with embroidered flowers adorning it. The colours reflected the sky and flowers of this strange place and when I was back in England I would look at it and always feel the pleasure of the sun again, even if it was raining and cold. I have never been in the habit of spending money since I rarely had any to spare, so this frivolous use of someone else's money was very enjoyable.

As I walked, I looked for the sign of an apothecary, thinking that there must be one in such a busy place, and it wasn't long before I found what I was seeking. The half door looked in on a dusty counter where a woman was weighing up what looked like herbs, but none that I recognised. She looked up at my curious face and beckoned me in. I didn't need inviting twice. I fingered the herb she was then handling and somehow managed to convey my interest but lack of knowledge of local plants. Between us we discovered a mutual understanding and she drew me into an inner room lined with shelves, many of which were loaded with baskets of dried material. On the opposite side of the room were jars full of liquids in all colours of the rainbow. Some seemed to contain pickled fruit but maybe not of the eating variety. Every basket and jar bore a label of yellowing parchment, in writing that might have been Latin. I spent some time with the woman, touching and smelling the various grasses and herbs. I fervently wished that I was more educated and wondered if it might be possible to learn Latin at this late stage in my life. I felt so confident of this young woman's knowledge that I purchased some of the dried herbs to add to my own when I got home. She wrote a direction on each packet for me to know how to use them. I felt sure that Dr. Grieve would be able to understand them.

When I returned to our cottage, I prepared for more arguments with Mrs. Campbell, sure that she was still refusing to see me as an independent person, but I was happily mistaken.

'Esther, when we get back to London,' she began as soon as I entered, 'I would be grateful if you would stay with me and Charlotte until we find a place to rent. I know you have reason to want to return to Lewes as soon as possible so I wondered if it would be better if we all travelled there together. I have no reason to stay in London. In fact, it is better for Charlotte and me if we go where we know at least one person and you have convinced me that the little town you have talked of is as good a place as any. Would you allow us to accompany you?'

I was quite dumbstruck at this suggestion and moreover the humility with which it was said.

'I would be glad to have you accompany me,' I replied readily, 'and of course I will help you find somewhere to live. Lewes is a very genteel town, if you have money. I am sure Captain Campbell would be happy to know that his wife and child were part of a good community.'

We had a light supper, prepared by Johanna, of different pressed meats. I recognised tongue but some of them were very heavily spiced and I selected cautiously, as I found them to be piquant and peppery, but very nice indeed once you adjusted to the spices. We were given a custard-type of pudding encased in a batter which was also quite unknown to me and I enjoyed it immensely. I reminded Mrs. Campbell to drink as much as she was able in order to keep her milk flowing, and our young friend prepared her a drink that the local women recommended for that very reason.

'Life is not very different for women, wherever you are, is it?' I mused.

A soldier called on us the very next day to say that a ship was expected in port which might be suitable for three passengers and a baby. We were to be prepared to leave at short notice. Later I hurried down to the port and watched a much smaller ship than the *Lady Charlotte* come in. She was rather trim-looking and did not carry as much rigging. I hoped we would be able to travel on her as she looked to be a faster vessel. She was certainly a lot newer and less weathered.

I visited Prickship again to see if he was comfortable. He seemed quite cheerful despite the dreadful situation he was now in, and I questioned him about what he was expecting to do once we got back to Britain. I had no idea if he had a family. I knew he was not married but he might have brothers and sisters or even parents still living. I wondered if they would welcome him into their homes for the weeks it would take for him to heal sufficiently to return to able work. He was quite reluctant to engage in the conversation, so I didn't press him on his plans. We sat together for upwards of an hour and every time I mentioned the future, he changed the subject to something more light-hearted. I wondered if his home life was not to his liking. I think a lot of sailors escape to the sea rather than live an uneventful or miserable life on shore.

Jones, whom I miss dreadfully, had had a lot to say on why men endure such a harsh lifestyle: for the general crew, it is often an escape route from trouble or crimes; while others are press-ganged onto fighting ships but transfer later to merchant ships, having got used to the seafaring way of life. His opinion of the officer class was never complimentary but he did concede, when I pressed him, that not all officers were bad, and that a good officer was vital in keeping the ship on course and safe. Men who became officers were often more educated and seen from the outset as leaders rather than followers. Others worked their way up into the officer class despite their lowly status and it was these men that Jones respected. I don't believe that Prickship fell into that group.

At last the message came that we, Mrs. Campbell and Charlotte, Prickship and myself, were to travel back on the *Lady Guinevere* and to be ready to embark in two days. We must be on board by six o'clock. The two prison guards who attacked Prickship, along with the two who were bribed, were to travel later - on a more suitable vessel, one with a lockup. I wasn't sorry, and I am sure Prickship wasn't either. I was overwhelmed with excitement and felt that at last I was getting my life back. I would soon be home to see Beth, whom I was convinced was with Cecilia and I was happy to have met Dr. Grieve again and to know that he would return to Lewes and to me as soon as he was finished with his military business.

The voyage back home couldn't have been more different. We were given spacious and richly-furnished cabins and there was a stateroom for dining. The captain, named Bowen-Brown, made much of us and I understood that the boat was of a different class, faster, and frequently carried paying passengers as well as luxury goods for the London market. Luckily for our little group she was not fully laden. *Lady Guinevere* was expecting to moor up in London and then take passengers and papers on to Amsterdam. There was some secrecy about its cargo but one of the sailors told me that the boat regularly carried large amounts of gold and government documents. I found myself able to relax and thereby seemed to need more sleep, so when I wasn't helping with Charlotte I stayed quietly in my cabin reflecting on all that had happened to me.

Part Four

Chapter Thirty-Four

A surgeon recounts the case of a 12 year old girl who vomited an 87 inch worm. He describes the unusual case of Ellen McCarthy, aged 12, whose symptoms include "disease or hurt, pain in the bottom of her belly, increased on pressure, abdomen hard and swollen, picks her nose, starts in her sleep, bowels constipated, pyrexia, tongue foul, pulse quick, skin hot, great thirst". She is first put on the sick list on15 June 1825, at sea. Her mother brought the Surgeon a 'lumbricus' [worm], 87 inches long, which the child had vomited. Later she has another "motion" and two more worms are found, one 13 ½ inches long, the other 7 inches.

Diary of a Ship's Surgeon

I t was an uneventful voyage with fair weather all the way until at long last we were nigh Dover. I had claimed back my life as Esther Coad, widow, mother of Beth, governess to Cecilia and John Elwoods' children and a midwife. I would no longer be seen as a convict in anyone's eyes or consciousness.

So near, but so far. We were stranded inside the mouth of the Thames. There was little wind and a deep wet mist engulfed us. Small wherries appeared through the gloom before returning the way they had come, the sound of their dipping oars muffled by a dense fog that had fallen. They carried letters from Captain Bowen-Brown to the shipping agent requesting accommodation for us as well as letters to the surgeon and the tailor and, most importantly, to my friends in Lewes. Prickship looked evermore gloomy and Mrs. Campbell seemed anxious at being near *terra firma*, as they call it. Apparently, she and Captain Campbell had rarely stayed put in one place and were more comfortable out at sea.

'But surely you take breaks or holidays between voyages?' I asked.

'Yes, but not in this miserable country,' she said. 'We prefer warmer climes. I particularly like Italy.'

Charlotte opened her eyes and looked all around her. 'She at least seems happy to be here,' I commented.

'As are you,' she replied shortly.

While we waited for tide and wind to carry us to London, I tried to contain my excitement, but the frustration of waiting grew beyond what I was capable of. We were enveloped in the thick, cloying sea-mist which clung to the rigging as mournful foghorns boomed eerie warnings. I paced the deck, my clothes damp, my hair dripping. It occurred to me that it would be quicker to get off the boat here and take a coach, and I suggested it to my companions. But they were not happy to change our method of travel. Prickship, anticipating rutted or mud-laden roads which would cause him pain; Mrs. Campbell, not wishing to expose Charlotte to other travellers who might have the temerity to breathe on her. They were right, of course, and I had to contain my vexation.

Days of becalmed weather tried my patience to its limits but finally a frisky wind filled the sails and we surged along with the tide, though still it took several days to reach the London docks where we could disembark. A carriage was waiting which speedily took us to a tall, elegant house some little way back from the river that catered for customers of the shipping agent. All our rooms were on the ground floor, which was helpful. I was told that it was unwise to wander unchaperoned, so the day after our arrival I stayed in with Prickship who was expecting the physician Dr. Grieve had contacted. I, too, was expecting a visitor: the tailor, whom I hoped would be able to furnish me as a matter of urgency with a heavy cloak, gloves and a hat.

Tailor Partridge was a dapper man but with an unfortunate stoop. He seemed physically unable to lift his eyes above shoulder height which struck me as a painful condition as his neck was not upright but laid at an angle near his shoulder. He suggested that he take my measurements to make a serviceable travelling outfit. Additionally, he promised to send one of his apprentices with a cloak and gloves and volunteered to buy a hat on my behalf from a milliner who worked in the same building. The bespoke dress would be sent on to me in Lewes as soon as possible. I was amazed at the speed, but clearly Dr. Grieve was a good customer as he would accept no payment from my store of guineas. When the cloak, gloves and hat duly arrived, I absolutely loved them, particularly the cloak which was of a good heavy weight; he called it 'midnight blue' in colour, with a paler blue lining. It was very pretty as well as serviceable.

As the business with Tailor Partridge was concluding, I was surprised to receive a young man at our lodgings. He introduced himself as 'Charley from the shipping office', handing me a note of introduction as soon as I had ushered the tailor from our sitting room.

'Captain Campbell says you will require passage on a coach to Lewes, Miss,' he said. 'I am apprenticed to the shipping office but me pa is a coachman on that route, and I am to accompany you and Mrs. Campbell until you be safely on your way.'

I sank into a chair with relief, having had no idea of how to go about finding a coach and booking seats. In truth, what I had so far seen of London was terrifying. It was all so busy, with people scurrying about their business, with no time spent tarrying nor passing the time of day; everyone seemed intent on some greater purpose.

'I am happy to meet you, Charley,' I said. 'I was wondering how to get to Lewes and where I would find the coaches.'

'If I might suggest, Miss,' he said, 'we could go to Blossoms Inn and book places for you, Mrs. Campbell and the nipper. Me pa will be there tomorrow. It is his day off and he likes to spend some of it with his horses. The inn is where some of the Lewes coaches stable their horses,' he added as an afterthought.

Charley told me to be ready by ten o'clock the following day and to bring money for the tickets. I asked him if we could book the whole of the interior of the coach as Mrs. Campbell did not fancy unknown company sitting alongside of her.

Charley clearly knew Mrs. Campbell of old, as he sighed, 'A lot of folks want to travel that route nowadays, Miss, and it ain't good business to turn them away, but I'll talk to pa and see if he can get someone suitable alongside of ye.'

I laughed at his grimace as he said this, replying, 'Don't worry if he can't, I am sure she will cope. Until tomorrow then, Charley.'

My spirits rose: new clothes and a coach to Lewes in prospect. Nearly home.

I was up bright and early the next day and sorry to see a grey sky threatening rain. As no-one else appeared, I breakfasted alone. Our landlady served up sausages from Kent and fresh baked rolls and I fell upon them with enthusiasm. The variety of food on offer was better than on board ship and the sausages were nearly as good as Mrs. Fisher's. I heard a knock and wondered if it was Charley though it was still some minutes afore nine o'clock.

The landlady was at the door. 'A letter for you, Miss. Can I clear away, or were you wanting something else?'

'Thank you, I am finished,' I said. 'The sausages were delicious.' I took the letter from her and read the direction. It was Cecilia's writing, though it was very unlike her usual elegant flowing hand. I tore at the seal, anxious to read the news she sent.

My dearest Esther,

We thank God that you are alive and safe and soon to be returned to us. We have feared the worst and in truth I had all but given up hope of ever seeing you again.

Esther, my dearest friend, I have terrible news for you, and though I would prefer to tell you face to face I think it best that you prepare yourself before you get back to South Farm. I am afraid that Beth has been lost to us since that dreadful day when you were both kidnapped. We have some recent information which leads us to think that she is alive, but she is not here with us and John and I fear for her as we did for you.

However, my dear, you have come back, so perhaps I

235

will take courage and put my dread aside and hope that she too will be returned. I am sure your old adversary Farmer Coad does not have her, and I hope that will comfort you. The trail on your aunt had all but disappeared though it was thought she was living at Coad Farm for a while. It was a great shock to hear that you had been put on a transport ship with her and we are all desperate to hear your story. I can't write more, Esther, as I am tired and weak from the strain, but John and I and all your friends are waiting here to greet you with love and compassion and it can't come soon enough. God speed.

    Cecilia

    P.S. We found Flossy and she is now in the stables eating her fill. I know that you will be relieved to hear this.

I felt sick and chilled as I read this shocking news. I had been so certain that Beth was safe. I sat there, unable to think or even cry. I kept re-reading Cecilia's words as I felt my heart thudding in my chest. Surely, I would have known if harm had come to Beth, or was it foolish of me to think that? I answered myself as no-one else would. Yes, I was foolish, and my certainties were not worth a penny piece. My dear friend was clearly unwell too, and I felt for her suffering. What a curse I was to that kindly family. They must wish I had never crossed their path.

Numbed with misery, I remained at the table until I was forced to respond to Charley's call. He accompanied me through the hectic streets to the Blossom Inn where we found his pa in the stables with a team of six fine sturdy horses. I had been around horses in Farmer Elwood's stables and I could see that these beasts were well cared-for and exceptionally strong, their great muscles rippling under a shiny coat as they were groomed with a currycomb.

Charley had explained that the coach was out every day with different coachmen and teams, the Lewes run being one of the oldest in the south. It took the whole day and the coach returned on the following. Lately, since the Prince of Wales had taken property in Brighthelmstone and started to build his palace, the traffic had increased hugely, with Lewes becoming a staging post before the coaches made their way over the Downs to the seaside fishing village.

There were four routes to the south and I was interested in the one that went to Lewes through Chailey. If that was not available, we could get there through Uckfield, but it would have to be with someone other than Charley's pa. I liked Charley's pa; he was a genial chap who promised to find us space on his next trip, likely to be the day after tomorrow. I paid for us all and asked whether there would be other inside passengers.

'One of my regulars, Miss. He be a lawyer and do occasional work in Lewes at the court. He is a quiet man and very knowledgeable, I count him as a good, honest man – you couldn't be in better company - and he is a good shot if things get rowdy.' He laughed loudly at the expression on my face.

'Why would they get rowdy?' I wasn't laughing.

'Drunks on top, scared passengers, fights between those as should know better, all sorts of reasons, Miss. But don't you worry none, I been doing this man and boy and I ain't lost a passenger yet.'

'Why are there scared passengers?' I persisted.

'Some people just got no bottle,' he said. 'First sign

of a man on a horse, they think they gonna be robbed or murdered.'

Charley broke in, 'You're scarin' the lady, Pa. Don't take no notice of him, Miss. There are two guards, armed, as well as pa, and as he says he ain't lost a passenger yet. The worst that will happen to you is being jolted to death or having to get out and walk up a few hills if there are too many outside passengers.'

I looked at this big genial man and saw a twinkle in his eye before I dropped our money into his calloused hand and put my trust in him. Returning to our lodgings, I suggested to Charley that we didn't mention the armed guards or highwaymen to Mrs. Campbell.

He laughed, sounding remarkably like his pa, before replying, 'They'd run away rather than getting a tongue-lash from her, Miss. She's been around and knows the ways, and most people round here knows of her. Be the captain well, Miss? We all hold him high and were right glad to hear he has a nipper.'

'He was well when I last saw him,' I replied, 'though he lost one of his key men, who is staying with us whilst his broken leg heals, and I worry for the captain on that long voyage.'

'Don't you fret, Miss, we heard he took on a new fella to take Prickship's place.' It seemed Charley knew everything, even the rude name bestowed on Mason by the crew.

We still had one and a half days to wait and Mrs. Campbell had some business to attend to, so I looked after Charlotte. Fortunately, the shipping office was not too far, so she was able to come and go around feeds. I left her looking after Charlotte herself on the following day as I wanted to see what London was like. I knew that if I didn't fill my time, I would just sit fretting about Beth, which did no good at all. I hadn't told the others my bad news - they were so preoccupied with their own business, they had no time or inclination to notice my mood - and in any case I would have found it hard to put into words without breaking down.

One area I'd heard about from Prickship was known as Wapping, where many boats were moored, and Charley accompanied me there, leaving Mrs. Campbell to her own devices. It was near a place called Execution Dock where smugglers and seafaring crooks were hanged. I had heard from my companions that those found guilty might be hanged on a short rope from a gibbet that was only just above the low water mark, so their necks weren't broken but stretched, giving them a long, slow death by suffocation; and as if that weren't bad enough, they were held by the river until three tides had covered them. Charley just laughed when I told him I didn't want to go anywhere near there. He seemed to think it was one of London's attractions.

Wapping was hectic with all sorts: black men, turbaned men, Jewish bearded men and Orientals as well as the local workers - all nationalities and every creed, attached to the many trading ships. The atmosphere felt a little menacing with all these people thrusting themselves forward to gain work or advantage of sorts, and not only men: there were women seeking to exploit men for their money - women who were not downtrodden and shy but openly relishing the trade of selling their bodies in public. I was shocked to see such low behaviour; these creatures were shameless, nor were their customers any better. Mrs. Campbell would have sneered at my distaste and reminded me of her earlier comments about men and their needs.

One of the things I found overwhelming was the smell. There was the ever-present effluent running down a middle channel of the narrow streets and the danger of a bucket of slop being thrown from an upper window. But also, as you walked past public houses, bawdy houses and warehouses where vats and cases overflowed, there was the pungent tang of beer, heady spices and coffee, as well as fruits - fruits that I had never heard of, let alone smelled. Then there were the barrels of wines and spirits, some of which had a bung that was easily loosened for tasting. The merchants in charge of these were more discreet as they hawked their merchandise to customers who were a cut above in their dress and manners.

I saw caged birds - from Africa, Charley said - screeching louder than the fishwives on most street corners. It was all so noisy, colourful and excitable that for a while you could forget the dreadful stink. Away from the waterfront, the streets were crowded and pitiful, with urchins constantly running between horses' hooves, carriages and carts in order to deliver messages and letters. Carters used sticks to beat their way forward, carriage drivers used long whips, and riders lashed out with their crops if anyone got too close. Somehow, they all got around each other, but I was unable to see what manner of preference there was; the carriages must have had the advantage, though, being bigger, smarter and having burly footmen to chase off anyone who got in their way.

There were lots of men in uniform, all very proud and most wearing swords. They had brightly festooned braid across their chests, round their necks and wrists; the eyes of the street women followed them, with many a bawdy comment thrown.

I pushed myself up against a shopfront, taking refuge from the mass of people crowding the walkway. It was a meat pie shop, and the aroma was wonderful, but suddenly it was all too much for me and I became fearful of the clamour. My eyes were gritty and strained, worst of all, my head had begun to ache. I was grateful to Charley for his company but asked him to take me straight back to our rooms. There I took a short nap before joining the others for a simple meal. Prickship and Mrs. Campbell were playing cards, rather noisily, which I found irritating. I looked in on little Charlotte. She was a delight: she fed, she slept and fed again, giving no trouble to her mother, which was a blessing. I retired to my room, but with Beth's plight tormenting me, struggled to get to sleep.

Chapter Thirty-Five

The George, one of London's great coaching inns is one of the treasures of London. It is the last remaining galleried inn in London and is now owned by the National Trust but leased to a private company who use it as a public house. The building was mentioned by Charles Dickens in Little Dorrit; it dates from 1677 and its rooms overlook a cobbled courtyard.

The Coach Roads to Brighton by Geoffrey Hewlett, 2014

I woke in a sweat and troubled of mind. Rising before dawn broke, I washed my megrims away before sitting by the window watching for the sky to lighten until, at last, we were ready to leave for the coach. Charley and another lad walked alongside us with our boxes loaded onto a hand cart. We had said a melancholy goodbye to Prickship who was very despondent at our leaving him, but by the time we got to the coach we were more cheerful, or at least Mrs. Campbell became so; I was anxious all the time about Cecilia's letter and the terrible news it contained. I kissed Charley goodbye and laughed at his blushes as I waved him off. Initially, we had the coach to ourselves, so we made it comfortable; if the gentleman lawyer was coming he had better make haste. There were four further passengers booked along the route at a place called Kennington, but they were not to be inside with us. At the last moment Charley's pa looked in and said we were still waiting for our lawyer but then, as a horn blew, he climbed up onto his high seat and gathered the reins - just as the tardy passenger clambered into the coach. We were off.

Our companion was very gentlemanly, doffing his hat and removing his gloves to shake hands. Mrs. Campbell thawed her gimlet eyes and chatted and simpered for all she was worth. His name was Sir Magnus Crisp. He was clearly an important man and we were reassured that he would be pleasant company – much more pleasant than if it were just Mrs. Campbell and me!

The coach lumbered through the congested streets, heading for London Bridge and as we crossed the great sullen river, I allowed myself a little hope for reaching Lewes safely despite the frightening pictures conjured up by Charley's pa.

Sir Magnus kindly kept us advised of all that was worth seeing and after we got used to the jolting and creaking, we settled down to watch the world lurch by at such speed that it made me feel quite woozy. We left behind the bustle of busy thoroughfares, and as we were then going through quiet and lonely woodland, we all stopped our chatter and I, at least, was looking through every copse and behind every bush for a highwayman. Sir Magnus had placed a gun in the luggage sack over our heads and I felt very anxious when he got up and lifted it down, putting it carefully on his knees.

'Nothing to worry yourselves about, ladies, but this area is notorious for robbers and it is best to be prepared,' he said. 'If you look to your right in a few moments, you will see the gibbet where the nefarious Jonas Pike ended his days. I should cover your noses if I were you - the air will doubtless be a little ripe.'

I tried not to look but my eyes were relentlessly drawn and I gasped in horror as I saw what remained of a man hanging in strips and tatters, his flesh shredded and mottled by scavenging birds and the weather. 'Ripe' was not the word I would have used, but even with my knowledge of putrefying flesh, I retched. Mrs. Campbell didn't turn a hair as she announced that she had seen it all before onboard ship when men had been hanged. Irritated by her manner and all the making-up to our companion, I cut in with, 'I can't believe your husband, Captain Campbell, would have left a man hanging until he dropped, Madam.'

She looked coldly at me before admitting that he would have been cut down as soon as he was dead. Sir Magnus Crisp looked from one to the other of us and a little smile played on his lips. After that, she didn't speak to me until Charlotte began to murmur and even then, it was with an acid tongue that she requested I hand down her changing things.

We stopped at Kennington and she took Charlotte into the public house to feed and change her clouts in the lady's lounge. The coach didn't stop for long, but it was long enough for the baby's comfort and to pick up the extra outside passengers.

After Kennington, the air cleared and the countryside was pretty, but we had not gone far before we had to alight for the first time to allow the coach easier passage up hill and down dale. We passed through the delightful villages of Brixton and then Streatham, but every time we had to get out, it meant walking in the draught of the dry road and rolling wheels, so were soon very dusty. The relentless jolting of the carriage was also having a bad effect on my neck and shoulders.

I noticed that our companion kept his gun by him and maintained a watchful eye whenever we passed through copses or thickets, which was nearly all the time. I could feel the increasing pain in my back, shoulders and neck and wished that I was anywhere other than in this shuddering contraption. Whilst it was dirty tramping alongside the coach, at least I could stretch the aches and stiffness away. We passed through Croydon and Godstone, stopping where necessary to water the horses and to allow us to buy some small refreshment at roadside inns, but there was always a sense of urgency to be on our way as soon as possible. After Godstone we left the heavy toil of the North Downs before heading to East Grinstead and our companion was able to describe the route and the nature of the towns and villages we passed through. When the coach was on hard, high ground we travelled at some speed; but it was when we dropped into valleys that had ghylls or streams at their base that we were liable to get stuck in deep mud, and again to have to get out of the coach while the men encouraged the horses to pull through the sticky clags; it was either that or dig us all out!

I was thankful to get through the worst of the highwayman's haunts and it was with great relief that we came out of a wet Ashdown Forest. Looking ahead, I could see the South Downs where the hard chalk surface would allow us to pick up some of the time lost while we were stuck in the mire. But as we came near Chailey, the ground dipped again into woods and bog; once more we were compelled to scramble to the ground. Well, Sir Magnus and I got out, leaving Mrs. Campbell to feed Charlotte as we picked our way alongside. Apparently, we were unlikely to meet with highwaymen there as we were now too far from the riches of London and the local people were too poor to be worth robbing. I was greatly relieved to hear this and, for all my anxiety, I couldn't help but feel excited. I began to talk to my companion of some of my recent adventures. He was quite taken by what had happened to me and made me promise to call on him, care of The Star in Lewes, should I ever be in need. I didn't know whether he meant his legal services or services in general. I felt him to be an honourable man and I agreed to stay in touch. At the back of my mind, once Beth was returned to me - as surely, she would be - was the thought that I might have to fight the Coads for her care. He said he would be in Lewes every six or so weeks and would send me word at the Elwoods if he had time to venture from his lodgings.

When we came to the tiny hamlet of Offham and the final toll house, I was sitting on the edge of my seat almost overcome with impatience. At last we pulled up at The Star in Lewes and our tortuous journey was over. I thanked Charley's pa for getting us safely home and hoped I would see him again sometime. Sir Magnus Crisp had already disappeared and once our luggage was dropped off into the hotel, I had a brief moment to look around and sniff the familiar and welcoming air of wonderful, wonderful Lewes.

Chapter Thirty-Six

The main bar at The Star was heaving with big, loud gentlemen who all seemed to be shouting, and I had to push my way through. As I did so, I felt my arm pulled and angrily turned to berate my accoster. It was Billy-alone.

'Oh, Billy, thank heaven!' I cried. 'I am so glad to see you.' I clutched at him, relief flooding over me.

'Me too, Miss, I be that glad to see you safe and back with us, an' you lookin' so different, like,' he said. 'I have the carriage waiting for you. Will you come now? Mrs. Elwood is beside herself and desperate to see you, and Farmer Elwood too. They been waiting for days - we expected you afore, like.'

He was looking hard at me and I suppose he was shocked at seeing my hair which, though partly hidden by my hat, was obviously shorter than when we last met. He had changed too; he was taller and didn't look so boyish. There were lines of maturity round his mouth and eyes and I was shocked to see a sadness in his look despite his warm welcome. I asked after Cilla, hoping that they were together still.

We struggled back through the throng and I pushed and shoved to make them move out of my way. I wasn't the meek and mild woman who had left this town.

'I have to settle Mrs. Campbell and Charlotte into rooms at The White Hart,' I said. 'We wrote from London to book, but I thought to bring them to South Farm first to introduce them.'

'Mrs. Elwood particular asks that you bring them with you. I'm to see their bags are taken to their room and say the carriage will bring them back later, like'.

'Billy, I have missed you so. How is everyone?'

'Mrs. Elwood wants to tell you everything herself, Miss. I promised faithfully to bring you home and not to chatter on the way.'

He didn't look at me, but I knew he was anxious, fidgeting and keeping his eyes on the floor instead of at me.

'Alright, Billy, I won't pester you,' I said. 'Let's get back home.' How I relished saying that word – home.

In no time we were away. The Elwoods' carriage was a good deal more comfortable than the one we had travelled from London in.

My heart quickened as the horses drew nearer to South Farm and as we clattered into the stable yard, I was so overcome that I felt almost breathless.

Billy jumped down and held the horse's heads as both Mrs. Campbell and I stepped out. Charlotte had slept through the last hours of our journey and was just beginning to murmur - I left them with Billy and ran to the front door which stood open and waiting for me. Cecilia and Farmer

Elwood were in the drawing room and as I ran in they rose and came towards me with their arms outstretched. We all clung together; I was so thankful to be back with them. Then I stood back and cried, great gulping sobs that wouldn't stop, full of relief that I was home at long, long, last, even though it was a home that didn't have Beth in it.

Cecilia crumpled into a chair and it was then that I noticed how white and dreadfully thin she was. I pulled myself together and knelt at her side, filled with fear for Beth and sorrow for what Cecilia had been put through. Billy came in with Charlotte in his arms and introduced Mrs. Campbell to Farmer Elwood while I tried to get some control over my emotions.

Farmer Elwood was speaking to Mrs. Campbell; I heard him welcome her and offer refreshments. It was late in the day and brandy and wines with small tarts were brought in but still Cecilia had not spoken. We just looked at each other; she unable to tell me how Beth had gone and I unable still to believe it.

'What happened?' I finally asked, my voice quivering.

John Elwood replied as Cecilia buried her head in her hands, her shoulders shaking.

'We went to Coad Farm, Esther, as soon as the stable boy raised the alarm. By the time we got there, and it was only an hour after you rode out of South Farm, they had gone and you with them. We found no trace of Beth or you. The place was deserted, the range was cold. We searched every room, every barn, every hayrick.'

I nodded and explained that I had only been there for a few minutes, which was all it took to bind and throw me into a cart.

I felt someone at my side; it was Cilla, with a small tray and a glass of brandy. I took it and hugged her.

He continued, 'We called in men from other farms, the justice's men and the constabulary, and searched the district nearby but it was as if you had never been there. We found no tracks. Flossy was found wandering down the river - clearly, she had been turned loose from somewhere, probably Coad Farm, but we did wonder if in fact you had never made it to the farm. Perhaps you'd been intercepted on the way, so we widened the search but still found nothing. We have been living in a nightmare ever since. My dear wife has been ill and at one point I feared for her life, she was so distraught. Esther, we thought you were dead, and Beth, too. Our only hope throughout has been that no bodies have been found, which made it seem possible you were both still alive.'

His face reddened and his eyes glistened. I could see how devastated he, Cecilia and the whole household had been for all the weeks I had been gone. It explained why Billy looked so sad. Farmer Elwood motioned to Cilla and she took the brandy round again to everyone in the room before he went on with his explanation.

'Lewes people searched for you both for miles around. Everybody knew the smugglers had gone too far this time and good, law-abiding folk have sought you up and down in every village, every barn and outhouse, even in Kent where there is another gang of smugglers. We received word from a Lewes man, who knows them, that it was not their doing. When we finally pinned down Farmer Coad and his sons, they flatly denied having seen you or being involved with anyone who might do you harm. They had alibis.' He swallowed another drop of brandy before going on.

'But then, we had a small breakthrough, and between then and the time we received your letter, Cecilia has gradually recovered her strength and we have all learned to hope again.' He pulled his handkerchief from a pocket and blew his nose loudly. 'That was the worst part – the loss of hope.'

I raised my eyes to his, my voice steady. 'What was the breakthrough?'

He turned to Billy. 'Would you tell Esther what happened, Billy?'

'Aye, yessur, I be out in fields one day overlooking the sheep. It were about three weeks after you disappeared. I saw someone creepin' 'long the hedge and I watched for a while afore I realised it be that young Coad boy. He was watching me watching him and then he legged it and I couldn't catched him. I went back to where he was first off and found a piece of a bill and on the back was some writing. It was tucked into your boots. I brought it back to Mrs. Elwood and she sent for the Master.'

'Here, Esther, is the piece of paper. Perhaps you would like to read it yourself?' Farmer Elwood passed it to me and I read it aloud:

Beth is with me and we be leavin'. They will kill us if they find me like they killed my ma. DON'T TELL. If her mama comes back I will know. She is safe with me. I asked a friend to writ this. He will tell me any news.

There was no name on the bottom of the scribbled note, but I could hear him saying those desperate words. I looked around, weary unto death and unable to move my limbs. Cecilia reached out to me and I collapsed into her arms and wept.

251

Chapter Thirty-Seven

Notice is hereby given that the Lewes One Day STAGECOACH or CHAISE sets out from The Talbot Inn in the Borough on Saturday next, the 19th instant. When, likewise, the BRIGHTHELMSTONE STAGE begins. Performed (if God) permits James BATCHELOR

Sussex Weekly Advertiser and Lewes Journal 1750/1806

I had been at South Farm for two days and I was still unable to comprehend how Job Coad could have spirited Beth away and kept her safe without anyone knowing or telling. His family - Farmer Coad and his two brothers - must have sought him high and low, wanting to get to him before he told everything he knew about their way of life, and their crimes. How could a young boy hide with a small child? How could he feed her, dress her and not be noticed by someone?

As I lay in my bed, unable to get up and unable to stop crying, I eventually concluded that he must have had accomplices and especially one that was female. Only a woman would be able to care for Beth in a way that would not draw attention; a woman perhaps who was claiming that Beth was her niece, or a childless woman desperate for one of her own. The idea pushed itself into every corner of my brain and I decided it was time to stop lingering abed and get on with looking for a woman who could harbour a child without raising anyone's suspicions.

I rose, washed and combed my short curls before heading for Cecilia's rooms, bursting in full of determination. I found her lying on her daybed. She was dreadfully pale, and it came as a further shock to realise not only how much she had suffered but how much she continued to do so. I rang the bell and asked Cilla to bring some of my special tea if there was any left, also requesting that Freddie and the baby be brought to us. It was time to get back some sense of normality if we were to make a plan and carry it through.

Freddie had grown since I was taken. He hid behind Mary-Jane's skirts at first instead of running to me as he would normally have done. I dropped to the floor and called to him gently before he suddenly rushed at me and put his little arms tight around my neck.

He smelled so good, my heart nearly burst with love for him as I stroked his blonde curls. Mary-Jane laid Felicia in a crib alongside Cecilia. She was fast asleep and only whimpered a little as she was turned; she was not so tiny now, either.

'Thank you, Mary-Jane,' I said. 'I am glad to see you are well. I will look after the children for now and call you when they are ready to return to the nursery.'

'Yes, Miss, happy to see you, Miss.' Everyone still called me Miss.

I pulled Freddie up onto my knee and when Cilla returned with the tea tray, he was very pleased to see the sweetmeats.

'How are you, Cilla? We haven't had a moment to talk. Are you and Billy still walking out?'

'Aye, Miss Esther, we have an understanding and my parents do heartily approve of Billy. It's good to see you up and doing at last,' she carried on. 'We have been so worried and poor Billy is blaming himself all the while,' Cilla spoke indignantly.

'Why is he blaming himself? He has done nothing wrong, far from it.'

'He do know'd that, but he thinks if he had run harder or sooner he would have caught the mongrel.'

'Don't call him that, Cilla,' I chided her. 'He has rescued Beth from his own family and is risking his life every day that he has her. They would think nothing of beating him to death and what would happen to Beth without him to protect her?'

'Me pa thinks 'e is long gone. No-one would 'ave put him up 'round 'ere, there be too many people looking for yer.'

Cecilia interrupted. 'That will do Cilla, poor Esther can't take on any more problems. No-one thinks Billy's at fault, so back to the kitchen now and tell him that from me.'

Cilla left the room and Cecilia said, 'Now Essie, we are alone, well nearly alone. We will make the tea and put our heads together. I so long to hear the story of what happened to you but I fear the telling will be long and we need to be thinking only of finding Beth.'

I agreed. 'Yes, I have had some thoughts and I think the likeliest plan is to find a childless couple who might have been persuaded to take in a little girl, perhaps being posed as a niece or grand-daughter. Young Coad was a delivery boy for my aunt's gang. He will know many people in the depths of the countryside and he might have told them that his father was behind the request to take the child.'

'Surely people wouldn't do that, especially with the hue and cry?'

'If they were part of the smuggling network hiding goods, why not hide a child, particularly if they wanted one of their own?' I replied.

'But wouldn't people question that?'

'Not if they had a good enough story: a niece maybe visiting whilst her mother recuperates from another birth?' I was warming to my theme even though Cecilia looked doubtful. I went on, 'Many people live in isolated places. It is those places where the smugglers hide their goods. They are unlikely to be able to read and it will be in their nature to be secretive and suspicious of strangers. Job Coad could have spun them a yarn and promised extra coin as well as a little girl to keep a wife happy.' It all seemed as clear as day to me as I expounded my thoughts but Cecilia clearly wasn't convinced.

'When did you dream this up, Essie? It is quite a theory.' She poured some tea before saying, 'I suppose you could be right. Now I come to think of it, some of the tenants on my mother's estates have never travelled, even to the next village. The only time they go anywhere is if there is a country fair or some such to draw them away from home, and that may only be once a year.'

'It is not unlikely - people are obliged to work hard and haven't got the time to be wandering about and it is possible only the men would go to a fair.' We both sipped our tea, each thinking of the possibilities. I carried on, thinking aloud. 'Women have to tend the animals and babies, probably in that order as the animals provide the food for all of them. It can't harm to make enquiries.' I looked up, before saying, 'Cecilia, can we look at the estate maps? And then we could ask your agent, or better still, Billy, what he knows about likely places. Billy would be a good source of knowledge. He seems to know everyone, or he knows someone who knows everyone.'

'Well, I know where they are, I'll go and get them.' She rose from her day bed with a new spring in her step which belied the pallor of her face.

I poured more tea and fed Freddie with extra sweetmeats. They were very good, so he wasn't too miserable at all the chatter and our ignoring him, and the baby was sleeping soundly. Two hours later, we had a list of all the isolated properties on the South Farm estate and the neighbouring farms as well. It ended up as quite a long list.

Mr. Harvey, the agent who had taken over from Wilf, was too recent an employee to have knowledge of all the people on our list but his willing help and good sense helped narrow the options we were exploring as, at our request, he drew up a document with three headings: family with children, yes or no; family with known connection to smugglers, yes or no; family, unlikely.

Seeing the places and names all noted down focused our thoughts and later, Billy and Farmer Elwood between them were able to supply details from one source or another. Towards the end of the day Farmer Elwood sent a message to the other nearby landowners requesting their help. A meeting of all parties, either owners or agents, took place early the following day at South Farm. Everyone seemed more than willing to help find Beth: they were all family men and must relate to the horror of what had happened.

I spoke at the gathering and explained my theory that Job Coad must have accomplices, probably including a woman. I also emphasised that the Coad boy was protecting

Beth, that he was not a suspect in her kidnap and must not under any circumstance be treated as a criminal. All the local knowledge quickly reduced the list, and with Mr. Harvey making all the corrections, it became much shorter. Several of the men were doubtful about my reasoning but as there was no other plan, they agreed to go along with whatever was decided.

While the meeting took place, Cecilia had a visit from Mrs. Makepiece who was upset that I had not been in touch. I heard her voice as I walked from the library to the kitchen and rushed into the drawing room to explain myself. Once she had been filled in with some of the facts of my return and subsequent collapse, and then the plan of how we hoped to find Beth, she was all for running her eye over the list which was now disappointingly small. I had no great hopes that she could offer something over and above the local men, but it wouldn't hurt to show her, and she at once pointed to a name that had meaning to her.

She looked up at me and said, 'If you are looking for a woman in all this, you should be asking other women for they know things that are closed to menfolk.'

The name of the family she pointed to was White and they lived up on the edge of dense woodland not too far from a great mansion called Sheffield Park.

'How do you know them?' I asked.

'The wife, as she is now, was a Lewes girl – pretty young thing she was,' she paused, before continuing, 'one of my boys was sweet on her. Unfortunately for her, she got into trouble and the father of the child, a travelling labourer who had taken advantage of her innocence, disappeared as soon as she began to show. Her parents were all for throwing her out onto the parish, but a man called Chalky White offered to take her off their hands, baby and all. Trouble was, he was not too far off the age of her own pa, so it wasn't a marriage made in heaven, was it? She, her name be Martha, was bundled off to his place and put to work collecting wood for charcoal-burning. She lost the child well into the pregnancy and every other baby that came along. To my knowledge she miscarried at least 5 times. I knew her mother well and she used to tell me what went on.'

'Is her mother still about?' I asked, breathless with excitement that this might be the family we sought.

'No, both her parents died, and I haven't seen Martha since she left Lewes. I was sorry for the lass, she must have had a hard time of it married to an old man and picked by him as cheap labour and bed warmer.' She grimaced at the thought of young Martha and her fate. I could see her looking back into her memories before she said, 'The loss of all those babies must have been terrible for her, they might have given her some solace.' She sighed again. 'My boy was sweet on her, as I said. I might have grandchildren now if he had been at home and persuaded to give the child a name, but her parents wouldn't wait and wouldn't take a bastard child as their own.'

'Do you think she could be helping the Coad lad?'

'Well, I don't know if her husband be one of the smuggling connection, but he lives set apart from all others. Martha's mother described him as a 'bugger' once she got to know him, but by then it was too late. I think she felt guilty to her dying day for forcing her daughter into such a miserable marriage. It is a lonely place up there and a child, like Beth, would be pure joy to poor Martha.'

I added Martha's name alongside Chalky White who was already on the list. 'Did she never come back to Lewes to see her parents?' I asked.

'No, never, she wasn't allowed to, and Martha's mother's only contact was via the tinkers who visited with their wares – that's how she got her information and then she would come and tell me. The father wouldn't have his daughter's name mentioned in the house and I became her confidante – she had to talk to someone!'

Telling us about Martha seemed to disturb Mrs. Makepiece and she left shortly after telling us her story. Suddenly, my theory seemed to be possible and both Cecilia and I were excited at this new bit of information, whilst feeling some sympathy for the unfortunate Martha.

After our midday meal, we all pored over the document and settled on a plan of action. Even though the names were few, they were spread over a wide area, so we would have to visit each in secrecy and try to ascertain whether Beth was there before going in with men and weapons. The smugglers or their accomplices were all heavily armed and would not be subdued easily and we could not afford for anyone to hurt or get rid of Beth; she was such a little thing and easy to hide, dead or alive. It was my fear that if anyone got wind of our interest, they would simply kill her and hide the evidence.

We decided that Billy and Mr. Harvey would go downriver to a place not far from Southease, where my aunt had lived and from where she had led the smuggling gang that I had helped to break up (with the loss of my cousins' lives), thus causing the enmity that had brought us to this unhappy state.

Farmer Elwood and several of the lads would go up to Martha's home, which was a good ride away but seemed the likeliest family to fit our thoughts of where Beth might be, and we wouldn't want her to be hidden just before we got there. Other trusted men would be sent to two other homes, all isolated and all fitting the bill in one way or another.

We agreed that everyone should be in place by mid-afternoon the following day when the men were most likely to be away from the home and the women preparing the meal. Everyone was sworn to secrecy and, all in all, I was confident that there would be no opportunity for Chalky White or the other families to hear about our activity before we were prepared.

Chapter Thirty-Eight

*On Thursday night last we have had a violent storm. Thunder,
lightning, and hail. The hail stones in general measuring two
inches or upwards round, by which great numbers of windows
were broke*

Sussex Weekly Advertiser and Lewes Journal 1750/1806

I went to bed early that night, willing the new day to
start when I would join the group who were going to
Martha's home. Farmer Elwood had no plan for me
to be with him, but I was determined and when he rode
out I followed closely behind on Flossy. I was well wrapped
against the wintry weather.

He reined in when he saw me and said, 'I suppose there
is no likelihood of you obeying me if I say go home?'

'No, none,' I replied. He nodded and we all trotted on,
trying to avoid places where there were people who would
gossip, particularly if we didn't find her. We eventually
came to a crossroads beyond which we could see the forest.
Skirting the boundary of the great mansion of Sheffield
Park, we plunged into boggy land that came before the
safety of brush and then tree cover. The ground was very
wet with some deep, cold pools for the unwary. Beyond the
swampy land there were higher irregular banks where deep
bracken beds were dying back and poor Flossy was soon
wet and covered in mud. Farmer Elwood's huge stallion

picked his way through the undergrowth as we all followed his lead, and when we came into the forest we found tracks through the wood. There were clear signs of industry, with wood chips and felled trees as well as ash pits. One of the men who was with us got down and walked deeper into the wood while I held his horse. I was shivering with fear along with anticipation that I might be just yards from Beth. In the distance, we could hear the occasional thud of an axe against wood, but it was far away from us and we were unlikely to be seen or heard by the axeman. It was some time before the stableman came back but when he did, he was clearly excited by something.

Not waiting for Farmer Elwood, I blurted out the question we were all wanting to hear the answer to: 'Have you seen her?'

'No, but there be a cottage and washing hung out,' he said. 'I reckon there is a child living there as grown men or women don't fit the size of clothes that is hanging.' My heart soared in hope as we all dismounted and tied the horses to some saplings nearby.

Farmer Elwood spoke as we gathered around him, 'We will get as near to the cottage as is possible without breaking cover and then, on my signal, all move in together.' He directed the men to surround the place but keep cover. 'Esther, you stay with me,' he ordered. Finally, before everyone disappeared, he said, 'I don't want anyone hurt, so no firing of pistols. We don't want the woodmen coming down on us with their axes. We don't know how many men use this place, nor if they are innocent of what we suspect.'

I stood behind a tree alongside Farmer Elwood, and after about fifteen minutes he stepped out from cover and raised his arm in a signal to converge on the cottage. A woman came out to see what was going on and I decided to slip inside the house while Farmer Elwood engaged her in talk. I had expected the woman to be still fairly young and attractive, as described by Mrs. Makepiece, but time had not dealt kindly with her. She was stooped and drawn in the face, her eyes shifting constantly. As I sneaked nearer the cottage, I heard Farmer Elwood demand her attention.

'Your name, Madam?'

Her mouth hung slack at the sight of all the armed men surrounding her cottage and she didn't reply but backed away into the safety of her doorway. I had got there before her and she was shocked to find me behind her and blocking her entry. I looked directly into her tired and frightened eyes, before saying, 'You have a child here?'

She was clearly terrified, but she nodded wordlessly.

'Where is she?' My heart was pounding.

There was a slight inclination of her head to the room behind me and I ran in.

The room appeared small and dark, but I could make out a deal table at the centre. I walked further in, adjusting my eyes to the dim light. I saw a small cot-like bed in the corner and on that bed was lying a form covered by a hessian sack. My heart was in my mouth as I lifted the corner of the sack. A child stirred and peeped from great dark eyes up at me. It was not Beth.

My hopes shattered, I couldn't wait to get away, to ride hard to one or other of the remaining dwellings on the list but Farmer Elwood was not satisfied with this setback and questioned the woman as to who the child belonged to. Once she had got over her shock, she became quite talkative and declared her to be the daughter of one of the nearby foresters whom she minded while the father worked. The child had no mother and this woman, Martha, was more than pleased to have the child spend the days with her.

I had looked around the room while she talked and saw no trace of any other child. Farmer Elwood insisted on searching the small cottage, which did not take long, while some of his men also checked the outhouses. Finally, we left and Flossy and I were in the lead as we trotted as fast as the terrain allowed back to the soft hills of Lewes. There was a thread of wind in my face as I rode and it drew tears to my eyes as I confronted the failure of our encounter. Behind me I could hear the men talk and they seemed as dissatisfied as myself with what we had found, or not found.

Later, when we were all gathered together at South Farm, we heard from each group. All reported a complete lack of success in finding Beth. I was devastated.

I was unable to sleep that night but despite all my sorrows I found myself wondering what had become of Mrs. Campbell and Charlotte. I had a nagging guilt at the back of my mind that I had abandoned them. I would ride into Lewes tomorrow and enquire if she was coping with the baby as well as finding rooms.

As I lay awake into the small hours, my thoughts continually returned to young Coad's note. He had written that he would know if I returned to Lewes so perhaps he would bring Beth to me if he was able. It was a small hope but sufficient to allow me to get to sleep for a few hours before dawn.

★★★

264

I went to Lewes the next morning and saw Charlotte. She was bonny and her mama quite happy with her accommodation. I apologised for abandoning them and Mrs. Campbell was gracious enough to acknowledge that I had more important things on my mind. Cecilia had sent her a letter of introduction to various people who might have rooms to rent and she had been enjoying herself looking around other people's houses. I proposed introducing her to Mrs. Makepiece and Mr. and Mrs. Jenkins who knew the town and people intimately.

My next trip was to Mrs. Makepiece. I told her all about our upsetting day yesterday.

'Are you sure?' she said, frowning in surprise.

'Well, of course I'm sure. We searched the cottage and an outhouse where wood was stacked. I looked around inside and there was no indication of another child.'

'If I had kidnapped a child,' she said, 'I would be prepared for callers looking for her.'

'Well, short of pulling the place to pieces, I don't know what else we could have done.'

'Personally, I would put someone on watch,' she said.

'For how long, though? They couldn't have known we were coming, we were extremely careful.'

'You of all people should know that smugglers have their fingers in every pie and they are no respecter of status. They must have known you were coming and planted a child to throw you off the scent.'

I sat down, a little spark of hope rising. 'Are you so sure that Martha is the one?'

'Yes, I am sure. The more I think about it, the more I am convinced,' she said emphatically, her lips pursed and determined.

'Let me think on it and then I'll decide what to do, without telling anyone!'

'Don't be foolish, Esther. You know who you can trust,' she said, sternly. 'Billy and John Elwood - keep them informed of everything you think of doing.'

I nodded, realising that she was speaking sense.

'There is one other thing, I feel guilty that I haven't helped Mrs. Campbell find suitable lodgings. She has been to a few places but hasn't found anywhere to suit her and Charlotte. 'May I bring them round to meet you and Miss Wardle as you know so many people?'

Mrs. Makepiece replied, 'I think it would be better if we met them at the inn. I take it they still have a ladies' lounge?'

'Well, I'm not sure it's called that but there is a room which the residents use for coffee and meetings. Anyway, it's separate from the bar that is always full of loud men. Shall we call in on her tomorrow afternoon, then? I have to look after Freddie in the morning.'

'Aye, lass, we'll see what we can find for them.'

I left a message for Mrs. Campbell and rode home on Flossy with Mrs. Makepiece's comments at the front of my mind. Had we given up too easily? Had we been duped?

Chapter Thirty-Nine

To Be Let, and entered upon immediately
A good Dwelling house, situate in Southover near Lewes;
consisting of a kitchen, hall, two parlours, three pantries, and a
brew house, five chambers, two large garrets, two gardens, a barn,
stable, coach house and a field about an acre of land adjoining late
in the occupation of the Rev........................
Sussex Weekly Advertiser and Lewes Journal 1750/1806

I n the days after we searched for Beth at Martha's, I kept trying to recollect all the details of that visit. Something had not been right but I didn't know what it was. Every time I tried to direct my thoughts elsewhere, a flicker of doubt would nag at me, but it had no clarity. It was a ghost of thought that didn't have body. I fretted endlessly over it.

I received a letter from Prickship that irritated me. I didn't want to think about anything other than Beth but here he was intruding on me. He wrote that he was going to move to Brighthelmstone to convalesce and asked if I would visit him there. No, I wouldn't visit him; I had no interest in his attempts to draw me into his clutches. I feared he wanted to build on our previous friendship and might propose. Such a thought was repugnant to me and I desperately wished Dr. Grieve would come back to Lewes and me. He would know what to do; he would understand my frustration.

I broke free of my unsatisfactory thoughts to focus my attention on Freddie, taking him to the nursery so we could play with the blocks the carpenter made for him. I built them up into a tower and his greatest delight was in then throwing them down; we repeated this over and over again, he never tired of it. Cecilia suggested that I go to visit my friends in Lewes in the hope that my spirits would revive and to let people, namely women nearing their birthing time, know that I am returned. I could see her thinking that if I got back into my midwifery I wouldn't have time to worry so much. I saw through her plans and agreed, if only to make her feel better, knowing that nothing except Beth's safe return would make me feel better.

I walked into Lewes in the hope that the fresh air and wide skies would calm me. I wondered how Captain Campbell was faring without his wife, baby and Prickship to help him sail his ship to the Australias and whether Jones was missing me. I also wondered if my aunt was still causing trouble.

Mrs. Makepiece had visitors and I was pleased to see Miss Wardle and Mr. and Mrs. Jenkins taking tea with her. My story was told again and in the telling I found I was not so cast down but reminded of how lucky I had been to survive such an ordeal. Whilst a fresh pot of tea was made, I brought the visitors right up to the present day by relating what had happened at Martha's cottage and the other places we visited in our fruitless search for Beth.

'Now you know as much as me,' I finished, glumly. 'But, tell me, how is Beth's grandfather? I must seek him out, or perhaps you could tell him that I'd like to see him?'

'Aye lass, he has taken all this very badly, and that wife of his is such a scold,' said Mrs Makepiece. 'He'll be that pleased to see you again. He'll take heart that if you have come back then Beth might do so, too.'

There was a knock on the window and I saw Billy-alone standing outside, twisting his cap in his hands. 'I'll open it,' I said. 'I think it's for me.' I stepped outside.

'What's wrong Billy? You're very pale.'

'I've found young Coad, Esther,' he whispered, 'and he is in a bad way.'

I didn't wait to hear the details, just flew inside to make my apologies and fetch my wrap.

'What's happened?' I asked as we turned down the steep cobbles of Keere Street.

'Pot, as works with the Jenkins, found him all but dead in a ditch off the river.'

'Where is he now, is he alright?' My heart skipped with excitement that Job had been found.

'We've taken him into Miss Wardle's piggy house. It's warm and cosy in there, 'n' she never comes down,' he said. 'He's been beaten, Miss, real bad, he's black and blue and very cold. He would have been taken by the tide if Pot hadn't spotted 'im. Did I do right to take him there?'

'Aye, Billy, but we won't mention it to anyone, at least until we find out what's happened. You say Miss Wardle doesn't venture down much?'

'Na, she do know I take care of piggies, even though Polly is supposed to, and she leaves me to it. I collect the slops from outside the scullery. I don't see her for days sometimes.'

'I'm sure she wouldn't mind, but if someone has thrashed him and left him for dead, it might be as well to keep quiet until we find out who and why. Pot won't talk, will he?'

'Not if I tell him not to, Miss.'

We made our way to Green Lane, which was the back entrance to Miss Wardle's house on St. Martin's Lane. We didn't meet anyone so were able to slip inside the gate unnoticed.

I knelt and entered the outhouse that had been Billy's home since he escaped the poor house.

'Miss Wardle is at Keere Street at the moment, Billy, so I think we can afford some light. Can you tie back the window covers and the door?'

He went outside and lifted the heavy pigskin flaps and tied them with twine so the light flooded into the furthest reaches of the outhouse. The poor lad was curled up on the straw-covered floor. The piggie, whose bed it was, was outside rolling in a mud bath that Billy had made for her some time ago.

'Let's lift him up onto your pallet, so I can see a bit better.' We both grunted as we tried to lift him, he was no lightweight.

Job was, as Billy had said, black and blue as well as bloodied about his nose and mouth, but what worried me most was that he was deathly cold and had a pallor I had never seen in a living person. I slipped my hand inside his clothing to feel if there was any warmth. He groaned as my fingers found his armpit.

'I think we have to warm him through first before we can look at what damage has been done. Have you any blankets or spare clothing, Billy?'

'Aye, Miss,' he nodded, 'I 'ave one blanket for me bed, like, and I've got them clothes that Cilla got from her ma and wanted me to wear when the press gang came by. I never did wear them; I'm not dressing like a lassie for no-one.'

I couldn't help but smile as I remembered Cilla's solution to Billy being pressed. As gently as I could, I removed all the boy's wet and torn clothing, lightly chaffing his skin where there was no bruising. I dressed him in the clothes Billy gave me and wrapped the blanket round him. His poor hands were bruised and bleeding but there was no broken skin other than on his face and hands, so I felt hopeful that he wasn't bleeding where I couldn't see.

'He put up a fight, Billy – have you got a drop of clean water or ale?'

'Aye, Miss, I alus keep some by, like, and I 'ave water from the well, I'll fetch some.'

'Drink up, Job, you're safe now,' I whispered to him when Billy came back.

'Where am I?' he muttered, struggling to form the words through his torn lips.

'Billy-alone has taken you in. Who did this to you, lad?' I said.

'Bruvvers,' he whispered.

'Did you say your brothers?'

He grunted, 'Aye.'

Then I asked the question that I was desperate to know the answer to. 'Where is Beth, have they got her?'

'Na.'

'Tell me, please, where is she?'

'In t' forest.'

'Is she with Martha?'

I thought he nodded, and at that point I realised what it was that had been nagging at me. I sat back on my ankles, ignoring the twinge of pain in my leg. The little bed! If

Martha was only minding the forester's child occasionally when he was at work, she wouldn't have owned a child's bed, nor would there be a child's washing on the line. It was surprising that there was a bed at all. Most poor families didn't have beds either for themselves or their children. I looked back at Job but his eyes were flickering in and out of consciousness, so I pressed him no further.

'Are you able to stay with him, Billy, for tonight at least?'

He nodded. 'I'll look out for him - there is room for both of us on the cot and I'll help him warm up.'

'I'll come back tomorrow, Billy,' I said. 'If he warms up and you can keep giving him some water, I'll bring him food from Mrs. Fisher's kitchen and we can see if he is mending. I'll come in the back way, so Miss Wardle doesn't see me.'

We stepped outside, and I pulled Billy away from the doorway.

'Can you come with me to the forest, Billy, to Martha's place - after we have seen to the lad tomorrow? I am sure Beth is there.'

'Do you think she is safe? If the brothers 'ave done this, what else might they do?'

'I don't know but it sounds like they don't know where she is either. He is a brave lad if he didn't tell them despite the beating, or, perhaps they were just trying to stop Job from talking about their smuggling secrets. They are not very clever - they just do what their father says.'

'Do you think they meant to kill him?' Billy asked, disbelief in his voice. 'Fancy leaving him there in a ditch full of water where the tide comes in. You wouldn't think they would treat their own brother like that.'

'I don't know, I can't put my mind into theirs. But it's too late to go now. I'd never find the way, so if we go early tomorrow we might catch Martha and Chalky White out.' I clutched Billy's arm saying, 'Don't tell a soul, Billy, and ask Pot to keep quiet about finding Job.'

He nodded but said anxiously, 'Shouldn't you tell the Elwoods?'

'I'm not telling anyone, except you, Billy.'

I barely slept a wink that night and was up before daybreak. I took some bread and scrape along with a dish of good jellied stock before leaving a scribbled note for Cecilia, saying that I had a hunch where Beth might be, promising that I would be back by four o'clock and wouldn't do anything rash. I also explained that Billy was with me and hoped he wasn't needed on the farm.

I saddled Flossy quickly and quietly and was away to Lewes before the birds woke up. I pulled her up at the bottom of Keere Street and hurried up the cobbles to leave a note for Mrs. Makepiece which said, 'If we don't return by four o'clock, we have gone to Martha's. Please do not raise the alarm until then.' I knew Mrs. Makepiece would keep my counsel but Cecilia wouldn't; she would have had Farmer Elwood charging after me. Billy and I would do this on our own, in total secrecy.

Flossy was safely hitched and I crept into the piggy yard. Billy was waiting for me and the boy Coad was warmed through. He was breathing evenly as I lifted his head and got him to swallow the stock; it was cold but still tasty. I whispered in his ear, hoping he was sufficiently conscious to hear me, 'I will be back later and see to your bruises. I don't want you to get up or talk to anyone. Don't go outside; you mustn't let anyone see you. Eat this, and if you can manage there is some bread to dip. We'll be back later.'

He grunted with a slight nod of his head.

We crept out of the garden and as we clambered onto Flossy's broad back, I said, 'I bet he is really hurting now, poor lad.'

'Where we going, Esther?'

'Near a place called Sheffield Park, beyond Chailey. It is a way, about ten miles, but I know how to get there.'

We kept up a good pace, taking care not to be seen, always pulling off the track when we glimpsed other travellers. When we finally reached the wetland, we both got off Flossy. I hitched up my skirts and skipped from clump to clump of the coarse grass - I didn't want to get my feet wet. Unencumbered by me, Flossy carefully picked her own way through but Billy wasn't bothered as he didn't have shoes anyway. When I thought we were near the cottage, I tethered Flossy and whispered to her to be quiet and not give us away. Billy had followed me closely through the woodland. Everything was quiet, too quiet, I thought, and wished the birds would start singing to cover any noise we might make as we approached the clearing. Smoke was rising fitfully from the chimney but otherwise there was no sign of life at all.

'I think we must sit and wait to see if anyone comes out,' I said. 'I don't want to blunder in until I know the husband is gone.' Billy nodded, his face pale and tense as we squatted down amongst the scrub, trusting we could not be seen from the cottage or the regular track that led to it.

The sun was well risen by now and it was uncommonly warm. Gradually the birds got used to us and piped up their notes as insects hovered and hummed all about us. I settled awkwardly on my haunches, wincing slightly as I did so, wishing that the door would open and Beth would run out; but as I pictured this in my mind, I heard voices. I touched Billy's arm and pointed to the track that led away from the cottage and deeper into the woodland. I strained to pick out first two, then three different raised, angry voices, as the two elder Coad brothers appeared, pushing a third man before them. The man was old, much older than the Coads. I remembered them as boys, but these were grown to be thickset and tough like their odious father. My mouth dried as I looked through the brush at them, remembering their petty cruelties and nasty ways. I could see how different they were to their younger brother.

They bullied the old man along, demanding to know if he had been hiding their brother and 'the brat'. My heart quickened that they seemed to know we had been there before, looking for Beth. Mrs. Makepiece had been right; you can't keep secrets.

Surprisingly, the old man didn't flinch at their bravado, even though they had the advantage of size and youth. He was a slight, stringy fellow and his physique was no match for theirs. As they got nearer the cottage, he shrugged them off and strode towards the door, shouting for his wife to come and show 'these scoundrels' that no-one was being hidden.

Billy and I both held our breath, desperate to hear and see all that was going on. After a few minutes Martha appeared, wiping her hands on her apron. The two Coads pushed their way past Chalky White, for it must be the same, and manhandled Martha away from her own front door.

They went inside, and we heard banging and crashing as they searched the little house. Their search took longer than ours but still they didn't find anything. When they came out empty-handed, and I thanked God they were, they blustered some more threats and warnings of what would happen if the couple were found to have helped their snivelling brother and hidden the brat. They left, going back through the woods the way they had come.

Still we sat peering as Chalky White went into his house with Martha trotting behind. I must have been holding my breath again, as I noticed that I felt quite faint with the fright of what might have been. After a while, he reappeared carrying a wood splitter and a long-handled axe before going back into the woodland. He walked quite normally and didn't look to right or left, appearing to be neither bowed nor bothered by the Coads.

We waited a while to be sure the coast was clear before we rose and started to edge towards the door which was standing partially open. My shadow must have appeared before me because as I reached to push it open, Martha jumped at me, pushing me out, trying to force the door closed. I jammed my boot in and suffered a jolt of pain. I leaned all my weight against her, forcing the door wide. I hissed, 'Where is she? I know you've got her, where is she?'

She saw me glance at the little, now empty, makeshift bed in the corner of the room and when I lifted my eyes to hers, I saw fear.

'Leave us be,' she cried, a note of terror in her voice. 'You don't know what he is capable of. We'll all suffer if you don't leave us be.' With that she shoved me hard and I fell backwards. I was so shocked by her sudden strength that

- with Billy dragging at my arm - I lost my footing as she bolted and barred the door against us. Beth was nowhere to be seen. Billy pulled me back to the cover of the trees and we dropped down again.

'She ain't there, Esther. They must have her hid elsewhere, or, someone else has her.'

Tears coursed down my face as I rocked and rocked. 'What'll we do – what'll we do, Billy? I can't go on like this. I want to die if Beth isn't with me.'

'We go back and get the truth out of the boy, Esther. We won't give up now,' he said, his arm thrown protectively round me.

Billy pushed me up onto Flossy and climbed up behind. He took the reins and as soon as we were away from the wet ground, kicked Flossy into a fast trot, all attempt at secrecy forgotten. My head was pounding and I still had tears in my eyes but we made good time, heading straight for the piggy house at Miss Wardle's.

I leapt off Flossy and rushed in to demand that Job tell us where Beth was being hidden but there was no-one there. No trace of him remained, nor of Billy's girl-clothes.

I cursed myself: I had let him get away from me, even given him the means to disguise himself, the one person who knew where Beth was. I, who thought I knew best and couldn't wait, had rushed off just when I should have stayed close to him. Billy was twisting his hat again and I hadn't got any idea what to do next.

'He's run away, Billy, he must distrust everyone, even me. Why would he do that? I only wanted to help him, surely he knew that?'

'He likely be frightened out of his wits. Perhaps he

thought we were going to get the law on him. Go home, Esther.' Billy sighed sadly. 'I'll stay here, he might come back. Go and tell everyone we are back before another hue and cry is raised.'

I nodded, and weary beyond belief, Flossy and I made our way to Mrs. Makepiece's house. She was not there but my earlier note was pinned to the door, it said: *At South Farm*.

I groaned. Now I would have to explain my stupidity to everyone and how it was all my fault that Beth was still missing.

Chapter Forty

We hear that there were two tons of Silver on board the Wreck, as mentioned in our last which is all saved and lodged at the Custom House, that the Captain died soon after coming ashore, and that one of the sailors was washed overboard and drowned.

Sussex Weekly Advertiser and Lewes Journal 1750/1806

Cecilia's face was white and drawn, while Farmer Elwood's was red and his eyes glinted angrily. Mrs. Makepiece started up eagerly as I went in but as soon as she saw that I was alone, she dropped heavily into her seat again. Farmer Elwood took a long, cold look at me and then walked out of the room, slamming the door behind him. I knew he blamed me for upsetting Cecilia, again.

I sank into a chair and wept. 'Billy and I had the boy Coad in our keeping,' I cried. 'He was beaten black and blue and dreadfully cold. We dressed him in all the clothing and blankets we had spare, even Cilla's mother's old clothes, but instead of waiting for him to tell me where she was, I rushed off thinking I knew. Now he has gone and Beth is still missing. I am so sorry to have worried you. I wasn't thinking about anyone else but Beth. Forgive me.'

After a moment of silence, Cecilia asked me where Billy was now.

'I left him at Miss Wardle's in case Job came back.'

She nodded and rang the bell for Cilla, instructing her to go to Billy and take him some food, and to tell him to stay where he was until we decided what to do.

She looked at me. 'Now Esther,' she said quietly, 'tell me what convinced you that Beth was at this woman Martha's cottage?'

'I asked Job if she was there and I thought he nodded,' I whispered. 'Also, I remembered that the first time we went there, I was in the main room, and there was a little bed in one corner. Martha has no children. She said she was caring for one of the forester's children while he worked. She wouldn't have a bed just for a visiting child, would she? Would she?' I repeated, desperate for them to agree with me.

'The boy, Job or Jo, or whatever his name is, did he actually say she was there?'

'No, he couldn't speak but I thought he nodded and agreed, and I suppose I wanted to believe it. He was so badly beaten and slipping in and out of consciousness – I just couldn't wait. His brothers had set about him and I worried they might get to her before me.'

Mrs. Makepiece chimed in. 'It were me that convinced Esther that Martha was the most likely person to want a child of her own.' She turned to me. 'But I didn't expect you to go there with just Billy, alone and unprotected. Anything might have happened if those boys, men, had caught you – you of all people should know that, Esther. You rushed off alone before and look what happened then.'

'I know, but I was convinced she was there and in terrible danger if the boy had given her hiding place away.'

Cecilia spoke calmly, 'Well, we have to think again and try to find this boy, as he is the key to it all.'

I nodded, thankful that she understood.

'I will ask John to make enquiries. We can send men round the public houses and drinking dens and down to Cliffe where it is easier to hide. He might even try to get on a boat, so we will tip off the customs officers.'

Mrs. Makepiece nodded vigorously. 'I will talk to everyone in the town and pass the word round.'

Cecilia was looking hard at me. 'I think you should go to your room now, Esther, freshen yourself and rest. I'll send one of the stable lads home with Mrs. Makepiece. We will get everything underway this evening and by tomorrow we might have some news. A badly beaten boy, even if he is masquerading as a woman or girl, can't get far. Someone will have seen him and if Martha hasn't got Beth, someone else must have. 'We will double the reward for her safe return and see if that flushes anyone out. Now leave me to talk John round to our way of thinking. He is a trifle cross, but he will do as we think best. Incidentally, did the clothing he was wearing include a hat and cloak? We perhaps need a description - I will ask Cilla.'

I nodded gratefully. 'Job has protected Beth all this time. I don't believe he will abandon her now.'

As I kissed Mrs. Makepiece's cheek, she gripped my arm and said, 'we'll find her, lass, count on it.'

I was in the kitchen when Cilla returned and there was a constant coming and going of farm and garden hands. Farmer Elwood took himself off to speak to the constable, demanding that there be another search party sent out and giving notice of a doubling of the reward for anyone who enabled the safe return of Beth, dead or alive, and a reward for finding the boy, Job Coad, possibly masquerading as a girl.

My heart fluttered in panic when I saw the handbill saying, 'Dead or Alive' and my stomach heaved. I retched before running to the scullery and vomiting.

Chapter Forty-One

*On Saturday last Richard Ade was whypt at the Cart's Tail
from the Bridge to the Market House, for the second time,
pursuant to his sentence at our last sessions, which was to be
whypt three times in the same manner, for attempting to commit
a Rape on a child.*

Sussex Weekly Advertiser and Lewes Journal 1750/1806

After another dreadful night, I was woken by a thundering knock on my door.

'Esther,' yelled Mrs. Fisher, 'Beth's grandfather be here to see you.'

I scurried around and dragged some clothes on, pulling a comb through my tangled hair.

He rose from his seat as I hurried into the kitchen. I was shocked to see how he had aged.

'Lass, you been put to more distress than it be fair for one person to bear,' he said. 'I cannot help thee, but I wanted you to know that you be in my heart along with our Beth. I make a promise to you, lass, that if we find the child I will make it my life's work to be as a father to her, no matter what my wife do think.'

I clutched his fragile, worn hands and nodded through my tears. I said, 'Beth could want for nothing more in a grandfather, and she loves you dearly.'

I sat him down alongside the fire and gave him a jug of

small ale. Mrs. Fisher offered some savoury tarts to tempt him.

The bell from Cecilia's room tinkled briskly and I volunteered to see what she wanted. As I ran up the broad staircase, I happened to glance out of the window and was stopped dead in my tracks by the sight that greeted me. There was a woman walking towards the house. She was moving awkwardly and looked on her last legs. Trotting alongside her I saw a child, *my* child. There was my Beth alongside this woman. It was Martha. My first thought was that I must be losing my wits but then I screamed and flew back down the stairs, dragging the great front door open.

'Beth, Beth, oh Beth!' I cried. I pulled her away from Martha, sinking to my knees as I clasped her to me, tears of relief spilling on to her matted curly hair. 'Oh, my lovely Beth, I am here, you are safe now.' She looked up through dish-sized eyes and studied me before she put a finger to my lips and whispered, 'Mama?'.

Still clutching her and crying, I turned to Martha who was swaying and looked to be on the point of collapse. Both her eyes had been blacked and her face was ghostly-white and still, like a mask. The apron she wore was covered in dark stains. Blood. Dried blood.

'What has happened to you?' I whispered.

She just looked blankly at me.

Suddenly, there were people everywhere: the stable lads, Mrs. Fisher, Cilla and the gardeners all came hurrying to see her; Beth's grandfather, too, tears coursing down his reddened cheeks. I looked up to the window and saw Cecilia carrying Freddie in her arms, flying down the stairs to the door. I raised Beth into her grandfather's arms and she put her own around his neck. I was gasping, great gulping breaths, overwhelmed to have my Beth back. The three of us clung together.

Beth was looking about her, not speaking, not laughing, just looking. She had grown and was wearing a smock that had been sewn with care. She looked so much older, no longer my baby. Her enormous eyes fixed on Freddie and when he reached out with his tubby arms and called her name, she broke into a small smile of recognition.

After all the hullabaloo had died down and the constable sent for, along with Farmer Elwood and Billy, I went to the kitchen where Martha had been taken and was being coaxed to take a drop of brandy in some hot sweet tea. She hadn't said a word and I could see that she was in deep shock. I fetched a blanket from my bed and wrapped it around her. She started to shake with great tremors wracking her careworn body. I knelt in front of her, my hands placed gently round her face and forcing her to look at me. 'Thank you, Martha,' I whispered. 'I thank you from the bottom of my heart.'

At last she seemed to hear me and focused her pale blue eyes on my face as if recognising me after a long absence. 'He'd 'ave killed 'er,' was all she said.

Cilla and Mary-Jane took Beth and Freddie upstairs to give them a bath together with an assortment of their toys. Cecilia was nursing Felicia and had retired to her sitting room, making me promise to tell her everything that happened, as it happened. Farmer Elwood came charging into the stable yard. He had been fetched from Lewes and brought the constable with him.

I tried to coax Martha to speak but she had retreated again, her eyes blank and fixed. I took her hands and found scratches and grazing, which I attempted to clean; her lip too was cut and oozing blood. Raising her skirt slightly, I saw that she was barefoot, her feet cut and bruised and looking so dreadfully sore. I wondered if Beth had walked barefoot all that way. Surely not - Martha must have carried her.

I whispered to Farmer Elwood, 'She is shocked and terrified, as well, I think. Perhaps someone should go to where they live and see if there are any clues as to what has happened. I think they must have walked here. It's a long way for Martha who can't have walked further than her garden in years, let alone for a toddler.' He nodded, and together with the constable, one of the stable lads and Billy riding Flossy, left at speed.

Mrs. Makepiece had been sent for as someone who knew Martha and might be able to coax her back into life. Both she and Beth's grandfather sat either side of her and tried to get her to eat some broth and bread, but she ignored them and said not a word.

I went up to see Beth and Freddie in the bathtub and my spirits sang to hear their giggles, for Freddie had found the Beth that we all knew and loved, and I cherished him for it. Once they were out of the water and running around the room trying to get away from Cilla and Mary-Jane with their towels, I caught them both to me and sat them on my lap. Breathing their lovely, clean baby smell deep into my lungs, I knew true happiness and was once again quite overwhelmed, but this time in a good way. I inspected Beth's little feet and could see that they were tender and bruised but not like Martha's. She must indeed have carried Beth most of the way.

It was nearly dark before Farmer Elwood returned with the constable. Cilla came upstairs to look after all three children while Cecilia and I prepared to hear what he had to say about the circumstances of Martha's flight from her home.

Chalky White had been found near the cottage with a long-handled axe embedded deep in the back of his head.

The constable insisted on speaking to Martha immediately, despite me telling him that she was incapable and completely unresponsive. I took him to the kitchen where she was still sitting and still staring blankly at the wall. He wasn't a subtle man and immediately accused her of murdering her husband, one Chalky Mark White. She didn't even blink. I don't think she even heard him. I butted in and told the constable that he could not know that she was responsible; the blood on her clothes might have come from simply holding him; perhaps she had even been trying to save him. I also told him that I had seen the two elder Coad brothers harassing him the day before. I moved in front of him. He was so aggressive and I felt protective of Martha. If she had plunged an axe into his skull, then it would have been either self-defence or in protection of Beth. I pointed to her black eyes and bruised face as well as the split lips.

He turned a look of withering scorn on me. 'People don't put an axe through the back of a skull if it is self-defence,' he flung at me. 'This woman stole your child. Why are you defending her?'

'I am not defending her,' I shouted at him. 'I am saying that we don't know what went on and until she speaks we shouldn't be accusing her of murder. We should be thanking her for bringing Beth back!'

Farmer Elwood joined us in the kitchen and I asked him if Martha could be held, under lock and key if necessary, in one of the storerooms rather than be sent with the constable to the gaol.

He wasn't very happy with my idea so Mrs. Makepiece volunteered to take Martha into her own home. 'I have known this poor lass since she were a child,' she said, 'and until you have some proof, or her own account, then I will keep and look after her. And, if that worries you, I will ensure that she can't escape.'

Reluctantly the constable backed down. Martha and Mrs. Makepiece were sent in the gig to Lewes, with the constable riding alongside looking most disgruntled.

Later, I went upstairs to Cecilia's sitting room and Farmer Elwood told us both how they had found White in his yard. An attempt to cover him had been made, but they found him almost immediately, with the axe still in his head.

'Would Martha have had the strength to do such a thing?' asked Cecilia, wondering.

'Perhaps it depends on the provocation,' I said. I told them what she had said to me when I tried to get into her cottage, and that her one and only comment today was, 'he would have killed her.'

I went on, 'When she comes back into her senses maybe she will explain, or perhaps she saw someone else attack him. Either way, it doesn't seem right to lock her up in the state she is in.'

I think Farmer Elwood thought we were a bit soft and I could see he was glad that Martha wasn't on his property.

Later, Mrs. Makepiece told me that the constable had made a great fuss over her locking her doors but then decided the next day that he was going to lock Martha up anyway. She had bathed Martha's feet and loosely bound them with some of her own hose before putting her to bed with a hot brick to warm her and some brandy in her ale.

Chapter Forty-Two

*Notice is hereby given that The Star Inn in Lewes in the County
of Sussex, which was late in the occupation of Mrs. Crips, is now
taken by James Jameson, from London, and is fitting up with all
the necessary conveniences to accommodate Gentlemen, Ladies and
others in the most agreeable manner and will be ready to receive
Company at the next races, where the utmost care will be taken to
oblige such as shall be pleased to favour him with their Commands,
by, their most obedient humble servant James Jameson.*

Sussex Weekly Advertiser and Lewes Journal 1750/1806

The following morning Martha declared herself to be Chalky White's killer. By the time I got to Keere Street, the constable had already taken her into custody, with a look, according to Mrs. Makepiece, of grim satisfaction on his face.

I felt dreadful. This woman had brought Beth back to me, almost certainly saving her life, and in doing so had murdered her own husband. What on earth had gone on in that household?

'I rose early,' Mrs. Makepiece told me, 'and didn't unlock the door as I would normally do. I took her up some bread and my best jam with a drop of tea. She had her colour back and was looking more like the girl I used to know. I sat beside her and gradually she told me her story.'

Chalky White was a hard man, only showing kindness

on rare occasion. He understood the pain of the loss of so many children but to him it was simply the loss of future labour. He expected his dues from Martha regardless of whether she was recovering from miscarriage or having her courses. She learned to do always as she was bid, and quickly, otherwise she would get a clout. He was a close man and hid his money from all eyes but what with the wood sales, the charcoal and the regular delivery of smuggled goods, which were hidden in a secret room below an outdoor scullery, there was money available. He fed and clothed her by buying material from the tinkers which she would fashion into serviceable workwear; she did not possess footwear. On occasion, he would unlock another secret store cupboard and in it were a pair of fine sheepskin slippers along with silk ribbons, some women's undergarments, all embroidered with the initials A.C. If he was in a good mood, usually after smuggled goods were collected and he was paid, it seems he would tell Martha to dress herself in the clothing and sit alongside him. He would gaze on her and drink himself into a stupor but never once lay a hand on her when she was dressed in this outlandish fashion.

This all seemed very strange to me, and it was Mrs. Makepiece's opinion that he had once had a sweetheart and these were her clothes, but as I have no experience of the carnal side of life, I didn't feel able to find a plausible explanation for such behaviour. She suggested that while Martha was kept in pregnancy or its aftermath on a continual basis, not to take her when she was dressed in this finery implied him feeling that such fine clothes would be defiled if he handled them. Perhaps they were his memories, or some strange fancy - anyway, something not to be tarnished.

I thought this all a bit unlikely, as I couldn't see a man like Chalky White attracting the sort of woman who would have such fancy garments. Cecilia's clothing was all monogramed, but she was a lady. I thought he had likely stolen them from someone he had worked for in the past; or possibly from the smugglers who were not above stealing during their lawlessness. Who knows, but clearly Martha had been made to suffer in all sorts of ways.

Back to Beth. I wanted desperately to know what had happened and bit by bit Martha had told Mrs. Makepiece that the boy Coad had appeared one morning and asked Martha and Chalky to take her in as their own, as a niece or relative. In return, he would stay nearby and labour for Chalky White in order to be close by his half-sister, whose keep he would pay for.

Chalky was not keen on the idea, knowing that the elder Coad might object to losing Job Coad's labour on the family farm, but he didn't like the Coads and it suited him to best them. Martha was desperate to have the child, if only for a short while, and when Chalky finally agreed, providing no-one else knew, Martha saw it as a rare act of kindness to her. They knew nothing of Beth's background, only that she was the boy's half-sister, and they chose not to enquire further. Their cottage was remote and visitors were not encouraged. The boy knew about them and their isolated manner of living because it was his job to deliver the smugglers' bounty to them until it was safe to transport up to London.

Once a month Chalky would walk or get a cart ride to Lewes or Uckfield to buy stores and it was following one such trip, a good month after the child came to them, that he heard the gossip about Beth, her mother and the Elwoods. He came home to Martha and said that the girl had to be hidden down in the smugglers' cellar. She could come up once it was dark or if the boy Coad was around, but at all other times she was to be imprisoned in the makeshift secret room which was well-hidden and its whereabouts unknown, even to the smugglers. At this point he began to regret sheltering Beth, but it was too late. None of us had found the cache because it was outside, and we had only searched the cottage and a woodshed.

Martha had done her best to comfort the frightened, tearful child, spending a great deal of time down in the cellar trying to play with her or, when Beth wouldn't play, just sitting with her and doing her sewing. Over time, Beth appeared to forget what it was that made her unhappy and she was allowed above ground more and more, usually when Chalky was in a distant part of the forest. Martha began to believe that she had a child of her own at last.

Then everything changed when the two elder Coad brothers first came looking for their missing brother and the brat. Martha, as instructed, swore to them that they hadn't seen him nor the child. They searched the house but couldn't find anything. The brothers left but had seemed suspicious and it was just a few weeks later that the Elwoods' search party arrived. Fortunately for Martha, on both occasions Beth was quickly hidden and threatened with a slap if she made a noise.

'Did they beat her?' I interrupted. 'Please God, they didn't beat her?'

Martha had said not, but Beth did witness White getting drunk and laying into his wife. She was becoming withdrawn and, with such violence handed out, she had learnt not to cry. Martha had tried to say that Beth was happy with her, that she would sometimes take her into the woods to find food and enjoy the warm sunshine; and I do believe she thought she was being a good mother to her. Anyway, after the Elwoods' search party called, Chalky began to mutter that having the child was more trouble than she was worth, particularly as the boy Coad had disappeared, and with him the money that he had promised for Beth's upkeep. Then the Coad brothers turned up again, even more certain that their brother and the child were somewhere about.

Martha was afraid. Chalky had threatened to take Beth into the forest and leave her there.

I cried. 'He surely wouldn't have done that?'

'Well, Martha thought he would,' said Mrs. Makepiece. 'When he came home from a visit to market, he had been drinking and started using his fists on Martha and threatening the child. She begged him to leave Beth be. He continued to drink and broke into a bottle of rum. Finally, he told Martha to fetch the child. No need to wrap her warm, the sooner she got cold, the quicker she would die. He found a length of rope and started to drag Beth out of the door.

Beth must have been terrified and I felt faint just hearing this terrible story. Mrs. Makepiece continued, 'Beth ran away from him but tripped on a tree root. It was when he reached down to pick her up that Martha ran at him with his own axe. He never saw nor wondered at her coming when she smashed the blade into his head.'

I was deeply shocked. 'I can't believe that he would be so wicked,' I exclaimed. 'For Beth to witness such things is even worse than when poor Wilf was shot.'

'But that's not all, my dear,' she said, giving me a look.

'The reason Chalky did not see Martha coming at him was because he was looking into the forest where a strange-looking woman had appeared and was leaping over the ground towards him.'

I gasped. 'Job! Dressed in Cilla's clothes?'

'Aye,' she said. 'Job apparently picked Beth up and then took her into the house where he washed her face and hands as tenderly as could be.'

Later Job had dragged Chalky's body to a wood pile, covered it in sacking and dropped a few logs on top. They barricaded themselves in the house in case the brothers came by again. The next morning, before dawn, Job and Martha took it in turns to carry Beth back to South Farm because they both knew they couldn't keep her any longer and it was time to give her back. They travelled through the woods and finally over the Downs and were fortunate not be spotted. Job was able to follow a route that was more direct than the one used by horse and cart, but still it was a long way for tender feet.

'When Martha was walking down to the house,' I asked, 'was Job nearby, watching?'

'Aye.'

'Do you think Job killed Chalky and not Martha?'

'No, Martha was adamant that she killed him on her own, in defence of Beth and herself.'

I sat with Mrs. Makepiece and we talked for a long time about the secretive world and ways of smugglers and the people who help them or just turn a blind eye when they were about.

I went to the gaol but wasn't admitted as Martha had been sent to Horsham to await the full force of the law for murdering Chalky Mark White and aiding and abetting the kidnap of a child. The constable lost no time in telling me that I would be required to give evidence at some point in the future, as well as the Elwoods and Billy-alone.

There had been no sighting of Job Coad and I hoped he was safe and well away from Lewes. If I could find him, I would thank him from the bottom of my heart for looking after Beth for me. I wondered if she would ever be able to tell us anything about what had happened to her; but other than mentioning 'Jo' on a regular basis, and always with a smile, she was not aware of the turmoil that surrounded her. She seemed happy to be back with us, and Freddie was a godsend in bringing her out of herself, but I still worried. This was the second horrifying event in her young life and who knew what repercussions there might be? In fact, it was the third event: the first being her birth and near-death when Becca, her natural mother, had put her in a reed cradle and floated her down the river to a new life. How I wished that Becca was still here with us. None of the horrible events that have dogged us since would have occurred. I watched Beth closely and, though quiet when Freddie wasn't around, she seemed to have settled back into the household at South Farm with no fearful memories. But, who knows what children think or what effect their experience has on their later life? I prayed that my lovely girl was content with being back in her home. Perhaps she saw the previous months as an inexplicable event of the sort that grown-ups arrange. It was I that clung to her rather than that she clung to me, and I felt I had to be very careful not to draw attention to the events in the near past. I think it is her personality to be a sunny child and not to dwell on anything too much. I thanked God for that but remained watchful.

The first few days after her return were filled with wonder as we settled back into our mother-child closeness. I gave her a lot more cuddles and kisses and felt real anxiety when she was not at my side, but gradually the household returned to normal and I began my duties as governess again.

One unexpected thing happened when I took Beth to call on Mrs. Campbell and Charlotte. I was much surprised to find them gone from The White Hart. A note was left for me saying that they were gone to Brighthelmstone where they had taken lodgings in the same house as Prickship! The note asked that I call upon them when my own personal troubles were resolved. There was a direction.

I talked about it to Cecilia at the same time as when, finally, I told her all that happened to me from the moment I was kidnapped to when I met Dr. Grieve. I didn't tell her about the renewal of our friendship and closeness nor why we had separated in the first place. After all, she didn't even know that there had been a connection between us. I couldn't quite bring myself to put into words what I felt about it all. I could see that she was curious and had looked most surprised when my new clothes arrived from the London tailor, but she didn't pry and was obviously waiting for me to tell her. I felt guilty, but if I talked about it and nothing happened, by which I mean if Dr. Grieve didn't come back for me, then I would be more able to cope with the humiliation and pain I would feel.

Chapter Forty-Three

Tuesday night about nine o'clock as a Gentlewoman and her daughter were coming over Moorfields, they were attacked by three fellows, who took from them what money they had, as likewise their bonnets and cloaks; and afterwards, upon one of the fellows attempting Rudeness of the young woman, the mother screamed out, whereupon the other two fell upon her, and by a blow they gave her struck out one of her eyes but some persons immediately coming to their assistance the villains made off.

Sussex Weekly Advertiser and Lewes Journal 1750/1806

At last Dr. Grieve returned. A short note arrived at South Farm, asking me to visit, alone, the following day. I said nothing to anyone. I had learned from my mistakes. I wouldn't rush in, I wouldn't assume; I would just be me, but a me that showed nothing but dignified restraint. I was firmly resolved on this.

I asked Cecilia if I could leave the children with Mary-Jane as I had errands to run in Lewes and I wanted to call on Mrs. Makepiece. She suspected nothing and smiled her agreement. Dressing carefully, I put on my new clothes which I then covered with the cloak I had been wearing when I returned to Lewes. No-one had asked where it had come from or who had paid for it. I asked one of the boys to saddle Flossy, and once mounted, I turned out of the yard going towards I knew not what.

The house welcomed me: its many windows, bright with sunshine, glinted down on me. I had missed it so. I knew the Jenkins were away and was not surprised when Dr. Grieve opened the door to me himself. He was dressed in plain, light-coloured breeches with a very smart military-style coat. Once we were in the drawing room, he took my hand and pressed it to his lips. For a moment, I wanted to fling myself at him, but I didn't.

'Esther, my dear, how are you and Beth?' he asked. 'You look very well, and I can see that being back in Lewes has suited you.'

I took a deep breath and asked if we could go into the garden as I felt a little unsteady and the fresh air would revive me. He nodded his agreement and we made our way across the grass. I looked up at him out of the corner of my eye but could discern no clue as to how our conversation would go. Carefully he handed me up some steps towards a stone slab seat; it was cold and lightly covered in moss, but the freshness of the air was invigorating.

'Dr. Crabbe and his wife, have they gone?' I asked, as I sat down, picking my way towards a conversation that might mean so much to me and Beth.

'Yes. I wrote to him giving notice of my arrival and they left last week,' he replied with a note of anger in his voice. 'I am sorry to say I was misled about his abilities and even more so his attitude - but that is all in the past now and I am sure I can smooth over all the feathers he ruffled.' He frowned, adding, 'I will not be resuming my coroner's duties for two months which will enable me to sort out the mess he has left behind.'

'It wasn't just me that he upset, then?' I didn't want to

talk about them, in fact I couldn't care less how he had upset everyone. I kicked at a pebble and tried to be patient. I could feel my fingers clenching and it was an effort to open them and make my hands lay still on my lap.

'No,' he replied. 'It seems he trampled all over some of my most needy patients and his ability was more in his opinion than in fact. I have much to do to right matters.' He turned and smiled broadly at me. 'Enough of such a disagreeable man. Now, tell me all that has been going on since your return. I only got back last night and Mr. and Mrs. Jenkins had prior arrangements to be away, so I am completely in the dark as to the events surrounding your sudden re-appearance. Cecilia must have been delighted and Beth, why Beth must have missed you so, though I am sure the Elwoods did everything in their power to keep her settled and happy.'

I took a deep breath and launched into my story, saying, 'I have so much to tell you, and the first thing is that I was entirely wrong in my assumption that Beth had been returned to the Elwoods. She was kept, in secret, by people who wanted a child of their own, and if I had not come back when I did, then I think she might not have survived for much longer - the Coads were looking for her and they would have found her eventually.'

Dr. Grieve looked so utterly confounded at my news that I paused for a moment, and when I resumed, my voice trembled. 'Do you remember me telling you about the youngest Coad, Job, who seemed so different from his elder brothers? Well, it was him who saved Beth. He took her after the confusion of my kidnap and found a family who would keep her safe. She was so well hidden that repeated searches by us and by the Coad brothers failed to find her.'

'Good God, you astonish me, Essie. Where is Beth now? I hope she is back at South Farm?'

'Yes, she is,' I continued. 'Everything came to a climax with the pressure of us searching for her as well as Farmer Coad and his eldest sons, which is not to say that searches weren't carried out before I came back. They were - to no avail - but then we had gained a bit of information that led us to rethink where she might be.'

I explained about the note left by Job, Billy-alone finding it and Mrs. Makepiece's suggestion of an isolated farm and its inhabitants. 'A woodsman, his name was Chalky White, who had her hidden, decided she was too much trouble and was on the point of getting rid of her - murdering her - but his wife, Martha, who had loved and cared for Beth, couldn't bear it and in the end, she took his own axe and killed him with it. Then, she and the boy Job, brought her back to South Farm.'

It was hard to relate all that had happened as it felt like I was reliving the torment that had almost ripped me apart. His arm went around me and with that I broke down. I sobbed into his chest as he tightened his grip and stroked my hair. After a few minutes I pulled away slightly and looked up into his horrified eyes. I made an effort to explain how terrifying it was to suspect where she might be but not find her; how Pot found Job left for dead in the brooks, and I not knowing if he had given the knowledge of where Beth was up to his brothers.

We sat for a long time in the garden as I told my story. The sun came out from behind the clouds and I stopped crying as I explained how badly the loss of me and Beth had affected Cecilia, how she had collapsed under the strain; and how Beth, though quiet, was now restored to us.

Dr. Grieve had listened carefully and, with just the odd word, encouraged the terrible sequence of events from me. As I talked, everything came flooding back, all the emotion that I had suppressed in my efforts to cope with the possibility of never seeing Beth again and of being shipped to the other side of the world with little or no hope of returning. After I had finished, I felt the strain I had lived with for so long begin to drop away and a glimmer of hope that at last the events of the past months were done with and we could be happy again.

At one point, I asked him, 'Can you do anything for Martha? She is in Horsham gaol and it is not looking well for her. I know she did wrong, but there were circumstances that made her act as she did. She did what she felt was right in the end, as her husband was dragging Beth away from her. She is not a bad woman, though they are calling her a murderess.'

'I will look into it,' he replied. 'Esther, your compassion towards this woman is a credit to you - not many would be so generous. I have good contacts in West Sussex and at the least I will try and ascertain how the authorities view it and then perhaps we can put forward some mitigating circumstances.' He looked thoughtful, before asking, 'What about the boy, Job? You say he has gone, disappeared. Could his brothers have taken him?'

'No, I don't think so. I think he returned Beth and then left the district, but I don't know. So many of my thoughts and ideas have been wrong, just plain wrong. I am not sure I can trust myself anymore.'

At the thought of the poor, lonely young lad, the tears started welling in my eyes again. But as we sat together, Dr.

Grieve took both my hands in his and I was comforted and reassured.

'My dear, I knew you to be a strong and resourceful woman - In fact, that is what drew me to you in the first place - but this tale is really quite unbelievable, and I deeply regret that my absence made things worse for you, and perhaps for the care of Wilf.'

'I don't think Wilf would have survived whether you were here or not. His injuries were too severe, and he sunk into a deep melancholy remembering his father's death at the hands of my cousins all those years ago - it affected him badly.'

'And Cecilia, you say she suffered, and I quite understand why. It must have been terrible for the Elwoods. Is she improving now?'

'Oh yes, she is indeed, and the house is joyful again.'

'I am relieved. I will call on them at the earliest opportunity.'

'Yes, do come. I haven't told them about us, so please don't say anything other than the coincidence of our meeting again. I am not sure I can cope with any more explanations or drama.'

'Esther, look at me. Now, dry your eyes and answer me plainly. I am sure this won't come as a shock to you after our talks in Gibraltar, but will you consent to be my wife?' He paused, looking down at my hand in his, before raising his eyes and studying my expression, 'I know I made a mess of this before in the most ungallant fashion, but I loved you then and I love you still - more, if the truth be known.'

I started to answer but he put a finger to my lips, saying, 'Let me finish, Esther. You must hear me out,' he continued.

'You are such a brave woman and I know I can't replace Wilf, nor am I as young and vigorous as he was, but I can offer you my love and security and I would be honoured if you would allow me to make a home for you and Beth.' He continued, 'I would not dictate to you. You could order your life around your midwifery and I would support you in everything you do. Please, just say that you will consent.'

Now that I had the chance to tell him all that was in my heart, I stumbled, my words didn't seem adequate to say what I was feeling, but as I looked into his eyes, I saw kindness and compassion and so much more: I saw love.

'Yes,' I whispered, 'I would like nothing better than to be your wife and for you to be a father to Beth.' I hesitated before adding, 'You know that I loved Wilf, but I am not sure now that we would have been happy in our marriage because we wanted different things. He didn't want me to work outside of our home and he had no compassion for people who were not close to him. You were right when you told me that my life would be limited by such a marriage, but I loved him enough to try, and it might well have cost me dear - but I wouldn't have given up on him.' I paused for breath. 'Now, however, I see things differently. I have grown up. I know my value, and I know you would cherish me and Beth. I would love and feel honoured to be Mrs. Grieve.'

He pulled me closer to him and I felt such joy as I laid my head against his shoulder and cried a little more with the overwhelming surge of emotion that took hold of me.

Later, as we talked more of his life since he left Lewes, he told me how exciting his adventures had been, but that he had also been made aware of the great injustices in the King's Navy. He was resolved to work towards making life better for all the unfortunate people who got caught up in the fighting with France with little or no thought by the authorities for their welfare or that of their families. He was considering resigning from his role of coroner and accepting a position in the King's service where he might be able to use his influence amongst those who ran the country.

As I listened to him outlining his ideas, I was struck again by how different he seemed now to the man who had left Lewes. He looked different, more vital and committed; and his views, which I had previously criticised to his face, had become more compassionate and thoughtful. Perhaps a life at sea had been a lesson for us both.

Chapter Forty-Four

Saturday se'nnight, a poor woman dropped down dead as she was gathering a few chips, two of her neighbours who observed her fall ran to her assistance but her pulse was totally stopped. On Monday she was put in her coffin and just as the joiner was about to do the last office, the corpse changed colour, and had all the appearance of returning to life; notwithstanding which, we are informed, they carried her to the grave and buried her.

Sussex Weekly Advertiser and Lewes Journal 1750/1806

L ater that day I returned to South Farm with Dr. Grieve at my side. I went to see Cecilia while he sought out Farmer Elwood. Cecilia was not greatly surprised by my news which was a shock to me.

She smiled delightedly, putting her arms around me and giving me a hug, before saying excitedly, 'I knew it, I told John that he was partial to you Esther. He used to listen avidly to you when we had our discussions round the dinner table and he visited much more frequently than he did before you arrived.' Her face clouded over a little as she continued. 'But, I must admit, I wasn't sure he would ever take such a big step as offering marriage, we knew him to be such a confirmed bachelor. So many ladies have set their caps at him and didn't appear to get anywhere. John and I discussed it several times but then he went away and we thought it had just been in our imagination, or, that the social implications were too great, particularly when you were so clearly in love with Wilf.' She paused, both of us remembering Wilf. 'Esther, my dear, I couldn't be happier at this news and I know John will be too, I can't wait to tell him.'

She rang the bell and when Cilla came in she asked for a bottle of the best Canary to be brought up along with any little savoury tarts that Mrs. Fisher might have. Cilla looked surprised but hurried back to the kitchen. I could imagine her telling Mrs. Fisher that something was afoot; the Mistress did not normally take wine, not even sweet wine, during the day. I smiled at the thought.

'Esther, this makes me so very happy. You have been such a dear friend to me, and with all the troubles we have endured, we have managed to come through it all safe and sound. I really can't believe that everything has turned out so well, especially after the nightmare of your aunt and her savage scheming.'

I was touched by her delight for me and Beth, but I would never forget that Wilf hadn't come through it all. It was a sorrow that I would bear, I think, for the whole of my life.

I chose not to tell Cecilia of the doctor's earlier suggestion to make me his mistress! It didn't seem right and I knew she would be greatly shocked. I didn't want to damage my future husband's reputation in her eyes.

My friends and the workers at South Farm have all been happy for me and Beth. But I soon realised that our marriage was not universally welcomed. Some in the town were critical of my elevation to a status to match their own. I discovered that Dr. Grieve had a sister whom he didn't see regularly as she lived in Scotland, and it transpired that she too was not kindly disposed towards me, having had correspondence with friends who still lived in the district. But we both ignored the gossip and bad feeling, and I hoped that I would be more accepted once the event had taken place. And, if I am not, then as long as it does not affect my future husband's ambitions, we won't care.

I felt so light-hearted as I waited for the day to arrive when I would become Mrs. Grieve. We planned a quiet wedding with just a few friends, not wanting to remind Beth of the earlier wedding. Things would be very different this time.

My news clearly had not got as far as Brighthelmstone because I had a letter from Mrs. Campbell with no reference to the wedding. It read:

My dear Esther,

I was so pleased to hear that your daughter, I am afraid her name escapes me, has been returned to you. I am writing this note to tell you that Charlotte and I have moved from Lewes to be near the sea, which I missed so, and for more stimulating company than was available in your little town. Mason (who I have heard you refer to as Prickship!) suggested that I be accommodated in the small pension where he now resides. This struck me as a good idea as he can be my chaperone when I leave Charlotte with her new nanny (a wet nurse who has admirable qualities) which leaves me free to enjoy the delights of this lively place. Mason is making good progress and will certainly re-join Captain Campbell on his return from the Australias.

In the meantime, do send my compliments to your employers, Mr. and Mrs. Elwood. Perhaps I might meet up with them again when I have been introduced into their circle of friends rather than just being an acquaintance of yours and, of course, there is always the prospect of meeting His Royal Highness, the Prince of Wales.

My good wishes, Esther, and I hope your days are now happy and fulfilled. Mason sends you his compliments and hopes that you will call on him. I told him that you would be very busy now the child has been returned, so, don't feel obliged.

Margaret Campbell

I laughed as I read this. As if the Elwoods or the Prince would be in the same circle as her! Vain, selfish woman, and poor Charlotte, to have such a mother. I wondered how Mrs. Campbell would react when she heard about my marriage. I would have the pleasure of writing to inform her, once I am wed.

On the same day as this letter arrived, I met Billy-alone in the middle of the High Street in Lewes. I had been visiting Mrs. Makepiece and Beth's grandfather who seems to spend more and more time at her home now and, I fancy, not only to see Beth. I wondered if his wife cared? Billy handed me a scrap of paper that had been pushed under the door of the piggy house at Miss Wardle's. The writing was the same as that on the earlier note when Job got in touch to say he had Beth.

Miss Esther,

I be glad all is well with you now you have Beth. I am taking the king's shilling and will be on a ship by the time you read this. There is no life for me in Lewes as me pa and *brothers are wicked men and will do everything they can to set me down.*

Please tell Beth that I do love her so and I will always be thinking of her and you together as is right. Do not try to find me. Maybe I will return one day when she be growed.

The note was unsigned but finished with:

I do rite this for the boy. He be a good lad and if I hear more of him I will tell. A friend.

My eyes filled with tears as I read this and clutched Billy's arm for support. 'He is such a good lad, Billy, and I hope he survives the seas, what with the French and all the privateers.'

Billy nodded. 'Aye, Miss, I do think he will. He knew how to look out for 'imself from his earliest days in that family.'

I vowed to keep Job alive in Beth's heart and wished him well in my own. I was quite certain he would return one day to see Beth. I wished I knew which ship he was on so I could send him a letter of reference, or introduction, to Captain Campbell.

Our wedding was a very simple affair, conducted by a kindly minister from St. Michael's Church. Only our closest friends were invited and, as we left the vestry and stood beneath the magnificent round tower that had played a small part in my earliest days of living in Lewes, I felt like I had come full circle. We escaped for a few stolen minutes as I took my new husband to see the tiny garden with its unusual gravestones. The herb I had discovered was still there and flourishing; I looked upon it now as an omen of our future happiness.

We all returned to South Farm where Beth would stay while we have a few days away. When we come back we will make our home in Dr. Grieve's house with Mr. and Mrs. Jenkins continuing as housekeeper and gardener. I looked forward to living a long life with a man whom I had come to love as well as respect. John and Cecilia Elwood have given Flossy to me as a wedding gift and I don't think I could be happier than I am now. I am even to take my table! I am going to give Billy and Cilla the beautiful bed that Wilf engraved for us. Farmer Elwood will put it in store until they are ready to marry and I will endeavour to find a carpenter who I will ask to try and carve their initials onto the headboard replacing mine and Wilf's.

Epilogue

Aunt Tilly survives the voyage to Australia as recorded in Captain Campbell's journal. No more has been heard of her. Through the shipping agent Esther stays in touch with Sarah who marries her sailor and settles for a life at sea. She tells Esther to keep her dress and promises to stay in touch once she has learned to read and write.

Smugglers still operate in the Lewes area and Esther remains wary of their power, fearing that another, with a score to settle, will either step into Aunt Tilly's shoes or that she will find a way to threaten them from afar. The Coad family remain a threat to both Esther and Beth.

Author's Note

This is a work of fiction and is not intended to be a true reflection of historical facts.

The following publications were of great value in the writing of this novel:

The selection of postings from *Sussex Weekly Advertiser and Lewes Journal* (The British Newspaper Archive) are entirely random and were chosen to give a snapshot of the times between 1750 – 1806. Clearly, then as now, newspapers only report newsworthy items, but they give an idea of the scale of hunger, violence and the activity of smugglers and other ne'er-do-wells. Britain was at war and times were very hard for those near the bottom of the social scale; so hard that there was need for a soup kitchen in Lewes. The snippets at the head of many chapters and the spellings and punctuation are as printed except for 's' printed as 'f' in the journals. I was greatly interested in the list of local smugglers and wonder if their descendants still live in the area.

(The Sussex Weekly Advertiser and Lewes Journal can be viewed as the forerunner to today's Sussex Express and County Herald).

The postings from the *Diaries of a Ship's Surgeon* are disturbing to read, particularly relating to the first wave of transportation. I have sorrow for the lives of those who suffered but, as always, you can find humour amongst every human condition. One of the postings from an eloquent physician made me laugh. It went along the lines of a man who had an ulceration of the penile gland. He was told in no uncertain terms that it would heal if he stopped continuously pawing it! The Diaries can be found online at: The National Archives: Royal Navy Medical Officer Journals (ADM101 Series).

The Convict Ships by Charles Bateson is a work of scholarship and a disturbing account, with specific detail of the transportation years: the squabbles between agencies, self-interest and instances of cruelty beyond belief. There are detailed lists of ships, crew and circumstance for anyone wanting to investigate their own family background. The early years of transport - the first wave - were tragic and the suffering endured by often petty criminals, whose crimes were theft, pickpocketing, soliciting etc., were extreme. It was amazing that any of them got to their destination at all, given the condition they must have been in. The first wave did not have a medical man on board and later some of the appointed medical men were worse than useless. Many of those transported looked forward to a better life and perhaps found it, but many died of rampant disease, cruelty, and man's inhumanity to man.

Midwives & Medical Men by Jean Donnison tells the history of women performing midwifery services in their community ranging from the worst that a Mother Midnight could do, to local women who were caring and knowledgeable from their own life experiences. Midwifery eventually became an honourable profession for certain classes of women but was then hijacked by male physicians who actively sought to dislodge them from their historic role in helping women give birth. An interesting book.

The Coach Roads to Brighton by Geoffrey Hewlett is also a knowledgeable and interesting read.